D1188093

HEAD
OF
GONZO
DAVIES

THE
HEAD
OF
GONZO
DAVIES

EDDIE
BUTLER

Gomer

Published in 2014 by
Gomer Press, Llandysul, Ceredigion, SA44 4JL

Reprinted 2014, 2015

ISBN 978 1 84851 873 5
ISBN 978 1 84851 914 5 (EPub)
ISBN 978 1 84851 913 8 (Kindle)

A CIP record for this title is available from the British Library.

This book is published with the financial support of the
Welsh Books Council.

Printed and bound in Wales at
Gomer Press, Llandysul, Ceredigion

Gonzo Davies sagged in the middle of a clump of players. From their shirts rose a cloud of vapour, and all their shades of colour were reduced to a uniform grey. The rain had been falling all afternoon. Nothing moved on the rugby pitch. Even the sound of a dozen pairs of sliding, slurping rugby boots had faded. Gonzo swayed in the heart of the mess, his chin lowered into his chest, one arm around the shoulders of his teammate, Capper Harris, the other hanging by his side. He was held upright by the squeeze of the bodies around him and, had he had the strength left in his legs, he could have lifted his boots and let himself hang, suspended in the human press. As it was, he was too tired to move and gently went with the feeble decline of the last action of the afternoon.

A memory stirred, an echo of a different trance. There had been a time when Gonzo slipped away to avoid the over-excitement of the international changing room ten minutes before kick off. He could hear a distant rumble, the sound of a stadium in full voice penetrating concrete to reach the innards of the sanctum. And in those depths sat Gonzo Davies in his prime, elbows on thighs, head bowed, eyes staring at red socks, scarred knees. He felt the tremor from without and sensed the rise of a vocal storm around him, as earlier reminders of the need for calm authority, cool heads and clinical finishing gave way to snarling imprecations against the enemy.

Curses and spittle began to fly and as they did, Gonzo floated away. He rose and hovered above his team. He looked down to see himself, sitting on the bench, mouthing the incantations of those about to play on the grandest of sporting stages. The spectral Gonzo was on his way to a quiet place, drifting out of the changing room, turning down one corridor and then another, weaving through the Millennium Stadium. He stopped outside a pair of grey doors, the police detention centre in the dungeons, and then went through them into a chamber filled with row upon row of fluorescent yellow jackets. Everything was bright canary plastic before him, except for one light brown coat. It parted the yellow jackets and stepped towards him. He floated towards it and they met, the red shirt of Wales pressed against the softest cashmere. Gonzo ran his liniment-soaked hands against a button and, seven minutes before Wales kicked off against England, the Welsh back row forward softly caressed the bare flesh of his Grace.

He had returned to his outer shell halfway through 'Mae Hen Wlad Fy Nhadau'. He opened his eyes to find himself on the field, before his audience, a television camera eighteen inches from his face. He had stared into it, unblinking, holding his lips together as the anthem soared. He had played brilliantly. Gonzo's finest hour.

But now, in this grey maul beneath the rain, his trance was born of weariness. His head hung low and his legs sagged. There was no Grace here; only his old mate, Capper the hooker, with his oversized dome of cropped stubble and ears as thick as fists. Suddenly the head moved, leaning into Gonzo. Its mouth opened and bit him on the ear. The maul twitched as Gonzo jerked his head away, and then convulsed as the ball was thrust from nowhere into his belly.

'Do something,' growled Capper.

The maul split in two and the curtain of steam parted. Gonzo burst forth and picked up speed, twenty metres from the posts. As quickly as the attacking break-out was made, the defence responded. A prop on the fringes of the maul lined Gonzo up, but as he bent into the tackle, the target shifted. Gonzo accelerated and shot out an arm, ramrod straight. The tackler was shoved into the mud.

Again the charger staggered, but rose as he ran towards the next in line, the outside half. Even though this was a mismatch of height and weight, there was no retreat by the defender. He leapt into the air, seizing the arm that was preparing for another hand-off, wrapped his legs around Gonzo's waist and slid one hand up his face. The referee saw a flurry of limbs, but had no idea that the fingers of the old recidivist, Paul Scrammer Morgan, were probing for eyes. As they worked their way up his cheek towards his eye-socket, Gonzo buried his chin into his chest, shut the threatened eye and lurched forward, carrying his tackler, his gouger, like a baby in a pouch towards the goal line.

Now he was slowing, weighed down by his cargo. A low tackle would fell him. The full back took aim at the approaching knees, but Gonzo crouched even lower, defying gravity, and then threw himself upwards, his legs springing, his back bending, to pick up the tackler. He covered the last three metres with two opponents clinging to his front, a burden that might yet prevent him from grounding the ball. As they crossed the line, however, Gonzo dipped to one side and then flung himself to the other, turning in the air. The two bodies were catapulted off him and he ended up on his own between the posts, delicately placing the ball on the ground, inches away from his face, where two livid scratch marks ran up one cheek, cutting through the mud that caked his head.

'You bastard,' said one of the tacklers, on his back three paces away. 'You bastard old man.'

Gonzo Davies breathed in the smell of the soil, then lifted his head.

'Living the dream, Scrammer,' he said. 'Still living the dream.'

He rested his head on the ground and felt cold water seep into his steaming shirt.

1

At the end of the dark street, the outside light of the clubhouse glowed with low-wattage optimism, a last beacon before the blackness of the moorland beyond. The street lighting in the uppermost parts of the village had gone out one night in the 1980s and the repair had remained on the council's list of jobs to do for nigh on forty years. The bulb flickered and died, and the pool of light around the 'RFC' part of the writing on the clubhouse front wall vanished. All the way along West Street, curtains were pulled tight, reinforcing the darkness and the silence.

The clubhouse door burst open and brightness flooded the uneven pavement and the untidy end of tarmac. A group of eight young men carrying kitbags came out in a tumble. They stepped noisily through the puddles on the small patch of scrubland between the gable end of the club and the moor. The engines of two cars that had seen better days were started and revved hard. With a couple of parps on the horn, the cars splashed out of sight, but could be heard all the way down Upper Street to the bottom of the village, past the rows of terraced houses to the roundabout they negotiated on squealing tyres, taking the exit that would lead them south, to noise and neon brightness.

Silence fell again in West Street at the top of the village, and as the clubhouse door closed with a click, darkness returned for few seconds. The bulb in its cracked holder, swinging in the wind off the mountain, glowed red for a couple of phases and then came back to life.

Far away to the west, across the entirety of the south Wales coalfield and deep into the dairy pastures beyond, it was the night of the Young Farmers' Spring Ball in Carmarthen and the revellers were heading into the middle of town. It had become a party piece to follow the dress code of Cai 'Floral' Thomas, a jocular dairyman from Llansteffan never reluctant to don a skirt, and for the men to dress as women. The spirit of the Rebecca Riots lived on in west Wales and the parade into Guildhall Square and the farmers' march into the tiniest of pubs, the Plume of Feathers, had become an exuberant display of tossed skirts and hairy thighs.

In the square were two women police officers, stationary in their patrol car, there to keep half an eye on a television camera on a long jib arm. An independent production company was making a history documentary about the election of Gwynfor Evans, in 1966, as Plaid Cymru's first Member of Parliament. The jib was sweeping up from street level to the balcony of the Guildhall, taking nocturnal shots of the spot where the successful candidate had stood and celebrated. The constables, warm and not in a state of high alert in their vehicle, were suddenly surrounded by farmers in drag. They laughed at first and declined the invitation to lend the lads their uniforms. But when their car started to be rocked back and forth, they grew alarmed and called for back-up. Within ten minutes, a larger police van had arrived and within twenty, truncheons were being swung, all the blows recorded in high definition in the outside broadcast truck, before the jib was toppled in the crush. It fell into the square, crunching into a deep bed of shattered windows, broken bottles and the occasional snapped high heel.

Gonzo and Capper were staring at a stain above the piano in the corner of the bar. For the past few months the patch of damp had been creeping down the wall. The flock wallpaper, hung in the last refurbishment of the clubhouse fifteen years earlier, when swirls of dark cream and pink over a beige background had appealed to Non, the wife of the club treasurer, the late Edgar 'the Piggybank' Parsons, was peeling off on one side of a seam. Here and there, salt crystals sparkled on the dark plaster beneath.

'That's new,' Capper said. 'Christmas decorations. Twinkle fuckin' twinkle...'

Three hours after the end of the game, there were seven players left – the regulars: Gonzo, Capper, the Professor, Mystic, Useless and the Twins. This pair, Tub and Town, were not related at all, but were identical in appearance: squat and round and slow. They played together in the centre. The Professor played on the wing and was worried about lasting metacarpal damage. He was very quick and was always injured.

'Well, he always thinks he's injured,' had been Capper's take on the day he first rummaged through the Professor's kitbag, not long after the newcomer's arrival – out of nowhere – at the club. Bottles of pills and tape and bandages filled the bottom of the bag.

'D'you mind, Capper?' the Professor had said, gently pulling his bag away.

'Sorry, Professor…' Capper had replied. 'It's just… how can I put this…?'

'He thinks you're a spy, Professor,' said Gonzo, looking over their shoulders. 'You know things. And you say you work in local government, which by his reckoning is just a cover. Import-export, management consultant, local government officer… could mean anything, couldn't they? '

'If I was a spy, Capper, would I tell you?'

'If you were a piss-poor spy you might. Up here might be the place they send useless agents. It's where useless people get sent. Isn't that right, Useless?'

Useless Jones was the only player from the club ever to have been mentioned, five years back, in a preview of the season by the *South Wales Argus*: 'Kevin Jones, a newcomer who promises to be a useful addition to the back three at the top-of-the-valley club not always renowned for attacking flair.' The promising newcomer had dropped the first two high balls that came his way and Useful Kevin had become Useless.

At almost the same time as the battle of Guildhall Square was breaking out in Carmarthen, two coaches were grinding to a halt on the M4, eighty miles to the east. One, full of Chelsea fans, was trying to travel east from Swansea back to London, but a minor accident in the Brynglas tunnels in Newport had stopped all traffic. The other bus was full of Cardiff City supporters, returning from Aston Villa. They were almost in sight of home when they were caught up in a jam on their side of the carriageway, caused by an unrelated crash in the roadworks ahead, by the High Cross exit.

For half an hour, the two buses sat in their respective lanes, perched above the Malpas Road. Then, a few Cardiff fans cautiously appeared and glanced around before running down the slip road to the roundabout below. In the shadows they began to relieve themselves. More fans began to appear from the other side and for a minute they all peacefully urinated against the concrete pillars holding up the motorway. As soon, however, as one side identified the other, insults began to be traded, a verbal prelude to actual violence. Once zips were fastened and buttons done up, the fighting began in earnest, a pitched battle of forty per side. Cars surrounding the buses were kicked and their occupants punched when they started to remonstrate. Other drivers and passengers stepped out of their vehicles, gesticulated furiously and started to scuffle. The fighting spread in both directions, its sound not unlike the usual roar of traffic on the motorway. The blue lights of emergency vehicles attending the original accidents became the flashing book-ends for this mile of road rage.

The opposition was long gone, having stayed for little more than an hour in the clubhouse after the end of the game. The younger brigade of the home team had not stayed much longer. For them, the clubhouse was but a starting point. To end any night there was, as they told the elders that remained, 'tragic.' They had drunk fast from the free barrel of beer, scooped up their kit bags from the mound carelessly formed in the corner of the bar, checked themselves in the mirror and were gone, down to the pubs and clubs of Newport and Cardiff, or the 'Deep South', as the cities were called up here, twenty miles up the valley and a thousand feet higher.

'Ay, off you go,' Capper had said to the youngsters. 'Run along now. This is no place for children after dark.'

Gonzo and Capper didn't remember much from their Welsh classes at primary school, but they did remember the morning routine.

'*Bore da, blant*,' Mrs Jones the Head used to say each day.

'*Bore da*, Mrs Jones,' came the children's chorus.

Gonzo and Capper called the youngsters of the club, anyone under 25, 'the *plant*' and named them accordingly: Daisy, Buttercup, Daff, Tulip, Moss, Buddleia, Blossom and Fungus – Capper's adaptation of Fungi – were the regular eight other players, now gone from the clubhouse.

'*Nos da, blant*,' Capper had shouted.

'*Nos da*, you bald old bastard,' all the children had replied.

Those that were left entered the period they called the lull. There were the seven players and a handful of other, even more ancient, regulars: George Prosser, Hayden Coles, Malc Phillips and Tony Moreton, all old enough to have worked in the pit, shut now for almost half a century, all frail enough to need walking sticks, that were placed in an orderly row against their table. They stayed together as a club within the rugby club, the Widowers. George and Malc had the proper credentials, but Hayden and Tony enjoyed weekend membership. They were still married – and happily enough as far as anyone could tell – but their wives had volunteered them for the Widowers.

'Being left for dead on a Saturday don't 'alf free up the rest of the week,' Jessie Coles had said when she gently pushed Hayden into the club.

The four men would be here to the end of the night, keeping the easy company of Meg Powell and Annie Thomas, ten years younger than the Widowers, each married and divorced twice. Meg and Annie made more noise on the touchline than the rest of the Saturday crowd combined. They went home immediately after each home game, but only briefly, to apply a generous coating of make-up and exchange their thick, long outdoor clothes and their waterproof boots for something short and high-heeled for the evening. The Widowers drank halves of bitter slowly, while Meg and Annie drank port and brandies copiously.

'The worst behaved 60-year-olds in the valley,' the Widowers said proudly.

For the moment though they all respected the lull, sitting together, talking quietly around their table. Meg would occasionally let out her trademark cackle of laughter and Annie would shake with the rich, lubricated cough of a heavy smoker, but they all patiently waited for others to set the pace of the evening.

Gonzo tilted his head to one side and held out his hand, tracing a finger around the edge of the stain. 'D'you know what, Capper? See the long bit at the top, then it cuts back in...'

'I see where you're coming from,' said Capper. 'It's a map of fuckin' Wales.' He ran a finger down the seam. 'That's the border, that is. Look at that. Typical. The wallpaper of England is holding. Not so damp over there.'

'It's not finished yet, mind,' said Gonzo. 'Over by us, we're sort of stopping at about… where's that, Professor?'

The Professor pressed a bag of ice cubes against his knuckles and looked up. 'Well, I'd say we're past Rhayader coming south… Builth Wells maybe. Yes, look, the latest patch could be start of the Black Mountains.'

'The stain of Wales, coming our way soon,' said Gonzo.

'More fuckin' rain like today and I reckon we'll be on the map soon enough,' said Capper. He reached up and put a finger on a dry part of the wall. 'Is that us, about there?' He dipped his finger in his pint and made a beery cross on the wallpaper.

'X marks the spot,' said the Professor.

The third incident took place far to the north, on the seafront in Rhyl. The members of Trelawnyd Male Voice Choir were milling around in their dinner jackets and bow ties on the East Parade, not far from the Pavilion Theatre, where they had just finished their annual charity concert. They were in a large group, adhered together in the fresh air as tightly as they had been on stage, at ease in close proximity to each other. The concert had gone well, a mixture of old favourites and new material they would carry forward into the summer eisteddfod season.

They were just starting to loosen as a group, giving themselves room to swing their arms, stretch their chests and keep warm – some humming in small groups, a few separating themselves and lighting cigarettes – when they all turned their heads towards an indistinct commotion further along the front. A woman, dressed for a nightclub rather than the bracing wind coming off the sea, was hanging on the arm of one man, and they were standing facing two others. All three men were in jeans and loose fleece jackets, and were engaged in an argument, most of whose sound was carried away on the wind. As the men argued, the woman swung herself into the middle, jabbed her finger into the chest of the tallest man, and screamed at him. It was her pitch that made the choir turn. The man being harangued calmly put a hand inside his jacket, pulled something out and clubbed the woman full in the forehead with it. She collapsed to the pavement.

Like a flock of starlings, the choir suddenly moved as one towards the four, but the tall man deliberately turned and pointed his weapon at them. As one, the choir stopped and ducked as the man raised his aim a little higher and fired off a round over their heads. As muffled as all other sounds had been, the scream and now this crack of the gun were loud and clear. Nobody moved until the tall man turned to the woman's companion and pointed the gun at him. This man held up his two hands. The gunman flicked the barrel in the direction of the woman and the other man lowered his hands, hauled her roughly to her feet and half-dragged her to a small van. He bundled her into the passenger seat, climbed in the other side and drove away.

The gunman and the fourth man started to walk slowly towards the choir. They each held out an arm in a calming gesture. The gun was lowered but remained visible. Suddenly there was a screech of tyres. The van had done a U-turn and was speeding back their way. Ten metres from the two men on foot, the van mounted the pavement and hurtled towards them. They threw themselves to either side of it and the van ploughed not into them but into the fringe of the choir. Black suits were sent spinning into the air. One was lost beneath the wheels of the van that swayed back on to the road surface and careered away. It vanished, and almost as quickly – and certainly before the first groans of the victims were heard – the intended victims had disappeared into the Rhyl night.

Gonzo was peering at one particular thin line stretching down from the main patch of damp, an advance party of crystals at the bottom right-hand corner.

'The River Monnow, Professor?'

'Close enough.'

'Funny that,' said Gonzo. 'I have dreams about the Monnow. Only ever been there the once, to Skenfrith, but for years there it's been, clear as anything in my mind.'

'You'd better tell us more, oh fuckin' great one,' said Capper, sifting through the notes of the kitty in the glass ashtray on the table. 'Get 'em in, Mystic. Gonzo's doing a dream thing.'

Annie finished a cough on the table of the Widowers and they all turned to the players. Twin Tub went and sat at the piano and while Mystic took the empty pints up to the bar he played a few gentle chords. 'About the right mood, Gonzo?' he asked.

'Play it by ear, Tub. Let me get started first. Not sure where this is going.'

Mystic, the second row who couldn't see a thing without his spectacles, came back with the beer. Gonzo took a deep drink.

'It's the border,' he said. 'The Monnow, that is. Between Wales and England. Quiet as anything, beautiful. There's a pub on the bridge at Skenfrith, called the Bell. And there I am, standing outside it, staring across the bridge. And on the English side there are police cars all across the road. And on our side, just me. This officer in a uniform full of sparkling medals shouts at me: 'Do not move, or we'll shoot.'

'Anyway, I take a step towards them and there's this huge explosion. The pub's blown up. And I'm thinking: 'Well, at least you lot never shot me.' And I'm just about to move when a piece of shattered window comes at me from behind. I hear this whooshing and suddenly my head's in the river. Sliced clean off by this flying saucer of glass.'

'Fuck me, Gonzo,' said Capper. 'There goes the happy ending.'

Gonzo took a pull on his pint and nodded at Tub who began to play some more chords, sadder now. Gonzo nodded. 'So, there I am in the river. Well, my head is. And I can still see trees, the sky above, or when I roll with the current, the riverbed below. Trout and eels down there, and cows blowing steamy breath from the bank over the water. And I'm turning, rolling, sometimes going fast with the current, sometimes slowing in a pool, snagged on roots. Sometimes bumping into the bank of England, sometimes kissing Wales... And that's it.'

'What d'you mean?' said Capper. 'That's all?'

'It's the start of a journey,' said the Professor.

Gonzo nodded again. Tub started to sing:

'So our Gonzo's in the Monnow,
Tumbling in the waters of sorrow ...'

And then he picked up the pace:

'And his head goes bobbing along …'

And everybody joined in:

'Bob-bob-bobbing along.'

Annie and Meg linked arms and held the final note longer than the rest of their table. They clinked glasses, threw the last of their port and brandies down their throats and banged their empties on the table for more. The lull was over.

2

Gwyn Seymour was singing in his bathtub in front of the kitchen range. He was also scooping handfuls of grey water over his head and working a finger into his ears and the corners of his eyes. The small terraced house rang to the sound of splashing and his medley of workers' anthems. He didn't have a good voice, but as there was nobody in the house to hear him, he bellowed out his verses, and the louder he sang the more water he spilt on the floor. He lifted his knees, took a deep breath and slid under the surface. He blew a quick blast of bubbles as a trumpet finale to his music before letting the swishing contents of the tub settle. And there he lay, silent and motionless, beneath the dirty water.

He could hear the tiniest beat as the galvanised tub rocked on the rough slabs of the kitchen floor, the floor where the Seymours had been sluicing away coal dust for generations, ever since Gwyn's great-great-grandfather, Claude, left

Coleford and his work as a sawyer in the Forest of Dean. The Seymours had walked down from the western uplands of Gloucestershire and over the border, crossing the rivers of Monmouthshire, the Wye and the Usk, and climbing the escarpment to the high treeless plateau where the south Wales coalfield rose almost to the surface of the moorland. And there they had started to dig, scratching away for coal and selling it to the small forges that sprang up around the giant ironworks of Blaenavon.

When their small surface workings were spent, the Seymours had signed up to work in the drift mines that went horizontally into the mountainside, and, later, to go down vertically with the deep mines. They moved from the crumbling cottage hastily built on the moor by Claude when he first moved the family to Wales, into new terraced housing near the pithead. Tucked into the village, here they still were, one hundred years later. Or at least, here he still was, Gwyn, the last of the Seymours, submerged and ever so slightly rocking on the flagstone floor of his kitchen in the early summer of 1935.

He was 23 years old and had been the last Seymour in the village for three years. His mother, Cath, had died at the age of 57 in the winter of 1933. Her life had been celebrated as long and full at the short service in the chapel at the end of James Street, parallel to their George Row. Gwyn did not think his mother's life had been so very long and, if full, only of toil and drudgery. She had buried three children before they reached the age of three, and a husband when he was 40. John Seymour had coughed himself to death, his lungs clogged with dust and blood. Gwyn, the sole surviving

Seymour was unmarried and if he was not always on his own in the house – sharing the second bedroom were two fellow lodgers, who were at work at the pit right now – he was on his own in life.

Beneath his dirty lukewarm water he was running out of breath, but just as he was about to come up for air he caught the muffled sound of singing. Not the deep rumble of miners on their way to work, but female voices. He paused, listening to the strange warble, and then he hauled himself up in the tub. He sucked in air. A wave slopped over the end of the tub. He knelt in order to peer through the window of the front room, causing a second wave to flood the floor. He was just in time to see a set of heads go bobbing past.

Without thinking, he leapt out of the tub, dried himself vigorously with the damp towel that he had forgotten to hang in front of the range, pulled on a pair of trousers and grabbed a shirt, buttoning it up as he opened the door to the street. The singing had stopped and the street was empty, but just as he was about to go back into the house there was a brief sound of laughter a street away, cut off by a heavy door shutting.

3

Our Marnie watched Gonzo rise unsteadily from his chair and scoop up the last of the kitty in the ashtray. She saw him do a bleary-eyed headcount of the conscious, stretch his back, flex his left leg and slowly move towards her. After a couple of steps he turned and limped back to the table. He picked up the empty glasses, stacking them into two columns that swayed as he set off again. On he came, never once raising his eyes until he placed the glasses with exaggerated care on the counter that separated him from Our Marnie. He put both hands on the bar and stretched his back again. He looked up and she saw the weeping scratch marks beneath his eyes, a different graze on his left cheek and other blotches and abrasions beneath his stubble. A thin trickle of clear liquid ran from his thickened right ear down his neck and into the top of his faded t-shirt. His brow glistened with sweat.

'You look good,' she said, handing him a dry cloth. He dabbed it against his forehead.

'Too old for this.' said Gonzo.

'Would that be you or me?' she replied, taking the cloth and tossing it into the sink under the bar. 'Given that we're the same age.'

'No, you look great,' said Gonzo. 'It's good to see you back. Here, again. After all these years.'

'After all these years, aye. Who'd have thought?'

Four of the Trelawnyd choir were killed instantly; five more would spend months in hospital, and of them, three would never walk free of pain again. Condemned as a drugs crime that had smashed into the lives of the innocent, the incident stayed in the news when the burnt-out van was discovered on a sink estate near Denbigh. The Hafod development was filled, as a letter to the *Daily Post* put it, with 'Scouse spillage', and showed what happened when Wales was treated as a dumping ground for England's undesirables.

The Rhyl tragedy also brought this turbulent Welsh night to a close. By the morning, it had been packaged together with Carmarthen and Newport, a three-pronged fork to jab at the nation's conscience. The debate was introspectively earnest until Doctor Meirion Owen Jones of Lampeter wrote a letter dripping with sarcasm to *Y Cymro*. '*Ai dyma'r Helyntion*?' he asked, suggesting that if cross-dressing farmers, football and drugs were the triggers of social upheaval, then what could there possibly be to fear in the promised land beyond? Revolution by full bladder was as close as he came to finding an ideology under the M4.

His '*Helyntion*' was nevertheless picked up by other media outlets: on Radio Cymru, S4C television and then in the *Western Mail*. Given the difficulties of pronunciation for the English-speaking readership there, it mutated, or at least shrank, into Hell, and by the time the putty was being applied to the last new square of glass and the Guildhall in Carmarthen was watertight once again, the Welsh Hell was firmly planted in the public consciousness, a madness leading only the devil knew where.

4

Gwyn opened the door of the chapel on James Street and slipped inside, gently closing the latch behind him. A group of young women was hard at work, running dusters along the pews, rubbing at the single brass plate on the wall, or rearranging the hymn books into neat piles. As they worked they sang a lilting song in a foreign language. They began a chorus that rose higher and higher until they all broke off and started laughing. They returned to their work in silence for a few minutes until one of them began humming and the others picked up on the tune and soon they were all singing again.

'Hello.'

Gwyn turned with a start to find a dark-haired girl sitting at the end of a pew.

'I am sorry,' she said. 'I startled you.'

Gwyn ran a hand through his wet hair, lost for words. 'I was in the bath…' he started. 'And I heard you.'

'We make a lot of noise, yes. Sorry to disturb you.'

'No, no, it wasn't that. I was under the water, see…' He paused, thinking this sounded ridiculous. The girl tilted her head to one side.

'It was like a dream,' Gwyn managed to say.

'So, you are following your dream,' said the girl. 'And here we are.'

'And here I am.'

'My name is Lena. I am German.'

'Gwyn. From here.'

'So, Gwyn, this is not such a dream. We come here to clean. It is our arrangement with the minister. He brings us lemonade where we do our other work, and for him we do one hour a week here.'

'What's your other work?'

'You are a miner, yes?'

Gwyn nodded.

'You have the hands.' Lena took one of them and inspected

25

the hard skin of his palm and then turned it over to look at the permanent deposits of black under the nails. 'Do you mind?'

Gwyn shook his head. She ran a duster over the hand. 'Some things in this chapel take more than one hour to clean.'

Gwyn smiled.

'You are a miner and we are the diggers.'

'You don't look like a digger.'

'And what does a digger look like?' Lena laughed and tapped him firmly on the hand. 'No, you are correct. I am not always carrying a spade. At home I am...' And she paused. 'I was,' she continued, 'a student. We are from the Volunteer Movement, and we are here for the summer, to make a sports field here.'

'Ah,' said Gwyn, 'I've seen the work.'

'Do you think it is a good idea?'

'I do, aye. Over in Brynmawr, with the lido and everything, people use it all the time.'

'Yes, that was us. Three years ago I was here to help. And now I am back.'

'Well, in times like these, things like that would never get built without help from...'

'From everywhere. There are boys from France and Switzerland. The girls here are from Switzerland, also, but I am from Berlin.'

'Well, welcome back to Wales, Lena.'

'Thank you, Gwyn.'

They sat there for a few seconds listening to the singing of the other girls.

'I must go back to work,' said Lena. She stood up. Gwyn took her hand and found himself without words again.

'Sorry,' he muttered and went to release it.

'No, it's good,' said Lena, holding on. 'You are finding times difficult here. Well, in my country it is not easy also. It is good to come to a country where my hand is held in kindness.'

Gwyn nodded. He was reluctant to ask but the question came out: 'Are you Jewish?'

'Yes, I am Jewish. Part Jewish. Jewish enough to be on the wrong side in Germany. How do you know?'

'We have meetings, at the Institute. International Affairs, every Thursday. We've heard what's happening. What Adolf Hitler is up to. Funny, isn't it? You're here to help us and we talk about what we can do to help you.'

'For the moment it is not too bad. My family is safe.' Lena looked down at her hand, still in Gwyn's. 'You must think this strange, meeting a Jewish girl in your Welsh chapel.'

'No stranger than finding me in this place,' said Gwyn.

'You do not come here?'

'Not since my mam died two years ago.'

'I am sorry.' Lena paused. 'Do you mind if I ask a question as direct as yours?' Gwyn nodded. 'Are you a communist?'

Gwyn looked her squarely in her dark eyes. 'I am. A lot of us at the pit are. I'm sorry, but...'

'Please, do not be sorry.' She withdrew her hand, but gently. 'I must go...'

She stood up and moved out of the pew. Gwyn remained where he was, but then rose quickly to his feet and strode after her.

'Can I… can I see you again?'

'Gwyn, the red miner with the wet hair… I would like that,' she said.

The singing had stopped. They turned to see the other girls staring at them and then breaking into a little ripple of applause.

'Come to the playing field,' laughed Lena as she slipped down the aisle and rejoined the group.

5

The weekend of the pouring rain turned into a Monday of grey scudding clouds. The tops of the mountains came and went. Gonzo and Capper were on their way out of the village, having handed over the keys of their latest house conversion to a young couple. He worked in Ross-on-Wye at a seed merchant's; she went to Cardiff every day to work at a dentist's. Towns and cities that for centuries had been beyond the reach of the village were now within an hour's drive. Commuters and students were the new villagers. It meant there was a demand for housing stock and prices were rising, another first for centuries. Gonzo and Capper, with their small portfolio of dilapidated properties, bought at rock bottom prices, were working hard. They had talked of taking on more workers but for the moment liked their own routines, finishing one project at a time.

The latest was a cottage on the moorland at the end of a twisting, dipping track. Gonzo was in the cellar that lay under one half of the ground floor. He was securing supports to the underside of an oak beam above his head. They had taken out all the joists that had gone from the beam to the end wall, finding that none had survived the removal of the floorboards. In fact, there wasn't a joist left on any floor, all of them having disintegrated in clouds of dust or snapped, and now there was bare space from the bottom of the cellar to the slate roof above. Capper stood above him on the solid earth that covered the other half of the ground floor, checking the teeth on a four-foot saw with a handle at both ends. The tool was one of their finds from the old days and they had brought it out now as a substitute for a power tool. Capper thought of it as a training routine, while Gonzo simply liked the idea of cutting oak by hand, feeling the sawdust on his face and smelling the rare scent of ancient wood. The problem with this beam was that its sweet-smelling goodness lay beneath five inches of rot. They had ripped through the damp, crumbling oak and had struck the solid core, as hard as iron. After quarter of an hour of rhythmic pushing and pulling – Capper was top dog and Gonzo beneath – the beam had begun to sag and pinch the blade. Gonzo finished screwing the supports tighter and they began sawing again, making too much noise to talk.

Gonzo was lost in history. Since his return to the village, he would sometimes spend Thursdays in the reading room of the Miners' Institute, the only part of the handsome old building still open. That it was still there at all was the legacy of his father, who had fought against plans to flatten it. Gonzo kept up the fight, maintaining the roof and windows. Time he had once devoted to running over the mountains was now given to a little upkeep on the outside and reading inside. Nothing heavy, Gonzo told himself, just a touch of belated self-improvement. He liked the warmth of this one room still open, heated by the boiler in the basement, a thumping beast that Capper serviced with love and hatred. Twice a year he beat it and he caressed it and somehow the boiler kept going. Gonzo liked the smell of the books and the leather chairs, and he liked to doze, leaning forward over the table, his head propped up by a pile of books. He no longer had the headaches, but in the days when he had struggled against them, he had found relief, at the first darts of pain behind his eyes, in sleep. And he still felt better now for a nap.

The tome currently on top, acting as a pillow, was about Sydney Gilchrist Thomas, inventor of the Basic Process of steelmaking at the nearby Blaenavon works in 1878. Gonzo was skipping through the chapters on the elimination of phosphorous in Thomas's process, but was intrigued by the trail of this inventor from England to the top of the mountain in Wales, where he and his cousin Percy were said to have spent their weekends firing up a home-made forge in a small cottage, and conducting the experiments that would lead to his Basic method, alchemy that would contaminate his lungs and lead to his early death in Paris.

When he had returned to the village, Gonzo had scooped up Capper from Dick Jones's – Jones the Other Builder – and they had gone back into business together. The first property they bought was this tumbledown cottage on the moors, a ruin they decided to mothball. There were easier projects to complete as the demand for accommodation on the flanks of the moor grew. The cottage had remained untouched, until now. They had started work at last on the property that was firmly fixed in Gonzo's head as Sydney Gilchrist Thomas's secret weekend workplace.

'You're frightening, you are,' Capper had said when Gonzo told him of this connection in his mind. 'Secret laboratories now, is it? Which makes you Frankenstein. And I suppose I'm what's his name...'

'Igor.'

'Aye, fuckin' Igor.'

6

It began with Gwyn and Lena, a young miner scrubbed up and dressed in his cleanest clothes going down to the playing field under construction to meet the volunteer worker, her long hair tied tightly back, her slimness hidden in baggy blue overalls. But soon there was a group of young men going with Gwyn down to meet the girls from abroad, and behind these boys came a troupe of girls from the village, trying to catch the eye of the foreign boys. Before long, a trail of couples formed, heading from the new flat space between the waste tips on the floor of the valley up on the old dram roads that criss-crossed the mountains.

One fine afternoon in this early summer of 1935, Gwyn was on his way to meet Lena, heading purposefully through the streets behind St Cadoc's church. He was passing the vicarage and let his fingers run along the black railing between the pavement and the front garden. A woman was kneeling in front of a rose bed, weeding between the bushes.

'Afternoon, Mrs Davies,' said Gwyn. 'See you've found a good use for the vicar's prayer cushions then.'

'Ah, Red Gwyn, how are you, my non-believer?'

Gwen Davies was the wife of the reverend Arthur Davies, vicar of St Cadoc's. She was from sound Church in Wales stock in the Vale of Glamorgan and was built like her background: solid, rosy-cheeked and cheerful. She worked as a part-time librarian at the Institute. The reverend Arthur, at thirty-three a few years older than his wife, called her his good egg and tended to pat her when he said it. Gwen looked forward to her stints at the library and discussing the woes of the world with the godless, like Gwyn.

'Please call me Gwen,' she said to him one day after they had disagreed on the cult of personality in Stalin's Soviet Union.

'I can't, Mrs Davies,' he replied. 'Even by talking to me you're letting Satan into your life. And anyway, think of it: Gwen and Gwyn. It's daft.'

They'd left it at that, Mrs Davies and Gwyn, she handing him newspapers, watching him devour pamphlets on social injustice and programmes for reform. Or he did until he met Lena.

'Haven't seen much of you lately,' Gwen said now. 'Although Arthur keeps me up to date on your progress.'

Gwyn looked puzzled.

'The reverend says he knows it's you at the head of the column going up the mountain. He thinks you're leading them all astray. He says no good will come of it.'

'And what do you make of it all, Mrs Davies?'

Gwen knelt back down on the prayer cushion, took a pair of secateurs from the front pocket of her pinafore, surveyed the red roses before her and snipped the stem of the biggest and boldest flower she could find. She held it through the railings. 'I say you should take that path as high as it will go, Gwyn Seymour, and see what light there is at the top of the mountain.'

7

Once the Welsh Hell became the headline of the moment it would not be shaken out of the media. News crews came from all over Europe to report on the incidents in Carmarthen, Newport and Rhyl and their ramifications. For a fortnight, there were satellite trucks going up and down Wales, moving from one prong to the next on the troubled trident. On their travels they found a snack-bar in a lay-by outside Welshpool, called Hazel's most weeks of the year, but now renamed Hell's Crossroad. Hazel Jones had rubbed out her own name on the blackboard, lacily scrolled in pink chalk, and splashed the new title in scarlet emulsion. It became the meeting point for even more crews on the move, with only the one topic of conversation. Hazel, larger than life, proved to be more than a purveyor of refreshment to weary journalists. She helped fill their airtime, too, and in an interview on Belgian television came up with the quote of the week: 'What you've got to understand about the Welsh is that we're only happy when we're miserable.'

8

Lena had unbuttoned her overalls down to her waist and had wriggled her arms out of the sleeves. She was wearing a coarse white cotton vest beneath the dusty blue outer layer and she flapped at it to let in some air. Now she lay back on the yellow grass, the sickly growth at the bottom of Gwenny Seven, one of the dozen ancient limestone quarries on the ridge. Each of the couples had found a similar place of shelter, the scars of industry re-used now for romance.

Gwenny Seven faced south, and in the far distance, beyond the moorland and between the columns of smoke rising up from the mines and factories in the valleys, the Severn Estuary shimmered, brown but sparkling. Behind the excavation there was more high plain, stretching away to the north, its vegetation barely greener than anything that could push through the barren floor of the quarry. Not far away in this direction, the moor fell off the edge of the escarpment. Vertically beneath the mountain face began the lowland folds of Monmouthshire, and only down there did the landscape glow with rich green fields on top of cloying but fertile red clay.

There was no wind in the small quarry and the sun still shone fully on its depths, a dozen feet below the surface. Lena picked up the red rose and twirled it in her fingers.

'So, my hero of the proletariat, I am asking myself when I must give in to your revolution.'

Gwyn was lying beside her, resting his head on an elbow, looking down at her, aching with desire yet not daring to touch any part of her, not even her hand. He spent his entire life with phrases and songs, chants and slogans spinning in his head, but he was always lost for words this close to Lena. He opened his mouth but she raised a finger and pressed it against his lips.

'Do not speak,' she said quietly. 'I know what you feel. And I feel it too.'

He took her fingers and kissed them one by one.

'But I must tell you straight …' she said.

'As you always do…'

'Yes, I must tell you that here is not the place. I see each hole on this mountain full of people like us, doing it…'

'Like rabbits…'

'Or maybe like some factory… what do you call it, a production line. A line where the couples are doing their production work…'

'Reproduction work.'

'Yes, reproduction. This may be good in your communist utopia, Red Gwyn…'

Gwyn rolled away from her and laughed. Away from the trap of her scent, he found his tongue at last: 'You're right. It's not Jerusalem, my Hebrew queen.'

'No, it is not. But when I find the place,' she said, rolling towards him, 'It will be special. I promise you.'

'I can wait,' said Gwyn, putting his hard, blackened hand against her cheek. 'Because I… I…' His tongue had tied and he groaned.

She placed her small, blistered palm over his knuckles. 'I love you, too.'

9

Capper, at the top end of the saw, was thinking less about the distant past, and more about the games of the past couple of weeks, and the near future. One of the reasons the team had been so poor on the weekend was because in the league they could reach nowhere higher than the middle of the table. Mediocrity had been set as the standard. Lethargy had crept into their performances, like rain through the cracked roof of the stand, unwanted but unstoppable. The knockout competition however was different. They were on a run, a roll. The late stages of the Babcock Cup were supposed to be out of the reach of the likes of them. Teams they called the Stalags and the Gulags were meant to be the contenders, but here they were, in contention – through to the semi-final. One Stalag, two Gulags and the village remained. You had to laugh. And Capper did.

Gonzo felt Capper lose his rhythm on the saw and looked up to see the hooker smiling, lost in his thoughts. Gonzo stopped the saw at the end of the down-stroke and Capper nearly fell into the cellar.

'Sorry,' Capper said, turning his arms to regain his balance. 'Just saw in my mind's eye that kid in the quarter final. Never seen anyone so ripped in my life. 'E could run like a stag, too, the pride of their fuckin' academy and coming straight at you, the old has-been they'd never heard of.'

Gonzo nodded. 'Maybe we did catch them a bit off-guard,' he said.

'Off-guard? He picked on you to make a point. Cheeky

young bastard. And you knocked him back eight fuckin' yards.'

'Two, at most.'

'Whatever. And then that other twat, the prop, tried to turn on me…'

'You were trying to strangle him, Capper.'

'He was a body-builder too, all muscles and big jaw… couldn't get my hands round his neck.' Capper chuckled again. 'Not such a big handsome fucker now, mind. Not after you put 'im on his arse. Piece of piss after that.'

'It was 12-10, remember?'

'Like I say, never in doubt. Now we've got that other bunch of pampered pricks. Stalag Two.'

'They'll be ready. Nobody will be taking us lightly this time.'

'Aye, but just think of it. Us, in the last four. And at home. The village'll go fuckin' mental.'

In Carmarthen the police decided to ride out the storm. The television images from the incident in Guildhall Square had exposed their heavy-handed response and they opted for a softly, softly approach. This was risky in its own right, for the respectable part of the town was insistent that something be done in the light of the flagrant breach of the peace and the breakdown in law and order. The police's more measured reaction seemed to chime, however, with the young farmers, who had hastily stepped back into their overalls and generally proved reluctant to talk to the media about the night of the riot, sensing there was an element of the embarrassing to the whole sorry night. The revolutionary trail went cold, life returned to normal and the media circus left town.

In Cardiff there was more pressure to do something about the M4 mayhem. The running battle up and down the lanes of the most public highway in Wales had been captured on all sorts of overhead cameras and hand-held phones, and an edit of the incident was 'most viewed' on YouTube for a full week. Thanks to the footage, the police were able to identify all those that had taken part. But once they began to assemble a list of the assailants' addresses at the Welsh end, they found that arrests would have to be made in areas of the city that they entered only with the greatest caution: Ely to the west, Llanrumney to the east. The computer revealed three addresses in the heart of the Somali community in the centre, and the police blanched at going there in any guise. It was a very delicate operation, as the assistant chief constable explained, fending off questions about nothing being done. *The Sun* ran a story that two arrests had been made and splashed a photo across page four, of a pair of Chelsea fans running away into the Brynglas tunnels. 'Charged with speeding offences,' went the caption.

Eventually the police decided to swoop and they piled officers into riot vans and set out for their various targets in Operation Bluebird. It was supposed to be a raid conducted with the utmost secrecy, but a convoy of journalists and news reporters fell in behind the police vehicles. For them, it was an anticlimax when no arrest was made at any of the premises raided. Not a single suspect was at home. 'The Bluebirds have flown', the papers wrote mockingly.

The ridiculed police were secretly relieved – and this they did manage to keep to themselves – that communications through the city's underworld had moved faster than their dawn raids, and that tensions within the city would not be strained.

10

It wasn't a major incident on Gwyn's night shift, but the roof-fall near the coalface trapped enough men for all work to be interrupted. It wasn't the first time everything had ground to a halt at the Garw Seam. In 1870, the Maplin and Garfield Engineering Company had produced a report in which they suggested that the Garw might measure a fat yard and a half. Since the average thickness of this, the deepest of the seams at the top of the coalfield, was thirty inches, there was something of a scramble to raise new capital and sink a shaft. Houses sprang up around the pithead and the village was born. It grew, but never into a town because the pit never expanded. The Garw had played one of its many tricks on the geologists, and even before the turn of the twentieth century the layer of black gold had shrunk below the average. Productivity throughout the 1920s and into the 1930s was officially recorded as low and by 1935 the international situation wasn't the only crisis under discussion at the Miners' Institute. Meeting rooms were filled with talk about what could be done to keep the mine open.

Below ground that night, the hewers crawled out of their cramped caves at the face, straightened up in the higher service tunnel, picked up their tools and patiently made their way to the scene of the collapse. They went about their routines: securing an air supply through the eight feet of fallen rock; digging out Tommy Rowlands, who had had a leg crushed in the fall; then tunnelling their way out. They knew their lives were not in danger, but they also knew that it was one more incident in the long chain that would one day leave them without work.

The fall also consumed Gwyn's time. By the time the rescue party and the trapped men reached each other, a full day had passed. When Gwyn next saw daylight, two nights and a full morning had passed. In his haste to see Lena he did not scrub himself as furiously as usual and was a still a little stained and damp as he made his way down to the playing fields, past St Cadoc's and the vicarage. As if expecting him, Gwen Davies was standing by the railings.

'Gwyn,' she said. 'I have…'

'Can't stop, Mrs Davies… not unless you're going to cut another rose off for me.'

'You must stop,' said Gwen. And the very seriousness of her voice did make him pull up. 'We heard about you being stuck underground.'

'No need to worry. We're all out. Tommy Rowlands broke his leg, but we're all above ground now. Have to be on my way…'

'No, you see, Gwyn, it's Lena.' And from the pocket in the gardening pinafore where she kept her secateurs she pulled an envelope. Gwyn took it from her and turned cold.

'I'll let you read it,' said the vicar's wife. She hesitated before heading for her front door. 'If you'd like to talk, please, I'll be here.'

Gwyn nodded slowly, holding the letter, not daring to open it. He leant against the railing and finally ran a finger under the flap of the envelope, leaving a faint smudge on the glue.

11

Rhyl had never attracted the same media interest as Cardiff. The story of a drugs trade that went wrong was obviously tragic, but all too familiar. North Wales Police, however, in what was possibly an attempt to show up the more timid approach of their southern colleagues decided to act decisively once their intelligence pinpointed the whereabouts of one of the pairs they were seeking. The public was warned not to approach Nathalie Coates and Ricky Watts, seen fleeing the incident on the seafront in a white van, nor Maris Plotkin and Nicholas Brampton, wanted in connection with supplying Class A drugs. The dealers, the police believed, had fled to Liverpool, but Coates and Watts lived on the Hafod estate near Denbigh, and a raid was planned for the early hours of the morning.

The Hafod was shaped like the head of a Celtic cross, circular with access roads going in straight from the four compass points. These four lines crossed streets laid out in rings. At the centre of the cross lay a last circle, a recreation area that was no longer a green space, but a scuffed dumping ground for all kinds of detritus from the estate. In south Wales, the Cardiff grapevine and the usual suspects of social media had passed on news of the police operations there quickly enough, but the network that protected industry on the Hafod was even sharper to respond to any threat to production. A fifth of all its houses held stashes of drugs, weapons or cash. The residents kept a 24-hour watch, and when four police vans crawled into the estate, one through each compass point, cars slid across the road behind them and stopped. The police were in, but could not get out.

Their vans moved quietly through the dark streets, the only vehicles on the move until a new wave of cars appeared. The first, with the head of its driver barely above the steering wheel, shot out and rammed from behind the van that had come in through the east gate. The police were about to leap out when a second car appeared, driven by another 14-year old, and drove into its side. The ramming was repeated inside the north, south and west gates. The police drivers shouted at their colleagues to stay in the vans and they shot off, screeching through the rings in ever decreasing circles, buzzed by a swarm of stolen cars, all seemingly driven by children. The vans were corralled into the centre, where they had to stop in a pen of charred cars. The police warily climbed out, listening for the helicopter they had summoned as emergency back-up. In front of them stood a small crowd of adults, all wearing a balaclava and all holding a shotgun.

'You have five minutes to leave,' said one of the men. 'On foot. Five minutes, before we start on your knee-caps.'

The police ran for their lives and the helicopter arrived

in time to film a pyre in the middle of the Hafod. Four police vans and a dozen stolen cars, slammed into a single pile, were burning furiously, while residents young and old danced in circles around the flames. The youngsters waved at the helicopter as merrily as children on a grassy bank used to hail passengers aboard a passing steam train.

12

Mein Liebling, my dearest Red Gwyn,

I have tried so hard to find you today, but know only that you too are missing. Please, please, be safe.

Word came this morning that my father has been attacked near our house in Berlin. We have been hearing for many weeks that new laws against the Jews are going to be passed, but now there has been a steep rise in aggression. The Nazi Party Rally in Nuremberg seemed to turn many people to violence. My poor father is recovering at home, but I must go to him. They are saying that there will be new passport laws and that Jews will not be allowed into Germany.

So, I must say goodbye. But I promise I shall do everything I can to come back. I have much digging to do in your village. And also I promised you our 'besonderer ort', our special place. But I do not know when. I know you cannot pray for me. But think of me. Think of this: Ich liebe dich.

Your Lena.

Gwyn never saw her again.

13

It took another half-hour to cut through the beam. By then, dark sawdust and shavings were stuck to Gonzo's head and shoulders by his sweat. His hair was thinning on his crown, but for a moment he had a full wig, the colour of oak. He rubbed his head vigorously and a shower of dust filled the cellar. He rested his aching arms on his thighs and bent forward to ease his back. He could hear Capper, equally weary, breathing heavily overhead.

'Maybe it wasn't so rotten after all,' he gasped after a minute.

'Maybe not,' came the reply from above. 'But it's a bit bastard late now.'

The beam was cut neatly in the middle, the two halves held up by the supports and still anchored in the cellar wall. Gonzo inspected where the beam went into the stonework.

'No, she's worse here,' he said. He went to the other side. 'Too far gone this side, too.' He stopped for a moment to catch his breath again and then ran his hand along the wood. 'Still a shame though,' he went on, 'to replace a piece of oak like this with a steel I-beam. Don't you think?'

There was no response from above.

'I know we've got one in the store that will fit. But, like I say, it's a shame.'

There was silence.

'Capper?'

Gonzo went to the ladder and climbed three rungs, to poke his head into the room above. Capper was staring out of the hole where a new window frame would soon be fitted.

'Capper?'

'You'd better come here,' said Capper, not turning round.

Gonzo climbed out of the cellar and went to join him. Standing by the garden gate that hung at an angle on a single hinge, was Grace.

14

Our Marnie and Gonzo had been friends at primary school in the village and as they progressed to secondary school in nearby Brynmawr there was an expectation by all who knew them that they would end up together. There was even speculation about their offspring, what issue might come forth from the black-haired, fiery Marnie O'Brien and Gonzo Davies, the gifted rugby player. It remained pure speculation. At first, it was Our Marnie – that was how she was known, mimicry in a Welsh accent of how an Irish father referred to his daughter – who refused to make a move. She resented how everything came a little too easily to Gonzo. How he never had to try too hard.

It was this innate idleness that prevented Gonzo being snapped up by the rugby academies of the land. The scouts from the south spotted him year after year in school games, upgraded their evaluations as he went through the local rugby club's junior sections, but none persuaded him to enter their regional trials, the only route, according to them, towards a professional career. Pressed by his teachers and coaches to look again, the development officers and youth coaches of the national set-up noted that every rugby-playing country was littered with potential never fulfilled; that you could heat the Valleys with all the energy wasted on trying to bring the best out of reluctant teenagers.

15

The rain turned the streets of the village silver. And in the stream of coal dust heading for the drains flowed dozens of sheets of paper. Nobody knew how the copies of *The Miners' Only Hope*, the pamphlet published by Oswald Mosley's British Union of Fascists, had made it into the Miners' Institute, but they were summarily thrown out of the windows and carried away by the storm water.

A meeting was called to see what could be done about what a second set of sheets promoted. Notices, posted against windows and boards throughout the village, advertised the BUF's forthcoming mass rally in Tonypandy. Blackshirt agitators had reportedly been seen in the pubs, whipping up trouble, preying on the minds of young families rendered vulnerable by all the talk of the closure of the pit. Rumours abounded in the summer of 1935 that Mosley's lieutenant, Tommy Moran, once a miner, had been put up for a night by old Mrs Lloyd in her lodging house. The fearless and toothless landlady had to face down an angry crowd that came to ransack her property.

'You're trying to find blackshirts in a mining village, you daft buggers,' Mari Lloyd shouted. 'It's strangers with scrubbed faces you want to be worried about. There's nobody clean in my house.'

The miners had left her alone, but the next day, a well-dressed Stan Davies, on a day visit to see his cousin, the Rev Arthur, had to run for his life. The trainee accountant had raised his hand – cheerily, he thought – to a group of miners, on their way home at the end of a shift, and suddenly they were charging at him.

More plausible was the rumour that funds for agitation in the area came from the pockets of Richard Cranshaw, the owner of the mine in the village and three others elsewhere, plus a brewery, a department store and three bakeries in Newport, and a mansion on the banks of the River Usk below the escarpment. He had recently married the young Lady Agnes, who was under the spell of Unity Mitford, a friend from her schooldays at St Margaret's in Bushey, Hertfordshire. Unity, like her older sister, Diana, was under a spell of her own, that of Adolf Hitler. Diana was married to Oswald Mosley, and Lady Agnes to Cranshaw, whom she quickly began to advise on the matter of profit. And since one filthy mine in particular provided none, he should, according to his young wife, shut it, preferably with all the wretches that worked there still inside.

The Cranshaws were patricians of the county, but had never been as uncaring as some other mine owners. They traced their line back to the Norman Conquest and, if not of Celtic stock, they nevertheless had deep roots in Monmouthshire. They were wealthy even before they began to exploit the mineral rights to what lay beneath their estates. Mining in the nineteenth century had made them rich, but Richard recognised the worth of more than just his money.

'We have a responsibility towards these people,' he chided his new wife. 'They are our people.'

'Then you'll be just as responsible when the entire country becomes part of the Soviet Union,' she replied.

16

Our Marnie was the opposite of Gonzo, driven in the classroom to attain the exam grades that would allow her to leave the village. She acted and danced in every school production, led the way on trips to the First World War battlefields of Flanders, or on outward bound courses on the Gower. She did laps of the athletics track in accordance with her research into the benefits of aerobic exercise, and inspired a whole year of boys to go the extra mile for her. She enflamed them, teased them and dumped them. They were left love-struck and frustrated but somehow proud to have gone out, however briefly, with Marnie O'Brien.

In her calculation of what she might need in her preparations for a life beyond the village, she decided that some genuine relaxation was in order and she fell back on Gonzo and Capper, calling it downtime with the dossers. She sat with them at lunchtime in school, or joined them in the village café for a hot chocolate. She stopped asking what they were up to, because they only ever replied: 'You know. Not a lot.' Instead, she settled into their easy routine of watching people as they came and went. Our Marnie could be short-fused, her energy acting like a chisel on her levels of patience, but Gonzo and Capper slowed her down. The trait in Gonzo that prevented her from fancying him at the age of sixteen also made her seek him out.

One Saturday morning she joined them in the café.

'Be with you now,' said Capper, as he and Gonzo stared out of the window up the street. 'Any moment…'

The bell in the tower of St Cadoc's Church began to strike eleven o'clock.

'Here he comes,' Gonzo said. And little Dario Aspetti appeared at the top of the steps, slumped on his crutches. Life for the disabled Dario was not easy, not even in the village where he had always lived. He sometimes still had to run a gauntlet of teasing. Skewed and hunched from birth, he tended to labour up and down the streets between his caravan just off the Garn-yr-erw Road and the village shops at the quietest time of the day. But at eleven o'clock on a Saturday morning, the thirty-year-old on his corkscrew body and withered legs went public.

Gonzo and Capper stood in the café and gave him the thumbs up. Dario nodded solemnly, raised his head and launched himself at the metal rail that ran down the middle of the steps next to the church. There were raised bumps all the way down, but with a twirl and a rapid plant of his crutches he raised himself over each obstacle and slid to the bottom, landing with an untidy dismount, arms and crutches held high above his head. He then resumed his more faltering progress, past the café, in front of which he turned his head to see Capper and Gonzo hold their judges' marks against the window: 5.9 and 5.8. His sad face broke into a beaming smile and he carried on down the hill.

'He's going to play for Wales one day, that Dario,' said Gonzo. They all laughed but Capper caught Our Marnie's eye and they both knew that unless something changed, Gonzo wasn't.

17

Gwyn Seymour at first had retreated into himself when Lena left. He was sure at first that just as her family had managed to reach her with news of the assault on her father, so might she be able to use the same route and convey news of herself to Gwyn, and provide him with some comfort. But the weeks passed and nothing came his way from Germany. He worked and he slept, but he lost interest in the affairs of the world and stopped going to the Institute.

His torpor ended when he realised that shutting himself away was allowing the enemy to advance. The forces that were determined to destroy Lena in Germany were at work in Wales. The time he had devoted to the joy of falling in love on the mountaintop he now used to plan and lead direct action, up and down the floors of the valleys. He was part of a cell whose mission was to disrupt blackshirt recruitment meetings. The dispossessed attended these drives, it was felt, out of frustration rather than conviction, and common sense could be knocked back into them before they were fully proselytised.

At the top end of the coalfield it seemed to work. Blackshirt recruiters soon found themselves addressing near empty halls. But in the build-up to the Tonypandy rally in the Rhondda, there was still enough zeal in the BUF to tap into all areas, and Tommy Moran was sent to address an open-air meeting in Beaufort. The weather was grim enough to keep the uncommitted away. In all, no more than eighty attended and they were divided unevenly into blackshirt minders and a larger contingent of anti-fascist protestors. As the heckling turned to pushing and pelting, and as the first fists began to fly, Gwyn couldn't help but watch Moran in action. Unlike his bodyguards, whose actions were entirely defensive, the former boxer took the fight to the protestors, landing punches with calm accuracy and decisive results. In the end, the numbers against him proved too great, and he had to be pulled away by his rearguard and driven quickly out of town, but a dozen on Gwyn's side were left dazed and bruised by their brief boxing lesson at his hands.

18

In the afternoon after the boys judged Dario's descent, Our Marnie went with them to the wasteland, where the pithead had once stood. A few of the old colliery buildings were still upright at the far end, and beyond them lay the green rugby pitch, but the boys were interested only in a black expanse near the heart of the village. White clouds scuttled across the July sky. School was over, once and for all for Gonzo and

Capper, whereas Our Marnie was mulling over her A level options. The boys were head down, scuffing the ground.

'Here we go,' said Gonzo all of a sudden. He ran into the nearest building. There was a bit of banging before he re-emerged with a pick, a long iron bar and a shovel. He threw the bar at Capper and gave the shovel to Our Marnie. 'Let's get at it.'

An hour later they had excavated three six-foot steel girders and hacked off the concrete that had once anchored them in the engine house. Our Marnie's hands were throbbing and she had to down tools before the boys levered the last of the steelwork out of the ground. Now they heaved the girders one at a time on their shoulders and carried them into the building. Our Marnie followed them into the darkness. At first she saw nothing, but she then made out Gonzo, who was prising up a heavy board. It rose and Capper grabbed its edge and together they forced it up and over. It fell with a thump. The boys peered into the void and then dropped the girders through the trap. Gonzo reached in with an arm, pulled out a torch and swung himself through the hole.

'Welcome to the pit,' he said when Capper lowered Our Marnie down.

Stretching the length of the underground chamber were neat piles of bricks, timber beams and concrete blocks on one side, and corrugated sheets and assorted pieces of twisted metal on the other. Gonzo played light on the bricks. 'We're going to build something one day with this lot,' he said. He turned the beam to the other side. 'And that is Capper's scrap. Try saying that in a hurry.'

He pointed the torch at the far end. 'Break through that

stone wall and we're into the bottom end of the old service yard. As soon as Capper's got his driving test we can start shifting this…'

'Well, haven't you two got a secret life,' said our Marnie.

She had glimpsed Gonzo and Capper's hidden salvage and now, just as abruptly, a trapdoor closed. The day after her visit to the wasteland that wasn't, she opened a letter from Loreto School in Dublin offering her a sixth-form day place, complete with a bursary worth half the fees. Since she hadn't applied to the school, this came as a surprise, nearly as big as the shock minutes later when her father admitted, not without embarrassment, that he had been interviewed as long ago as the previous May for a job with the brewery in Dublin and that his appointment had just been confirmed.

'I'm sorry I didn't tell you. But I didn't know myself what was going to happen. It's a tough call, I know, Marnie. But look, this place is on its arse,' he said. 'In Ireland, though, things are happening. It'll be a fresh start, you'll see.'

There was barely time to say goodbye. After the long wait for news of the job, suddenly there was a rush and the O'Briens were whisked away from the high village in Wales to the far side of the Irish Sea, part of the reverse migration, the chance for Ireland's absent sons and daughters to come home and join the charge of the Celtic Tiger. Our Marnie, initially numbed by the suddenness of it all, allowed herself to be swept along. Soon she had new friends and a change of accent in her school in Dublin. She then spent a year doing voluntary work in Botswana, an experience that helped on her application to do a nursing degree at Manchester University.

After two years there, something of the feisty Marnie O'Brien rose up against the disciplines and routines of nursing and she paused for thought. For no good reason that she could think of at the time, she found herself in the summer of her confusion stepping off the bus, with all of twenty pounds in her purse, in the square of the village in Wales that she had once wanted so desperately to leave. Within a short space of time, she had taken a job behind the bar at the rugby club.

'It's only until we appoint our steward,' Edgar Parsons had told her.

'I'm only here for the summer,' said Our Marnie.

'Can you start tonight?' asked the treasurer.

Taking advantage of the steady drop in house prices in the village, the club had bought up the adjoining property, knocked through on the ground floor to expand the social facilities and had plans to convert the upstairs into accommodation for a steward. Unfortunately, the money ran out and the committee asked Capper and Gonzo, who had just finished their first project – the renovation and sale of a tiny terraced house three streets away – to help.

'Keep it in-house, like,' explained Edgar to the players. 'You do the building and we'll run the bar till you're done. Then we'll get a steward.'

Upstairs, all went well. 'It'll be a bloody show home, boys. Brilliant,' said the club treasurer. Downstairs, his committee's devotion to duty was slightly wobblier and Edgar the Piggybank was soon counting the cost of the volunteers' rota system. The odd tenner missing from the till was one thing, but it all came to a head when Brian

Hopkins collapsed at the end of his shift on the best day of the summer, the July barbecue. As the committee pulled one of their own up into a sitting position, notes spilled out of his pockets.

'Very kind,' old Hoppy mumbled. 'Just an 'alf, thanks. You know I'm on bar duty.'

Our Marnie was given the job of temporary steward and a place to stay in the new flat. Edgar had told her it was ready, but what he meant was that the shower and toilet could be used and there was a mattress on the floor of the bedroom among the bags of finishing plaster. For a few weeks it didn't matter; it was good to be home. By day, the three old friends made up for lost time, the temporary steward fuelling the builders with food from the clubhouse kitchen and helping paint the walls and ceilings wherever the plaster was dry. By night, they would cook for her in their second project, a slightly larger terraced house. And between day and night, Gonzo and Capper would train, pounding the roads and the mountain paths, heaving weights, forged by Capper from his piles of scrap, up and down. It was as if self-employment had converted them overnight into disciples of hard labour.

It became one of the rituals of village life to take the air of an evening as the light began to fade, and check on the gap between the two forwards as they returned from the Keeper's Pond on top of the Blorenge mountain – the small lake whose contents used to be drawn off to fill the tank in the water-balance tower of Blaenavon's old ironworks. Gonzo, the back row forward, increasingly left Capper, the hooker, a long way behind.

Meg and Annie, in those days not long past forty, were never far from the head of the promenade of admirers.

'Here he comes,' Meg would say as Gonzo galloped into view on the home stretch, glistening with sweat, the muscles of his thighs juddering with every stride. 'Trouble if ever I saw it.'

'Aye,' said Annie, 'But too good for us, girl.'

'And too good to be here for much longer,' said Meg.

Gonzo would see the pair and raise a hand.

'Never mind us, Gonzo Davies,' they'd shout. 'There's half a stone still to come off that arse.'

19

However much Richard Cranshaw was naturally inclined to agree with his wife that socialism could only be contrary to their family interests, he did nothing to promote the force that opposed it at the other extreme. Agnes may have dressed in a black silk blouse for parties thrown by the Mitford sisters, but to his mind there was something distasteful about their attempt to make Britain part of some Wagnerian opera. Agnes on the other hand had money enough of her own to fund a barracker here, a heckler there, a thug anywhere to mete out a beating. She ordered flunkies up the mountain to distribute cash to her converts. It was a careless process, hard cash handed from stranger to stranger, most of it spent on beer not counter-revolution – and thereby destined to come back as profit to the brewing Cranshaw. He none the less did not approve of what his wife was up to and when word inevitably reached him through his own network of agents – informants paid more discreetly to keep the ruling class up to speed with events on the mountain-top they rarely inspected for themselves – he set off to intercept the givers and takers of his wife's rash generosity.

He ordered his driver to speed the Daimler Double-Six away from the banks of the Usk, over the Brecon and Monmouthshire Canal at Govilon and up the side of the Blorenge towards the ridge above Blaenavon. There, the conspicuous luxury vehicle turned into a pull-in by the Keeper's Pond. The Daimler stopped in front of three men who froze in astonishment. Cranshaw opened the door before the driver could do it for him. The driver assessed the group ahead and began to follow his master.

'Stay there, Philpott,' said Cranshaw. He began to walk towards the group, aiming his words at the smallest of them. 'And you, Trott, get in the car. With the money, boy.'

The stable lad from the Cranshaw estate lowered his head and, holding a small leather bag, crawled into the front of the car.

20

Gonzo was on too much of a fitness drive to imbibe much in the week, but on the first two Saturday nights of the new season he and Capper still tried to drink the barrel dry. Our Marnie was due to return to Manchester in late September. She was going to carry on with her nursing degree, saying that she could put up with it now that she seemed to have rediscovered an anchor in her life. On her third and last Saturday of that month, Gonzo was once again the subject on the lips of everyone that came back to the clubhouse: a revelation, unstoppable. The player himself on this Saturday night, Our Marnie noticed, was for once not intent on drinking himself stupid. Instead he spent the whole time looking at her in a new way. She didn't spot how he managed to get rid of Capper but at the end of the evening he and Our Marnie were left alone in the bar.

'I suppose you could come back to my place,' said Our Marnie, 'It's not as if it's far…'

Gonzo kissed her before she could finish. Locked together, they stumbled into the store room at the back of the bar. Gonzo undid her blouse and Our Marnie arched her back. Gonzo leaned against her and they pressed against a box of crisps that resisted, yielded and then exploded beneath their weight.

Outside in the street a chant began: 'We know what you're doing, we know what you're doing.'

Our Marnie and Gonzo looked at each other. 'Bugger it,' she said, doing up her buttons. Gonzo nodded, stroked her face and left.

21

Gwyn had decided that he would match Tommy Moran pound for pound, blow for blow, and he set about making himself as fit as possible. He was lean and taut from his work underground, but he needed stamina, more air in his inefficient lungs. He pushed himself on punishing runs on the dram roads above the village and across the moorland, stretching his chest, expanding his mileage. It was while on his longest run yet, a slow climb out of the village and then straight over the moor to the edge of the escarpment, that he came to the Keeper's Pond. His intention was to keep going past the water and complete a series of shuttle runs up and down the dram road that linked the industries near the top of the Blorenge with Llanfoist Wharf on the canal below, but as he raised his head at the end of the last pull up to the little plateau where the pond sat, he saw Richard Cranshaw's Daimler and the man himself talking to two people he recognised.

The Crabb brothers were known to Gwyn well enough, a pair of wasters who had been sent packing from just about every town and village in south Wales. They arrived on their Triumph motorcycle with sidecar and before long they left the same way. They had done a turn in the village a few years before, offering their services as odd-job men but more interested in petty theft and picking fights with anyone that stood up to them. But where Gwyn had seen them recently was in the place that offered them a true home, the bosom of the BUF. In every back room of every pub where the BUF had reached out for members, the Crabbs had never been far away, shadows in the background. On bigger occasions they had been allowed on stage, muscle for the protection of the blackshirt speakers.

And here they were, in conversation with Richard Cranshaw by the Keeper's Pond, confirming all the rumours that linked the mine owner to right-wing extremism. Or so it seemed to Gwyn as he looked down on them, until he saw that instead of engaging with the Crabbs conspiratorially, Cranshaw was remonstrating with the brothers and that they were resenting whatever was being said to them. Cranshaw made a final point, jabbing a finger at the two men, and then turned on his heel. Only then did the Crabbs look up and see Gwyn, thirty yards away. Cranshaw looked up and saw him, too. For a moment the mine owner in his light overcoat and shining shoes took in the collier in his dirty, sweat-stained vest and battered boots. He turned back.

'This is what I mean,' he said loudly. And he pointed at Gwyn. 'A consequence.'

22

It was one of those rare days in early October, when the sun could still warm the moorland and create a shimmering haze over it. Our Marnie had gone back to Manchester. Capper, with the obsession of the convert still fresh to the rewards of physical fitness, was planning the route of a Sunday morning run. He suggested they should end with a dive into the Keeper's Pond. 'Think of it as a cold shower, Gonzo,' he said. 'You know, stop you thinking about your girl. Keep your mind off... her, in her nurse's uniform, like.'

They had nearly completed the work on the clubhouse flat, and were half a day away from washing the emulsion off the last brush and putting the lid on the last tin of gloss. It felt empty without Our Marnie. And yet Gonzo couldn't help but feel slightly relieved that she wasn't there. He hadn't talked to her at length after the night of the crushed crisps and certainly hadn't managed to share an intimate moment. Even though it would have been easy to turn up and see her at any time of the day or night, he had avoided doing so.

They were both in their running kit and Capper was doing some stretching exercises. Gonzo was taking a pair of scissors to a straggling pigtail, all that was left of his thick mane of hair, over the kitchen table. His opposite number the day before had taken a handful of his full locks and tugged his head backwards in a desperate attempt to bring him down. It hadn't succeeded. Gonzo had scored two more tries for a tally of six and the club had won their fifth league game. On the way home on the bus, his teammates had been joking about the incident.

'Serves you right, Gonzo,' said Twin Tub, 'for looking like a tart.'

'Aye, maybe it is time for a change of style,' said Gonzo. 'Next week...'

Before he could finish, Mystic, who had taken a cue from Capper and removed his spectacles, Useless and Twin Tub had him pinned down in his seat. Capper reached into the bottom of the Professor's bag and pulled out a pair of nail scissors.

'Let's make a fashion statement right now,' said Capper.

By the time they reached the club, Gonzo was shorn except for the pigtail, with an extra couple of nick marks on his scalp, where the shearers had jabbed the victim as he struggled. In the warm light of the morning after, he checked his appearance in the mirror and sighed.

'As I was saying, you dope... Our Marnie,' said Capper, trying to break into the reverie. 'In her uniform.'

'I don't know,' said Gonzo, making a last snip. 'Maybe it was just that one night. Something was weird, coming back to the club and hearing everyone talking about me, slapping me on the back. Gonzo this, Gonzo that. Maybe I let it go to my head.'

'You let it go a bit lower than that, I reckon,' said Capper. 'Maybe you saw her and thought she looked great and it might be now or never, what with her going off again. And you went for it. And maybe, because it was Our Marnie, that we've known for ever...' And here Capper hesitated, checking that Gonzo was ready for this: 'Maybe it was a bit like kissing your sister.'

'Don't know about that,' said Gonzo. 'Jesus, look at me. As if she'd look at me now. Anyway, what did you call it? A cold shower? Let's call it an ice bath. That's what they all have now – the professionals, isn't it?'

'I suppose it shows you can't be in love,' said Capper. 'Not real love. Boys in love can't run through a paper bag.' Capper pulled him away from the mirror. 'Fuck me, Gonzo, you think you look bad. Think how that bloke you handed off three times in three minutes must be feeling.'

And with that they set off on this late Sunday morning for the Keeper's Pond, staying together as they eased themselves through their aches and pains, before Gonzo started to pull ahead.

23

Richard Cranshaw took one last look at Gwyn and stalked off towards the Daimler. He climbed into the back and slammed the door. Philpott the driver retreated, carefully keeping an eye on the Crabb brothers and the stranger. He took his place behind the wheel and turned the car, to carry his master and the stable boy off the mountain. Of those that remained at the Keeper's Pond, none moved. Thirty paces separated left from right on this barren moonscape by a glinting stretch of water. Finally, one of the brothers took a step towards Gwyn, only to be held back by the other, who half-turned him to mutter in his ear. When they looked back, Gwyn had disappeared behind the mound and was on the move. The brothers ran to the tump, but found nobody on the other side. They darted in and out of the shallow trenches, checking every hiding place. They stopped and cursed loudly before making their way a little further back to retrieve their Triumph.

'Damn it,' shouted Richard Cranshaw from the back seat of the Daimler. 'Philpott, stop the car.'

They glided to a halt on the steep road down to Govilon,

having just crossed the tree line. They now sat in the gloom under the canopy of the beech trees.

'Trott, get out. You can bloody well walk home.'

Gwyn darted in and out of the waste mounds, running down the gentle slope that led to the tunnel at Pwlldu. He heard a motorbike being kick-started. With a roar the brothers shot down the hill towards the Rifleman's Arms on the edge of Blaenavon. Gwyn waited until the roar faded, but instead of breaking cover, he continued down the track towards the old tunnel. He half-walked, half-jogged, stopping every now and again, as if knowing that it was not safe to re-emerge. He almost nodded to himself when he caught the sound of an engine coming back out of Blaenavon. The noise grew and the Crabbs on their machine flashed between the mounds in the distance.

Alfie Trott, the forlorn stable boy, stood as the car whispered away. There was a long straight and he watched the Daimler go all the way down the steep incline, before the brake lights come on for the S-bend at the bottom. The car disappeared. Alfie began to trudge down the hill. After a minute, he heard the sound of a motorcycle behind him and turned to see a headlight pierce the darkness of the tunnel of trees.

24

At the same time as Gonzo and Capper headed out on their Sunday run, an old Mazda sports car was heading up the other side of the Blorenge. Grace Courtney had left home with mist off the Usk settled as a deep blanket over the eighteenth-century house that her mother, with a sparkle that soon died, used to describe to her friends in London as their gentleman's residence in the sticks. That was what Mary Courtney called it until she decided to leave home and family, and return to the closer company of those friends in the capital. And in particular the embrace of Gordon McArtney-Hall, far more her age and twenty years younger than the husband she left behind and on his own in the appropriately named – no hint of irony required now – gentleman's residence.

In Govilon, Grace stopped to fold back the soft top and now her hair streamed behind her as she powered up the mountain, rumbling over the cattle grid on the tree line and bursting into sunlight on the other side. It was not a road she knew well. The Courtneys regarded the mountain as a splendid but seldom visited accompaniment to the river that ran to the side of the house. The Usk offered movement and sound, while the mountain was a silent, towering backdrop to the garden. Here they did spend time. On the lawns of summer Grace's father played bridge with those that remained of his chums and took gin.

Captain James Courtney was ex-Royal Navy and did not go above sea level. He fished for trout and salmon, occasionally bringing a catch up the lawn. He fought against the weeds on this sward aboard his antique Atco mower, worried about the house, and he thought of his ex-wife –in that order and all on his Navy pension. Now in his seventies, he wondered how it could be that the two boys who only yesterday, it seemed, were diving into the river and climbing the tallest trees, had left home for London. Will was trying his hand at ceramics, a passion that did not seem to involve making any money; Godfrey was in the City. Grace the youngest, his darling late arrival, was still in the house, but her father was alert to the possibility that a girl in her early twenties could only stand so much living with a creaking single parent. She seemed to be on a mission to exhaust the world's stock of notepaper with her reminders to him about doctors and appointments and pills. What also made him wonder was that, just like Will, he did not appear to have a penny left in the pot. The house was falling down around their ears and if it weren't for top-ups from Godfrey he would probably be living in a caravan. With Grace, no doubt, banging on the door and telling him every half hour that he needed to take his medicine. Damned ticker. Dearest Grace.

In the opinion of Captain Courtney, then, her new chap, Martin Guest, was something of a mixed blessing. The chap had money, no question. It was new money, which wasn't always to be trusted, but made from steel, which was of proven worth in Monmouthshire. Steel-Ag. The captain would try to remember to ask him about his company's name. Guest had experience of life, which was another way of saying he was ten years older than Grace. He had charm when he chose to display it, and had certainly done some impressive groundwork at the Trostrey Ploughing Society Ball, which he had sponsored. And apparently he was starting to be active in political circles. But there was something about the chap that the captain could not quite put his finger on. Grace, he supposed, as she tended to do, would work it out for herself. Life, the captain thought wistfully, would not be easy without her.

25

What was left of Alfie Trott wasn't discovered until the spring. Saplings had broken his fall down the escarpment the previous summer and brambles had wrapped themselves around his body in the last weeks of the growing season. The falling leaves of autumn had then covered his body, with its split skull, and it wasn't until the sharp frosts on the north face of the Blorenge cracked this shroud apart that nature released her grip on poor Alfie's remains. Heavy spring rains then dislodged him and he rolled into the view of a woodcutter one morning in April, 1936.

26

Grace was thinking about Martin Guest, too. Good-looking; only as old as her brother Godfrey, who was still a laugh. He was of means, which God knew couldn't be a bad thing. But why was the thought of him making her drive at 70mph up an almost vertical B road? She slowed down. Perhaps it was because she felt summoned on this Sunday morning. Not asked nicely or wooed or courted, but somehow expected to say yes to what was in effect business, in a rugby club of all places and in a village she'd barely heard of, although Martin had said it was a couple of miles at most over her head. She considered it all to be a million miles from home and up a bloody steep road. She was going too fast again and now she saw that the temperature gauge of her dear old sports car was up in the red zone.

Suddenly there was a hiss. Steam was pouring from under the bonnet of the Mazda, obscuring what she could see through the windscreen. Grace slammed on the brakes and skidded into the car park of the Keeper's Pond.

'Damn it,' she said.

For a moment she sat behind the wheel, gripping it as tightly as she could. Through the hot mist she saw movement and she stood up. With trainers, socks and a pair of shorts strewn across the mound over which he had just appeared – and now running towards her while peeling off his vest – came the otherwise naked figure of Gonzo Davies. He finished removing the last garment, flung it down, saw Grace, veered to avoid the Mazda and threw himself into the cold water.

27

Richard Cranshaw had informed the police of the boy's disappearance two days after Alfie failed to reappear at the house. If the mine owner felt he had played a part in Trott's vanishing act his remorse came second to his annoyance at having to replace a talented, if gullible, worker, one who was undoubtedly good with the animals. In the view of the master, Trott had slunk away because he couldn't face the consequences of being revealed as Agnes's little go-between.

The police had recorded Mr Cranshaw's notification of a missing person in September and were slightly surprised to find out that when the young but very decomposed Trott turned up in April, there was no mention in the original report that Mr Cranshaw and his driver had deposited the boy, very much alive according to them, on the side of the road not far from where the woodcutter made his gruesome discovery. For his part, Cranshaw decided that the political situation had calmed sufficiently after the routing of the blackshirts in Tonypandy for him to be able to reveal at least part of the truth about his meeting with the Crabbs. Not the whole truth about Agnes's foolish meddling; just that he had warned the brothers off. Besides, they too had vanished. As far as his informants could tell, they had last been seen speeding out of the Rhondda on their motorbike in a hasty retreat.

Implicating the Crabbs no doubt lightened the faint shadow of suspicion that fell on Cranshaw, but as a further insurance he thought it prudent to appear as co-operative as possible. And in that light, he remembered the stranger standing on the mound as he was ticking off the good-for-nothing brothers. And so it was that the police began to search for the sweaty onlooker, a further witness they wished to eliminate from their inquiries. Moving with extreme slowness, given the time that had elapsed since the deceased met his untimely end and given the lowliness of his rank, it took the investigating officers several weeks to identify the stranger as Gwyn Seymour. But when they did, a sense of urgency entered their work. Gwyn was known to them. It was with another screech of tyres that the police in no-nonsense mood arrived at his house and banged on his door in the high summer of 1936.

28

Gonzo, chiselled and shivering, was standing in the pond with the water up to his waist.

'Hello,' said Grace.

Gonzo was conscious of his cropped head, complete with its fresh nicks. 'I'm heading for the rugby club in the village,' said Grace.

'Left out of here,' Gonzo said. 'Down the hill to the Rifleman's, turn right and keep going, through Garn-yr-erw, look for a left and then on for a few miles. Until you hit the wilderness. That's where the village is. The club's up the hill at the far end of the last street. Can't miss it.'

'Thank you,' she said. She looked down at her steaming bonnet. 'I don't suppose you…'

Gonzo looked down at his nakedness and shrugged his shoulders.

'Yes, I see...' said Grace.

At that moment, Capper appeared over the top of the mound, with his running clothes on, panting and carrying a bottle of water. He strolled over to the car and miraculously pulled out of his pocket a roll of gaffer tape.

29

'He's not here,' lied Malc the lodger.

'We've checked his shifts,' said the constable. 'We know he'll be in. Regular as clockwork, you lot.'

'He swapped...'

'Obstructing the police, is it? We'll add that to the list.'

'And what list would that be, then?'

'The list that starts with the deep trouble that Gwyn Seymour is in right now,' shouted the first policeman, not at Malc but over his shoulder and up the stairs.

Gwyn took advantage of the minute that Malc was buying him to pull on a shirt and some trousers. The greater the distance in time since Lena had left and the fitter he had become, the more militant his views had grown. And the more carefree he was now with his fists. Sympathy originally shown him by the local bobby – when Gwyn, say, was the last to obey an order to desist from causing an affray – had long worn thin. For officers in the wider area, who knew nothing of his personal circumstances and cared even less, he was fast moving up their list of trouble-making undesirables.

Gwyn knew he was on something of a last chance. What he did not know was that in this instance he was an innocent caught up in the suspicious circumstances surrounding the death of Alfie Trott. Even if he had been aware, he might not have hung around to argue the toss. He had a knapsack already packed and a couple of weeks earlier had run a plank from the window in the rear bedroom to the roof of the outside toilet, and a ladder from there to the small backyard's brick wall. On the other side lay the alley, one of a small maze of rat-runs through the houses. Gwyn's haste was interrupted only by the need to open the bedroom window silently. He pressed his cheek against the dirty pane and eased up the sash frame.

'Let us in,' said the first officer.

Malc felt the current of air from upstairs on his back. 'Just to be sure, now,' he said, pushing for another minute, 'Would you be needing a search warrant, like?'

'Just to be sure,' said the second officer, reaching for his truncheon, 'how much would you like to feel the full weight of the law?'

Malc stared at them for long as he dared, counting the seconds. He reached five before he was jabbed in the chest and the officers barged past him.

'You'd better come in then,' Malc said.

Gwyn was gone. He had teetered along the wobbling gangplanks, jumped off the wall and was now running with all his new-found energy through the alleyways of the village to the open moorland beyond, destination unknown.

30

For the Welsh Hell to become truly troublesome, it needed Caernarfon to stir. Or, if not the town itself, somewhere in the Welsh-speaking heartland had to react. The triangle of the north-west had to be engaged. A couple of youths from Bethesda did go out with the aim of setting fire to a cottage, but they were chased away by an Englishman's doberman. 'Snowdonia, too wet to burn,' was tweeted.

But just as the correspondents from the continent were starting to pack their bags and leave Wales, and as Hazel in her lay-by café was thinking of turning her blackboard back to its original lacy pink, there came a leak from Broadcasting House in Llandaff that made them all pause. BBC Wales was about to publish in full the findings of the review carried out by the Roberts Committee into the 'The Viability of S4C in an Age of Cuts', when an email, a précis of the report, was sent to the *Western Mail*. It came from 'a valued and reliable source within the broadcasting organisation', according to the newspaper, which shrank the content again to make their headline: 'BBC to slash programmes in Welsh.'

BBC Wales hastily filled the airwaves with explanations that this was not entirely accurate and that the Corporation was fully committed to making and commissioning programmes in Welsh for both radio and television. But the facts could not be denied. And the BBC could not but confirm the report's findings into viewing figures, and had accepted the conclusion that in many cases, and in television in particular, audiences remained 'stubbornly and disappointingly below expectation' and that it was sadly inevitable that programme output in Welsh would be reduced. English-language programmes, subjected to some crude pruning of their own in the years after S4C was absorbed into BBC Wales – or 'subjugated by the state', according to *Y Cymro* – would not meanwhile be affected.

In Caernarfon, a protest meeting was called. It took place in Castle Square, in the shadow of the great grey monument, the giant symbol of invasion. Caernarfon – the only 'v' now allowed was two fingers to the language crushers – began to move. It was so spontaneous that nobody was really ready for it, but the protest became a march through town and then somebody with a loud-hailer shouted: 'Shall we march on?' At this point numbers fell, but only because the protestors went home to pack a rucksack. By the time they entered the foothills of Snowdonia, the marchers were not necessarily numerous, but were certainly loud enough to have news crews from all corners of the land heading their way.

'Where are you going? What do you want?' they were asked.

'We're going south. We're going to create hell.'

If the march from Caernarfon set off in anger it soon settled down. Through the Snowdonia National Park the movement was cheered in every village, and children waving Welsh flags took the sting out of the rage. The children kept a tally of the numbers and posted them on banners: 36 out of Caernarfon, 52 into Llanberis, 78 in Capel Curig and 103 in Betws-y-coed. Food was delivered at every mile-post and at every junction. Some of the marchers took up the offer of a bed for the night along the way, but far from disappearing, they would reappear the next day, often with reinforcements. The mission statement remained the same, to throw off the yoke of the 'Welsh Not', but there were so many expressions of thanks that the tone softened. Raising hell became a peace march, and was all the more popular for it.

At Betws-y-coed the march halted and there were fears that it was the end of the road, a suspicion that the purest of Welsh speakers dared not break out of their Snowdonia citadel. But they were only waiting. On the second day, a convoy of four black funeral cars bearing four empty coffins rolled slowly into town. Behind the cortege were tractors pulling trailers and on these stood the Trelawnyd male voice choir. Rhyl had responded and was on the move, too. The marchers from the north-west now had a motorised escort from the north-east, and together, at walking pace, they set off along the A470, singing every inch of the way. The next tally-banner, embroidered by the schoolchildren of Blaenau Ffestiniog, showed 247, carefully stitched in red.

Cars that beeped by way of support were allowed to pass through the march. The only vehicles that snaked in and out of the walkers without a sound were Hazel's snack caravan and the battered old Land Rover Defender towing it, driven by Hazel's husband, Brian, from Blackburn. Four times a day, Brian and Hazel leapfrogged the column and put a few miles between it and themselves, sufficient distance for them to restock the shelves and the fridges and heat up the water and be ready when the march came through. Brian was supposed to be retired and enjoying his fishing and the occasional puff on his pipe, but he found himself driving from a wholesaler in one town to a cash-and-carry in the next. He didn't understand a word of what the marchers were going on about, but Brian was having the time of his life.

The only bad odour on the march came from the Defender. The pistons on Brian's old Land Rover began to wear and the walkers found themselves following a trail of smoke. The problem disappeared outside Builth Wells, where the marchers found Hazel's van parked not behind the Defender, but hitched to a brand new Nissan Navara, picked up on a diversion by Brian to Llandrindod Wells. The leaders of the march viewed this purchase not as profiteering by their caterers, one of whom they found having a snooze behind the wheel of his new pride and joy with *The Angling Times* in his lap, but a reflection of the growing strength of their ranks.

The long pull through mid Wales had been expected to see a drop in numbers. Instead, the throng grew. At first the gains were slightly dry and dusty: a few academics over from Aberystwyth and a small posse of rather stern representatives from the University of Wales Trinity Saint David in Lampeter, including the letter-writing Professor Meirion Owen Jones, all drawn to the movement by the news that members of BBC Wales's senior management were on their way up from Cardiff to meet the leaders. The new arrivals came with a serious tread, but from the other direction came youngsters by the handful, and behind the professors came hippie troubadours, who brought a new music to the march. The manly strains of Trelawnyd were supplemented by the floating harmonies of the western woods and if there was now a narcotic fragrance to the evening air it was soon swallowed up by the smoke from Hazel's burger grill, a new addition to her facilities. Word spread, and iphotos proved it, that something was happening on the road, and that people had to be there to believe it. A steady trickle came in under banners of Welshpool and Newtown, heading for the party on the move and the carnival that awaited the march in Builth Wells.

The senior management of BBC Wales requested a meeting with the leaders of the march in the BBC pavilion on the Royal Welsh Showground across the River Wye from Builth, in Llanelwedd. When the column reached the entrance, on the A470, it wasn't just the head that turned left. The body of the snake and the tail followed it through the gate and spread out over the main arena. The schoolchildren of Builth divided themselves up into groups and did a head-count: 423 flashed up on the arena screen.

Across the river, the townsfolk of Builth looked rather anxiously at the showground. A scouting party was sent over the bridge to see if the march had come to a full halt, or was pausing. Without a fixture that weekend, Builth Rugby Football Club had been preparing the stalls for their eighth annual real-ale festival when they heard about what was heading their way. With a swift call to arms and a word with the licensing authorities, they decided to bring forward the opening of their 'Aprilfest' by 48 hours and turn it into a four-day festival, not two. The scouting party was about to break open the packets of circulars, promoting their event, when the message reached the marchers on the showground that Builth was a town awash in beer. Within half an hour, the only people left in Llanelwedd were the dozen heavyweights of Welsh broadcasting and the language, meeting in the BBC pavilion, now overlooking an empty arena. The big screen was turned off. The protest march had snaked back out, crossed the Wye and would not budge for four whole days.

31

The most important person in the life of Martin Guest was not Grace Courtney, even if the owner of Steel-Ag had to admit that she was the most striking partner to have been paraded on his arm. Grace was too new in his life to be indispensable. No, the person Martin needed most was the Professor, who was like no other in working through the labyrinthine regulations that governed planning and grant funding. Martin could place him in a unitary authority, have him seconded to the Welsh Assembly Government, send him to a meeting with a bureaucrat in Brussels, with a community councillor in a pub in the back of beyond, or simply order him to the library for the day, and the Professor would come back with the information required: the land that could be acquired, the official that could be persuaded to go with a proposal, the money it would cost to grease that palm and, above all, the greater reward that could be wrung out of all the systems. The Professor was king of the systems of sub-national government. The Professor was a genius. And it helped Martin no end that the Professor was gay.

The secret was out. Clive Jones, from Alloys, hadn't been able to resist spreading around the Steel-Ag boardroom in Cardiff what he had seen the Professor doing in the lower folds of the great sand dune of Pyla one summer. It was, the gossip merchant hastened to add, not by design that he had stumbled upon this indiscretion. Clive happened to be on holiday in France, with his girlfriend it went without saying, and was romping with her to the top of the beauty spot overlooking Arcachon Bay, when they chanced upon the Professor, wrapped in the arms of a bronzed man. For somebody known at Steel-Ag as Mr Guest's mystery man, the Professor had rather given his game away.

The next thing Martin knew, the Professor was in his office begging him to make sure this went no further. The Professor was a genius, but he had a weakness for rugby and somewhere in his great engine of a brain he had the notion firmly planted that his beloved club would never be able to stand the outing of their wing three-quarter.

It was not exactly a coincidence that the Professor was playing his sport in the very place where Martin was toying with the notion of building a production unit. The entrepreneur had heard that any scheme to bring industry to the top of the Valleys would be viewed favourably. A small-scale specialist works might fit into his plans for expansion. It all depended on the start-up money available and the price, if any, of the land up there on the edge of the world. The Professor's research took him up there, and there he had remained, stuck in its high desolation, devoted to the sorry place, or at least to its rugby club.

Strange, Martin thought. But he liked the Professor and he needed him. He had a sharp word with Clive, exacting a vow that the scurrilous story would not be repeated. And to lighten the spirits of its victim, his most important man, and to promote goodwill all round, he had proposed a Sunday meeting at the rugby club when he would unveil a sponsorship package, modest by his standards, sizeable, he suspected, by theirs. And he had invited Grace to be there, because he liked her too.

Martin had always thought of himself as classless. His father, George, had been a toolmaker at Longbridge in Birmingham, a skilled worker in the tail-end years of mass car production in the country. When he was finally laid off, he went into the guesthouse business in Bromsgrove with his wife, Kitty. Martin's mother was devoted to George, but was always reluctant to expand their family. One son, and never an easy one from conception to delivery, was more than enough. Happier in adult company, Kitty helped George run the Guest guesthouse, and shared his mirth at the name, until they discovered what hard work it was.

One day during the school summer holidays when he was 14, Martin was listening to George dealing with an awkward customer, a rep who had complained about everything in the Guest establishment from the moment he arrived. As he was leaving he naturally had queries about the bill and George patiently explained that, yes, sir had ordered a second bottle of wine on the third night, and a third on the fourth night, when he had dinner with his district manager. But he calmly deducted the price of a bottle of the house Rioja from the bill.

'He cheated you. And you let him get away with it,' said Martin. 'You work like slaves and he's robbed you.'

George went to the small window by the front door and turned the sign around, to show No Vacancies to the outside world.

'The slave says he's taking the day off. Come on.'

They walked out of the house at a brisk pace, past Sanders Park, all the way to the M5. They stood on a bridge over the motorway, watching the traffic streaming beneath them. Lorries and buses went past with a roar, sending a blast of air upwards, but it was the cars that interested George.

'Wonders of science, Martin,' he said. 'Even the ones made in Longbridge. And heaven knows we did our best to make them badly.'

Martin had noticed that his father's Birmingham accent had softened with the move to Bromsgrove. They were still in the West Midlands but his voice was less twanged now. His mother had never had a Birmingham accent. She was from Dundee.

They watched a Porsche go flying down the outside lane and brake sharply behind a queue of slower traffic.

'Nice car that,' said George. 'German, of course.' He put his hands on the railing and looked straight down. 'In the December after my sixtieth birthday I'm going to make my last repayment to the bank. Your mother and I will own what we have one hundred per cent. That's our goal.'

The move to Bromsgrove was not the last George and

Kitty made in their new career. They built up their business there through reps and lower-tier management on upgrade courses, and then sold and moved west to Ledbury, pursuing tourists less bound to their *per diem* expense accounts. And then they exchanged the attractions of the Malvern Hills for the Wye Valley, buying a B&B not far from Ross. And from the far reaches of England they made one last move, into Wales, buying their last small hotel, two miles from Crickhowell on the River Usk. Each new hotel cost a little less than the one they left behind, but soon it was worth more as they grew the new business. They chiselled away and over the years took regular, small chunks out of their debt. The Guests worked tirelessly and uncomplainingly. At each new place, George lost a little more of his accent. By the time he reached Crickhowell, he was neutral of voice, the classless father of a classless son. And the former toolmaker and card-carrying member of the Amalgamated Union of Engineering Workers was now a stalwart of the Crickhowell Conservative and Unionist Club.

Martin was, according to his father, thoughtful. To Kitty, he was remote. He was not bad academically at his various schools, and quite good as a midfielder in their football teams. Where he came into his own was at work in the holidays. He never worked for his parents in their guest houses, but found jobs within cycling range until he learned to drive. Everywhere, he improved systems and productivity. In Ledbury, he worked in the Pultney Furniture workshop and changed the way materials came in and finished goods went out. Within a week, the Pultney store went from being chaotically cluttered to never more than five-sixths full. The extra capacity was there for peak periods, like Christmas. Every item was labelled and catalogued as never before.

At the Stoneham Bakery outside Ross, he changed the routine for lightly oiling the tins before they went into the oven, and even as the family were congratulating him on saving them ten minutes, enough to grab a cup of tea at half past five in the morning, he was preparing a bike tour of their customers. By the end of his second week, he had increased orders for sandwich loaves by eight per cent.

He saved every penny he made, left school after securing a C in English at A Level, a D in History and an A in Economics, the only subject that interested him, and bought himself a van which he packed with meticulously researched and carefully purchased items, mostly to do with spare parts for agricultural machinery in the Crickhowell area. He sold the lot, item by item, to farmers who were notoriously canny with their money. They had a good deal, thinking they had edged the whippersnapper in the negotiations, and Martin doubled his money. By the time he was twenty-five, he had bought his first factory, making cheap suitcases in Tredegar, and by the time he was twenty-seven he had sold it and owned three more factories in the Valleys, and was an investor in a specialist steel plant in Cardiff. When he was thirty and about to sign the documents that made him the sole owner of Steel-Ag, Martin phoned his father on Christmas Day.

'Can I ask you, Dad, if you made that last payment you once talked to me about? Are you the outright owners of the Guest guesthouse? Are you going to be well-off and respectable now?'

There was a long pause at the other end.

'I'm dying of cancer, son,' said George Guest eventually, with a hint of Birmingham back in his voice.

Two months later, Martin went to the funeral and awkwardly embraced his mother and told her that if she needed any help with the sale of the guest house, he was there for her. She told him she was sure she could manage. He was back in the Steel-Ag boardroom for a meeting by two o'clock.

32

Sunday lunchtimes at the rugby club were busy now. The day that used to be dry in Wales now produced the best bar takings of the week, although with Our Marnie's departure, the committee were back behind the bar and nobody expected the announcement of a bumper profit. George Prosser, Hayden Coles, Malc Phillips and Tony Moreton were not yet called the Widowers, but they were on their way, persuaded by the upturn in the playing fortunes of the team to add this extra Sunday session to the time they spent in each other's company. It allowed them to discuss the previous day's game with the benefit of a good night's sleep behind them. Gonzo's form filled their analysis, but today there was something else on the agenda, and they had to sit in silence for a time. Martin Guest was speaking and everybody was listening. Even so, when Gonzo came in they all nudged each other and chuckled.

'There's a plucked chicken in the house,' said George.

Gonzo thought he'd be able to sneak through the club and go up to the flat to finish off the last bit of painting. Martin, casually but expensively turned out, paused as this unkempt shaven-headed latecomer in spattered overalls held up his hands in apology, shuffled across the floor and went up the stairs.

Grace watched him go. She smiled as a few more teasing rumbles about hair followed Gonzo out of the room, and felt for no more than a second an urge to take her hand away from where Martin had placed it, on his arm, as he broke the good news of his sponsorship of the club. The committeemen, behind and in front of the bar, could not have looked more delighted. Upstairs, Gonzo was dipping his brush into the last pot of brilliant white emulsion when the clapping and cheering started.

Dario Aspetti was passing the clubhouse on his crutches. The club sat at the end of its street and beyond lay the moorland. A gate led to it and was also the start of a path down to the rugby pitch, on the other side of the old pithead. Dario had taken a right turn and had spent an hour sitting in a little windbreak of rock on the moorland, listening to the landscape, watching the clouds bring their stories in from the Atlantic. Back on West Street, heading for the same caravan off the Garn-yr-erw Road – but with a few more holes in the floor now – he heard the applause and the cheering. He quickly crossed the street. He feared a crowd spilling out of the bar and sending him flying, but all went quiet again.

He hobbled away, wanting to be back in time for the Welsh derby on S4C. Nobody else in the village took any interest in professional rugby. Everyone naturally supported their own club and went down to Cardiff on international days to pledge their blind faith to the cause of Wales. But for the rugby between the village and the national team they cared not a jot. The politics of the middle ground left them cold, the number of regions didn't matter, what competitions they played in was irrelevant, the comings and goings of overseas players were of no interest, the departure of the best Welsh players to clubs in England, France or even Japan was unimportant. Dario worried – strange, he admitted, for a man who had never gone further than the edge of the escarpment – because he did not believe the village could shut itself off from the outside world. The occasional rugby away day in the league or the cup did not count, in Dario's eyes, as interaction with planet Earth. It was merely one bubble floating to another bubble. Dario had no logical explanation for why he worried so. Why did he cross the road, he wondered, away from the sound of cheering? Perhaps he felt it was the duty of someone unable to make a traditional contribution to the story of his home – a tale based entirely on manual labour – to be its sentinel. To know things that might protect the uninquisitive. He swung himself towards his caravan.

Gonzo finished painting and lay on the floor staring at the ceiling. Our Marnie's place was finished at last, but instead of thinking about her, Gonzo listened to the rumble from the bar downstairs, the buzz of the aftermath of the visit by Martin Guest. The girl on his arm, was she his wife? He thought of her staring at him as he ran into the Keeper's Pond. Him, with no clothes on and his head freshly chopped and scarred. He stood up, rinsed the last brush and picked up the last tin of paint, closed the door of Our Marnie's flat and turned the key. It would be many years before it was unlocked.

Dario had tucked his legs under him on the threadbare sofa-bed in his caravan. He had a finger of shortbread halfway to his mouth when the game stopped. Television directors were sometimes reluctant to show rugby's more extreme injuries, but the collision had seemed innocuous. In slow motion, however, the unnatural movement of the limbs was revealed. The knee of the number 8, Kevin Mulwinney, could be seen bending to the side as he was tackled, while the ankle of Sparks van der Linden, one of his fellow back-rows, was trapped when the same tackler who had just ruptured Mulwinney's anterior cruciate ligament fell heavily to the ground. Van der Linden's studs were planted in the ground, but his body twisted as he fell over. The number 8 was left clutching the middle of his left leg, the wing forward staring at the end of his right. His foot should by now have been pointing at the sky. Instead it was at ninety degrees to his shin, lying against the ground. It took eleven minutes to secure the limbs and carry the two players off on stretchers, oxygen masks over their mouths. Dario groaned when he saw the replay, not because he was shocked at the sight or reminded by the pain of others of his own disability, but because he knew what this might mean.

The following Saturday morning at eleven o'clock, he stood at the top of the steps in the square and looked towards the café. Meg and Annie were sitting at a table by the window. Meg looked up at him and waved. Dario struggled down the steps and pressed his face against the window.

'Bloody hell, Dario,' he could hear Meg say through the glass. 'You look like Capper Harris ready to go down in the scrum.'

Dario backed off an inch. 'They'll be coming for him,' he said.

'What's that, love?' shouted Annie.

'You mark my words,' said Dario in a louder voice, 'They'll be coming for him.' And he scuttled away.

That afternoon, two strangers stood on the far side, opposite the small grandstand and near the uphill 22, as the line was called on the slightly sloping pitch. The village were playing a league fixture against a team struggling to stay in existence.

'Aye, aye,' said George Prosser from his seat in the stand, nodding towards the visitors. 'Looks as if Dario could be right.'

'They could be with that lot,' said Hayden Coles, with a gesture towards the twenty or so away-team supporters who were leaning against the railing on the far side, a few yards nearer the halfway line.

'No way,' said Malc Phillips. 'They've got big city written all over them.'

'There goes Dario,' said Hayden, spotting the little figure edging conspicuously towards the strangers. 'He may frighten 'em away.'

'Aye, but here comes Gonzo,' said Tony, as Gonzo scattered three tacklers out of his path and crashed over. 'He might make 'em stay.'

The game was over before half-time. Gonzo scored another try and could have scored a lot more, but chose to pass the ball to others. In particular, he supplied the Professor, whose confidence always needed a little boosting. The strangers did not stay long, but as they left after half an hour, there was a shuffling in the stand to make way for Martin and Grace.

'Sorry we're late,' said the new sponsor. 'So, how are we doing?'

'We're winning easily,' said Edgar Parsons. 'Which may or may not be good news.' The Piggybank, too, had seen the strangers.

They came back the following Wednesday and met Gonzo in the house he and Capper were renovating. Gonzo wanted Capper to stay, to help him ask some awkward questions, to help him find a way to stay, but the hooker shook hands with the strangers and left.

'Those boys who got hurt,' said Gonzo, handing the pair a mug of tea and sitting down on a trestle. He wished he could remember the names of the players. He wished for that matter he could remember the strangers' names, but despite having been introduced to them only five minutes earlier, his head seemed to have turned soggy. 'Those boys,' he managed to continue, 'They were international players. An All Black and a Springbok, right?' The strangers nodded. 'Don't you want a player of that experience to replace them?'

The first stranger took a cautious sip from the mug that wasn't spotless. 'We'll be frank with you. You've probably heard there's a bit of a row going on. The regions and the Welsh Rugby Union. Same old story, except it's coming to a head. And right now, let's put it like this, it's in our interest to pull a home-grown player out of the hat.'

Gonzo, wishing he had Dario here, didn't know anything about regions and rows. But he tried again: 'If you want home-grown then why not go to your academy? You've got the best of the Welsh youngsters there, haven't you?'

The second stranger spoke. 'Well, not right now. Not in the back row. It's partly our fault; partly… look, it's all part of the same thing. The same row, about funding and who controls what. Strictly between us…'

'They're obsessed,' picked up the first, 'with controlling the next generation. 'Give us the child,' they say, 'and we'll give you the grand slam'.'

'And we want to say to them that there are players who develop late, that only we can find… in places like this.'

'Except you don't come here,' said Gonzo.

'We're here now.'

'I'm not some, what d'you call it, some pawn in a game, am I?'

'We're all pawns in our game, Gonzo.'

Dario watched the strangers drive away. He judged their speed, the care they took over the potholes and went to the café.

'They've got him,' he announced. And the heads of Edgar and Meg and Annie, George, Hayden, Malc and Tony, who had been coming here and sitting in silence over a cup of tea at this time in the afternoon for three days, dropped.

'We must congratulate him,' said Edgar, head still bowed. 'Send him on his way with our best wishes.'

There was a murmur of miserable agreement.

'In the old days,' mused Malc at last, 'They used to come up here and flash the cash in a suitcase. I remember my father telling me about the scouts that knocked on the door of Don Quidgeley. Lived in squalor up on George Street, apparently, but had plenty about him on the field. They showed him the money and off he went. Packed a bag there and then and jumped in the car with 'em. 'Don's gone North,' they'd say. And that was the end of him. Up to rugby league, and not allowed back into the club in his home village.'

'Not officially,' said Tony.

'Never allowed to play in Wales again.'

'Different now,' said Hayden.

'Aye,' said Malc, 'Gonzo's gone South.'

'Don't be so soft,' said Capper when Gonzo said he didn't fancy life as a pawn. 'This is the chance of a fuckin' lifetime in rugby and you can't afford to worry about playing fuckin' chess. And don't tell me I don't get it. I do get it. It's simple: you're a player. So play. Fuck the politics.'

Capper allowed Gonzo to give him one hug.

'Right, bugger off now and let me get on with this brickwork.'

And that was his last line. Gonzo left him at work and headed down the valley and over to Cardiff. He moved into a rented flat in Cardiff Bay, and a car, second-hand but with low mileage, was put at his disposal. He was asked to share both his accommodation and his transport with the other new signing on a probationary contract, a giant called Gareth Mewson from the academy. Almost as soon as Gonzo arrived, however, there was a fresh outbreak of feuding over funding and the Mewson deal fell through. Gonzo found himself a single player covering for two injuries on a probationary contract. But after he had been seen in action, he was swiftly upgraded to a full contract. Gonzo had truly gone South.

33

Gwyn arrived in Bilbao in the autumn of 1936. He had set sail for the Basque Country from Cardiff a week after listening to a speaker in the Cine-Variety cinema in the city tell of the uprisings by large parts of the Spanish army and their Nationalist cause to overthrow the Republican government. Spain was involved in a civil war. Gwyn was aware that he had spent the last year doing nothing but shout and brawl in recruitment meetings, and here he was, hanging on the every word of this man selling the International Brigade to him. He volunteered immediately, his justification to himself being that, since he was on the run anyway, he might as well keep going. Spain's fight against fascism was an extension of what he had been fighting at home.

34

Gonzo found professional rugby easy. He no longer had to do everything, no longer had to make up for the inadequacies of teammates not as accomplished as himself. With the region, he was in the company of players who did their own job without assistance and it was now a question of how they might bring out the best in their new recruit. His fellow forwards threw him high into the air at the line-out with an efficiency and power he had not felt before. For a short time, being new helped. Gonzo was an unknown quantity and was able to make an immediate mark as a runner. He was up against stronger tacklers and better defensive systems, but he was also given the ball at more opportune moments, at angles that allowed him to burst through contact.

The coach, Murray Collins, was from Gore in the deep south of New Zealand. He had played down there, it was said, but had vanished off the radar, resurfacing in Carcassonne and Béziers in France, as a coach. He had coached in the Pro2, the French second division and it was part of the French rugby folklore of Languedoc that he had knocked his supposedly untameable forwards into order, using only his own bare hands. He knew about domesticating animals and thought he had a similar project on his hands with his new recruit. Except Gonzo never lost his temper. He stayed unnervingly calm in the sheds, as Murray still called the changing room, before going out and cold-bloodedly knocking bad people out. He was yellow-carded in his first professional game for clouting Brendan O'Mahoney, a pest of an Irishman who had had it coming, no question, according to the home crowd. They thought their team had been a soft touch for too long and took to their new signing immediately. Gonzo, slightly perplexed at being sent to the sin bin for ten minutes for nothing more heinous than a punch, left to a standing ovation. In the coach's view, it was all very well, but not if it cost the team his services during that period.

'Mate, you're not in your redneck village now,' Murray told him. 'There are cameras and citing officers watching out for people precisely like you. You'll become a liability if you carry on like this. You'll be targeted because other teams will work out that if they prod you, you'll retaliate. That means you're predictable and in my book there's nothing worse.'

In the village and on its rugby field, fighting had been an entirely acceptable way to sort out an issue. Gonzo had no reputation at all as a thug. He was seen at home as a purveyor of swift, fair justice. Now he had to keep his fists down. He kept them low until he saw Caddie Larne, a second row whose own coach did not appear to have given him the same lecture, take down Sam Harris, one of Gonzo's partners in the back row, with a swipe from behind. Sam fell down, joined a second later by Caddie, blood pouring from his nose. Gonzo was heading for the sin-bin even before the referee brought out the yellow card. The crowd roared its approval again, but Murray fined him half a week's wages and told him that next time, he'd find himself back with his cavemen on the mountain.

Three games later, the coach was going through the analysis of a much improved performance by the team in the European Cup, when he paused and replayed an incident where Gethin Hughes, his hooker, jerked his head out of a scrum and pointed to his eyes. The referee had a stern word with the two captains, giving Gethin time, Murray noted, to confer with Gonzo. The referee than delivered a strict lecture to the two sets of front rows, who stared at him with blank innocence before re-engaging in the scrum. Five minutes later, a maul ended with Jean-François Beaujoire, quite the most terrifying enforcer in the European game, sprawled on the ground. In the style of a boxing referee, the crowd counted him out. The referee consulted his touch judges and had a word with the television match official, but nobody had seen a thing untoward. Murray sifted his way in slow motion through the action between the eye-gouging scrum and the exit of the monstrous Frenchman on a stretcher and found nothing either. He went up to Gonzo the next day in training and squeezed his right hand hard. Gonzo, just for a fraction of a second, winced, but then returned the coach's stare without a flicker. Murray squeezed harder still.

'Good game, mate,' he finally said. 'That's more like it.'

When Gonzo became known for his more legitimate skills, and his running with the ball in particular, opposition teams began to pay him special attention, analysing his angles and lines. He remained an elusive step ahead of them, devising ways to avoid the clusters of tacklers now bearing down on him, largely by broadening his range of skills as a passer of the ball. 'A Gonzo' entered rugby parlance, describing a pass at the point of contact, when every other forward was devoted to smashing the life out of defenders and themselves. He had to be durable because to give a pass while taking a tackle left his torso exposed. But he seemed to pick himself up every time. 'Gonzo's got a good chin,' became a chant whenever he, but not the ball, disappeared beneath a whirl of defenders.

35

In Bilbao the volunteers of the International Brigade came and went on the dockside, moving back and forth under orders that took them nowhere. There was no parade through the streets, but people from the city did come to the quayside to hand out bread and cheese to the groups that stuck together according to nationality. After half a day, they were all reassembled and then divided up again and taken to the stores. They were given rifles, some of which were brand new, others ancient. Ammunition was counted out sparingly by a Belgian volunteer at the stores and distributed.

'Mes camarades, please do not waste these bullets,' said the armourer, putting his hands together beseechingly.

Gwyn found himself heading west in the company of Canadians and Americans. They talked, but their conversations soon dried up because the unknown ahead dominated their thoughts and they did not wish to share their fears. They trundled their way by train and lorry into the coal valleys of Asturias and then found themselves without transport. Their last order was to climb southwards, up towards the high plateau and the regions of Old Castile and León, which had fallen to the Nationalists.

One day, when the complaints about blisters and the

lack of food were at their loudest, a shout came from the rear and they turned to see a pair of trucks in the distance behind them. The men fanned out from the middle of the road and watched intently, until a figure opened the door on the moving lorry in front, leant out and gave the salute of the International Brigade, a raised arm with fist clenched. Gwyn's group re-formed and they waited for the lorries to catch them up. A Spanish officer in the brand new Regular Popular Army invited them on board and untied a sack, full of bread and ham. They drove for half a mile and stopped to take their fill of water from a pump in a small village. They set off again immediately, the uphill road twisting and turning. In a swirl of dust, they advanced slowly towards the front. After ten miles the lorries stopped at a crossroads on the rough road and the officer, in broken English, divided the group into three. Two groups of Americans climbed back into the rear of the lorries and the driver of the second, with a grating of gears, turned the vehicle to face west. Once in position, he stopped, waiting for the order to leave. The Spanish officer climbed into the front seat of the first lorry – that was facing east – and looked down at Gwyn and the ten Canadians.

'Please,' he said, pointing straight ahead.

'What do you want us to do?' asked one of the Canadians.

'Go. Look. Report.'

'On foot?' asked another Canadian.

'I am sorry,' said the officer. He looked to the west. 'That way there is fighting.' He turned to the east. 'This way there is fighting. We must go with speed.'

'And this way?' asked Gwyn.

'We do not know, compañeros. So, please, go, look and report.'

He gave the driver a nod and the lorries headed off in opposite directions. Gwyn and the Canadians were left at the crossroads, alone in an arid land. A couple of the group started to reach for their rations. Gwyn stepped forward.

'See that ridge ahead?' he said. 'How about we stop for a bite up there? Admire the view. Walk and look. That'll make us a patrol. Proper soldiers.'

36

The games rolled on through the autumn and when the pitches grew heavier, Gonzo grew less committed to delivering adventurous passes, but instead pumped his legs through the mud. He played against Callum Browne and Stuart Craig, Scottish back row players who had become something of a double-act in the tackle, the one going low from one side and the other going high from the other. They were the first to make a mess of Gonzo in his professional career, Stuart smashing into his ribs and Callum simultaneously chopping him down below the knees. The ball went loose and was scooped up by the tacklers' teammates and carried thirty metres downfield.

'So, that's a Gonzo is it, pal?' said Callum to the player he'd helped tackle.

The next time Gonzo had the ball he deliberately stepped into the space guarded by the two specialist tacklers. He jumped out of Callum's tackle and handed Stuart off so hard that the Scotsman's gum shield flew six feet into the air. And the third time he went into their space, and as they came at him even harder to settle the score, he slipped a ball to Gethin the hooker, who ran away to score.

'No, that's a Gonzo,' said Sam Harris.

It took another week to answer the last but one question posed in the *Western Mail*: 'He can pass, but can he run?' In the game against the league leaders, Gonzo ran in a try from fifty metres, and the few who had doubted his speed at the outset of his professional career now had to admit he was fast enough to play in the three-quarters. Whole sections of the rugby programmes on BBC Wales and S4C were devoted to his power and gait. The last question began to be asked: how long would it be before Gonzo Davies played for Wales?

37

The only people Gwyn and the Canadians met on their first day of walking were small groups of civilians coming toward them, walking away from the war. There was no flood, no mass exodus, but an irregular procession of silent refugees. After an uncomfortably cold night under the stars, the patrol set off again and this time they were on their own. They passed through the front line without knowing they were now in enemy-held territory. There were no trenches, no artillery barrages, no shots, no flags flying from the highest tower to say which side a village was on.

They knew they had reached the war zone only by the pile of corpses they came across in the square of the village of Villaobispo de los Pozos. Five minutes earlier, the patrol had been strolling across open fields; now they stood stock-still before naked death. The bodies of twenty men and women had been stripped and mutilated, piled high and left deliberately on display. Inside a house on the square, one of the Canadians found half a dozen children, all dead.

The only people alive in the village were old women. The patrol found them by following the sound of shovels, scratching away at the soil in the cemetery. The women looked up at the soldiers with eyes so vacant that a few of the Canadians said later it was the worst thing about that day in Villaobispo – the eyes of the survivors. At the far end of the cemetery, a line of twelve men stood. They had been shot, but could not fall to the ground because they were tied by wire around their throats to nails, driven into wooden posts. Gwyn thought there was perhaps one thing worse than the unseeing eyes of the women: the smell of decomposing corpses in the village.

38

Wales were not at their best in the autumn internationals. They played a warm-up game against Georgia and scrambled to a win, but then faced New Zealand at the Millennium Stadium, and all the confidence instilled by the Six Nations campaign of the previous season evaporated in twenty minutes. It did not provoke a crisis because this was a tale often told, of Wales thinking they had a chance against the All Blacks, only to see it come to nothing. It did, however, prompt a rethink in selection for the last game of November, an awkward encounter against Argentina. The name of Gonzo Davies was pitched into the debate and then put to one side. He was still inexperienced, too raw to be thrown into international rugby. He hadn't, moreover, been selected for the national squad and hadn't been in camp with the top players.

When Albie Thomas, the experienced reserve number 8, felt a twinge in his hamstring, however, Gonzo was invited to join the squad for training. It meant he would be holding tackle bags for the senior players as they were given a vigorous workout, a reminder of the good habits they seemed to have forgotten, before the last Test. For two days, Gonzo was bounced around on bag duty and his mind was sent into a spin by all the calls and moves. The coach told him not to worry and the players did their best to explain, but Gonzo found himself thinking he'd be relieved when the match-day squad was announced and he could go back to Cardiff.

The virus then struck and six of the team were ordered to take to their beds. The medical staff hoped it would be one of those twenty-four hour afflictions and that everybody would be fit in time, but by Wednesday nobody had emerged from under their covers. The announcement of the squad was delayed until the Thursday. Three were still running a fever and at midday the name of Gonzo Davies was included in the Wales team to play Argentina.

39

As they made their way back to the valleys of Asturias, Gwyn and his group were absorbed into a heavier flow of refugees on the high plain, families fleeing the Nationalist zone for the slice of Spain in the north still loyal to the Republic. There was urgency now in the retreat. It was no longer a trudge along the road, with belongings piled high on carriages and handcarts, but a flight with nothing heavier than a small hastily packed suitcase. After them came the enemy, under orders from General Franco to relieve the siege of Oviedo, where the garrison had risen in favour of the Nationalists. Republican Asturias was falling fast and the flow turned into a flood as they descended into a greener landscape on the coastal side of the mountains.

Two days after reeling away from Villaobispo de los Pozos, Gwyn's group came across a large old Citroën, painted with a red cross, by the side of the road. The driver of this temporary ambulance was changing a punctured tyre and, while the refugees walked quickly past in silence, Gwyn talked to the injured soldiers, three Frenchmen and an American, who had been placed in the sun by a ditch. He described to them what they had found in the village.

'It's what they do,' said Frank Sumner, his arm in a sling. He had taken a bullet in the shoulder during a skirmish near Barruelo. He asked if Gwyn had any spare water and took a careful sip from the flask held out to his good hand. 'They send in the regular troops to take a village or town. If they succeed, they flush out the Reds and shoot them. But the regulars only stay until the reserve arrives, and if it's the mercenaries, then the place is in big trouble. They're real bad. It's all about terror. This is a war of terror, and they want people – including their own people – to know it.'

They wished each other good luck and the group set off again. Soon, they arrived at the small town of Almancillas, a crossing point over a tumbling stream. The town's narrow bridge was now a bottleneck and the refugees were already backing up on the approach road. Those at the back continued to shuffle forward, pressing against the crowd in front. Everybody was encouraged to be patient, then ordered sharply to hold their nerve. They quietened down, and their resigned silence allowed them to hear the distant, but approaching, rumble of aircraft.

All the bombs from the single pass missed the target. All bar one that struck the middle of the bridge. The entire structure folded into the ravine. When the dust cleared and the sound of the bombers had faded, the refugees cautiously made their way back to the ravine, checking the skies for a second wave. They peered over the edge and a young boy jumped down and plotted a course over the pile of rubble. Men and women followed him, clambering down the steep side, grabbing a branch or clinging to a fallen block of stone, handing young children from to adult to adult. The climb up the other side was even more exacting. It was a slow process, and fear spread among those waiting on the upstream side.

Suddenly there was another low moan, but not from the air. Somebody in the long line had turned to look back up the valley, and on the distant skyline had seen lorries. The groan of despair became a roar of blind panic and there was a rush towards the stream. People were pushed over the side if they hesitated. The ravine was filled with screaming and the sound was carried upwards and outwards, echoing all around the valley.

Gwyn was studying the road they had come down through binoculars. Between the lorries at the top of the pass and Almancillas there was a small village. He rounded up the group and pointed to the way they had come. They all set off, back up the mountain. A huge cloud of dust filled the air above the mayhem in the gorge, but a smaller cloud broke away and moved uphill as Gwyn and his group ran to face the enemy. There were only eleven of them, but they had all worked out that in Spain war was not always fought on the grand scale. Besides, when they reached the small square of Santa Engracia de Sozuelas, their numbers grew to fifteen. Frank Sumner and the three wounded Frenchmen were sitting in the shade of an oak tree. The ambulance, now with two flat tyres, was parked at the side of the square. Of the driver, there was no sign.

'Thought we might use this as a barricade,' said Frank, pointing at the ambulance and then at the entrance to the square that faced the skyline to the south. 'But then we thought there's probably a Geneva Convention saying we can't do that. And you know how they respect the Geneva Convention in these parts.'

'So, we meet again,' said Gwyn, shaking the American and the Frenchmen by whichever of their hands was still working. The Canadians passed around their water bottles. 'Anyone have a plan?'

40

Gonzo was losing control of himself. He had to adapt to the ways of the international team – his team now – but his head was spinning. He had three of his teammates from his region here, Sam and Gethin and Huw Martins at full back, who all seemed relaxed and did their best to make him feel at home, but the routines and schedules and instructions were so alien that Gonzo could not think straight. He had been spiralling out of control for a whole day, ever since his name was read out and the texts and calls started to pour in. He had never ever felt nervous, not once in his entire life, about rugby, until these past few weeks. First the decision to go south, and now this. His brain had turned soggy at his first meeting with the strangers from the region. But now he had full liquid mush between his ears. He feared something foul-smelling was going to seep out of his head. He fumbled with the keypad on his phone and managed to send two texts of his own, one to Capper, to say that he was on his way up to the village, and one to Murray, saying he was losing it.

'Losing what?' Murray had texted back.

'It. Big time.' replied Gonzo.

He was in camp, not far from Cardiff in the Vale of Glamorgan, but as soon as the final captain's run was over, he headed for the car. Before he reached it, he saw Murray striding towards him. And then his phone beeped.

'Stay 'kin put,' Capper texted.

'Who's that from?' said Murray bluntly.

Gonzo held out the phone. 'An old mate,' he said.

'Is he a caveman?'

Gonzo nodded. Murray glanced at the message.

'Seems pretty good advice, for a Troglodyte,' said Murray. He pulled Gonzo away from his car and they began to walk slowly around the car park.

'I could give you a right bollocking for letting all this get to you. But you know something? It happened to me. I was picked for an All Black trial. Hell, it was almost on my bloody doorstep, in Dunedin. It was like a dream come true for two days. I was tough as old boots and this was my destiny. But the day before the game, I couldn't get out of bed. I lay there in some kind of bloody trance. And I played like it the next day. The day of destiny turned into my day of doom. I never played again. I became so involved in trying to analyse what had happened that before I knew it I was coaching. And you know what? I still don't know what flipped in my head. But it's not going to happen to you, Gonzo. You're going to breathe and say to yourself that it's only a game of bloody footie, which, mate, it just so happens you're bloody good at.'

Night was falling fast. Murray held out his hand.

'And keep this to yourself,' he said, shaking Gonzo's hand and giving his fist a final squeeze. 'No bloody fighting. Now bugger off before you catch bloody pneumonia. That'd be the only excuse I might accept for you not playing well.'

Murray's words had kept Gonzo going through an almost sleepless night. He had eventually dropped off in the early hours of Saturday morning and had awoken early. He was the first down to breakfast. Time crawled for him through the late morning of his first international, and he was glad there were meetings and more meetings to keep the clock ticking. He was still not one hundred per cent confident, however, that he had fully absorbed the moves and plays. He had to finger through a painfully compiled list in his head, rather than have them automatically come to mind on command. He was worried not so much now about the grand occasion of the afternoon, but was bogged down in the detail of his job.

In the changing room he was replaying Murray's every word in his head, but, minutes away from the start of the game, he was still fighting a rising panic. He sucked in the air so hard he felt a pain in his ribs. He tried to draw inspiration from the red shirt he held in his hands. But even a flush of pride seemed to be the wrong chemical to throw into the mix of hormones surging through him. He felt sick. In fact, he was sick, and rushed to bend over a toilet bowl, thinking as he retched that this was no way to frighten an Argentine forward. And thinking of them made him feel worse and he lowered his head into the bowl again. With a taste of bile on his fingers, he pulled the shirt of Wales over his head.

The crowd of 35,000 filled less than half of the Millennium Stadium, but their noise was still a physical barrier and he seemed to bounce off it. He had never heard a sound so loud and it seemed to scramble his brain even more. He didn't hear the anthems, but stood in line and forced himself to concentrate, to think of what he had to do. 'It's only a game of rugby, Gonzo,' he repeated to himself over and over again.

The game started and a new roar split the air. Twenty minutes passed and he did nothing. He thought maybe five at most had elapsed, but was horrified to look up at the clock on the big screen and see that a quarter of the game had disappeared and the only thing he knew was that he was so exhausted he could hardly draw a breath. He had thought once the game was underway he'd be fine, he'd settle down and find his feet. But his chest was quivering uncontrollably and his hands were shaking. He had been thrown to the ground by players twice as strong as any he had ever come across. As he was looking at the screen, he saw himself projected on it, a giant close-up of wide-eyed helplessness.

41

The aim was to buy enough time for the refugees to escape to the other side of the ravine. Three hours might do it. They did not have the ammunition to hold out for longer. The plan after that was to run like hell. The moment Gwyn said it he knew there would be a problem with the wounded. Frank held up his good hand.

'Let's cross that bridge when we reach it,' he said. 'If only we had a bridge to cross…'

As far as they could tell, the village was empty. They thought about using the church tower but decided that concentrated fire from a group would be more effective. Besides, they had a clear view from ground level, all the way up the road to the top of the valley. So, they stayed together and kept watch.

They didn't have to wait too long before the lorries, three of them, began to lumber down the road. The group waited for Gwyn's command, and he in his turn waited and waited.

'Steady, steady,' he said calmly. When the lorries were so big that the defenders could see the face of the leading driver, he almost whispered his last command: 'Fire.' Gwyn's first shot shattered the windscreen of the lorry. It slewed to a halt.

The fusillade caused the second lorry to crash into the back of the first, but with a scramble in the seats and a crashing of gears, all three vehicles reversed out of range without further casualties. The next time they came forward, they had covering fire from mortars. Explosions shook the ground beyond the village. Nobody inside it was hit. Soldiers followed on foot behind the lorries. Three fell when they tried to leave their cover and storm the square. The lorries reversed again. The next time they advanced, they stopped further away, drawing fire. It was as if somebody was doing a calculation about the strength of the defence, saving mortar rounds. The lorries edged forward again, drawing more fire. And then reversed. And so it went on until the lorries approached the square and stopped, and not a bullet came their way. The defenders were out of ammunition.

Gwyn ordered the four wounded into the ambulance. If they could set it rolling it might freewheel, even with two flat tyres, down the hill. They were all pushing the heavy car towards the square's exit at the rear when a line of soldiers appeared there and raised their rifles. The ambulance stopped in the middle of the square. More soldiers appeared from the front and at the sides. The defenders were surrounded. Slowly, they reached for the rifles slung over their shoulders, dropped them to the ground and raised their hands. They had held out for four hours.

42

It clicked for Wales in the second half. Having stuttered and stumbled through two and a half games, the champions of the Six Nations rediscovered their rhythm, and they began to play fluently. And swept along in the flow was the new cap. Instead of going across the field, or being rocked on his heels, or thrown down unceremoniously, Gonzo began to run straight and true. His confusion cleared and his lungs responded, expanding, letting him suck in the air of the stadium and be uplifted by the atmosphere. Wales ate away at the 12-point deficit until the scores were level. And then they scored the winning try – or rather, Gonzo Davies all on his own scored the winning try, picking up a ball off his toes, one-handed and at full speed, and selling a dummy to the last defender, a feint that he himself described afterwards as 'ridiculous.' He dived for the corner and planted the ball, still in one hand, an inch away from the corner flag.

Nobody moved for a minute in the square of Santa Engracia de Sozuelas. And then the door of the church opened and a priest, no older than thirty, stepped out. An officer – a slightly older captain – stepped out of the ring of soldiers and walked towards him. The soldier knelt before the priest, kissed his hand and stood up. The man of religion reached out and embraced the man of war. Behind them, through the same church door and holding their hands up against the sunlight, came a small stream of old women, dressed in black. They walked straight past the priest and the captain, through the ring of soldiers that shuffled aside to allow them through. The women slowly approached Gwyn and his group. Frank and the Frenchmen hauled themselves out of the Citroën and joined the tight circle, right in the middle of the square. An old woman went up to one of the Canadians and spat in his face. The other women came forward, eyes blazing and spitting at all the men. One picked up a stone and threw it at a Frenchman, hitting him in the chest.

The priest stepped forward and put himself between the women and the prisoners. The casting of stones stopped. Soldiers roughly tied the hands of the prisoners behind their backs. The priest and the captain put their heads together for a short conversation. The captain held out his hand as if to invite the priest to do the honours. The priest turned to the prisoners and surveyed them. He eventually held out an arm encased in its black cassock and pointed at Gwyn. He curled a finger, indicating that he should step out of the group. Gwyn hesitated and the captain stepped forward.

'Better do it, buddy,' muttered Frank over his shoulder.

Gwyn reluctantly left the others and the captain waved him over to the shade of the oak tree.

'You see this?' said the soldier, looking up into the oak tree. 'This tree is a symbol of the freedoms of the people of the Basque Country. The oak.' He spoke English almost without an accent.

'This isn't the Basque Country,' said Gwyn.

'Very good, very good. You know a little about my country. You are English?'

'I'm from Wales,' said Gwyn.

'Ah, another oppressed people. I know England. My family sells sherry to the English. I do not know Wales.' He patted the thick trunk of the tree. 'You do not belong here, man from Wales.'

He raised a finger and the priest stepped out of the way of the women. They picked up stones and began to pelt the prisoners. If any man tried to escape he ran into the butt of a soldier's rifle and was driven back into the circle. The women did not have the strength to keep throwing for long and their supply of stones was limited, but after ten minutes all the prisoners were lying on the ground, bleeding from the face and head. The captain made a slight indication with his finger again, and three junior officers stepped forward, removing pistols from their holsters. They picked their way through the fallen and shot each one twice in the head. The priest stood watching, crossing himself as the shots rang out.

The captain turned to Gwyn when it was done.

'You are lucky to live. You are unlucky to see this.'

He flicked his head and a soldier untied the prisoner's hands.

'Now you may go.'

Gwyn could not move.

'Yes, go. Go and tell the world what is happening in Spain.'

The captain bent down and picked up a small stone.

'One last thing,' he said. And he lobbed the stone at Gwyn, who instinctively reached out and caught it in his right hand. He was immediately seized from behind. He dropped the stone and his catching hand was pressed against the trunk of the tree. A soldier then placed a metal spike against the back of Gwyn's hand and with the single blow of a mallet drove the spike into the oak. Gwyn sagged.

'Look how strong it is, this tree,' said the captain and he held out his hand. A heavy cleaver was placed in his palm by the same soldier, the quartermaster of torture. The captain took careful aim and with a backhand stroke swung the blade. Four fingers fell to the ground. The captain eased the cleaver out of the trunk and handed it back to the soldier, who wiped it clean and slid it into his backpack. The soldier then grabbed the spike and yanked it out. Gwyn collapsed. The soldier wiped the spike and put it away, too.

The captain bent down and almost gently wrapped a cloth around Gwyn's stump. 'You must go now,' he said. 'You have five minutes before the women are turned on you.'

43

Our Marnie didn't give Gonzo another thought after their grope in the store cupboard. It had been a laugh, what friends get up to all the time; one of those things that happen when the night is a little more charged than usual. The one single night. It wasn't even as if anything had happened, anyway. It was all over in three minutes, whatever 'all' was. 'All' was nothing. A kiss, a snog, a fumble. She didn't mind that he hadn't said anything but 'See you, Our Marnie,' after it, whatever 'it' was. It was less than nothing. See you, too, Gonzo bloody Davies. No, she didn't mind at all. She was on her way back to Manchester, thank you very much, a world away from the bloody village she'd been planning to leave for years. So, why should she give anything or anyone from the bloody place another thought? She was Marnie O'Brien and she was looking good.

In Manchester she found herself a fine fellah in no time, a rugby player, Tom, every bit as tall and strapping as anyone else she might know, and probably just as good. And when Tom turned out to be a bit of a bore she found another, Harry, who was definitely the star of the team. Even when he was dropped because he wanted to spend more time with her, she went with it for a while, because Harry made her laugh. And then he didn't, and she met Chris who was... she didn't know what Chris was, except he wasn't Gonzo bloody Davies. Who, by the way, didn't even text her to let her know he'd left the village and was Mr Professional Gonzo bloody Davies now. It had been left to Capper to do that: 'Gonzo's been nabbed by the pros. Hope it hurts. All well here, except we're shit.'

Now Capper, he was different, and if she was ever going back to see anyone it would be him.

'Gonzo's been picked for Wales. We're still shit,' he'd texted at the end of November.

Or the Professor. She liked the Professor. He was kind, unlike some. In fact, she'd be happy to sit down with the Professor, or Capper, and tell him, or them, why it was that she hadn't given Gonzo Davies another thought.

The Professor was always uncomfortable about having Martin Guest in the village. It was a clear marker, a reminder of control. Nobody in the rugby club, the Professor's haven, knew about the new sponsor's association with the player, but it mattered to the Professor. Martin was trespassing on his privacy. What he knew hung over the wing. He began to play nervously, his hands and legs responding to the uncertainty in his mind, and refusing to behave with the co-ordination required of the team's leading try-scorer. He faced a choice. On the one hand, he could leave the club, which he was reluctant to do. Confidence, bolstered by the Steel-Ag sponsorship, had soon returned to its normal proximity to pessimism when Gonzo left. A couple of defections had followed and the Professor did not want his to be the one that brought the club down.

On the other, he could fabricate some findings that showed the village to be totally unsuitable for the specialist steel-making sub-unit Martin had in mind. He hardly had to fabricate anything. A case to build elsewhere, anywhere closer to the M4 motorway, was easy to make. The Professor stewed and he fumbled a try-scoring pass; and then he was caught from behind by Mel Price, a winger the size of a bus, a prop wearing 14, whom the Professor had been skinning for years. Furthermore, there seemed to be a perpetual niggle in his hamstring, and he was sure he was about to go down with tendinitis in his achilles. The Professor's head dropped, going in the same direction as the team in the league.

Grace Courtney was dragged along to a couple more rugby matches in the village to which Martin seemed strangely drawn. It was a little unfair to say she was dragged, because they were all terribly sweet, despite their language which, to put it mildly, was a little ripe. But it was all a bit peculiar. It didn't strike Grace that this was Martin's type of place at all. The team was certainly not very good, which made it all the more surprising that he should take any sort of interest in them. He was passionate to the point of obsession, it struck her, about excellence, and yet here they would come, late as usual, shuffling through the spectators in the stand, who would half-rise in their rickety hinged wooden seats to let them pass, without taking their eyes off the play. They were glued to their sport, even though it was clear – even to Grace, unversed in the unfathomable ways of rugby – that there was only going to be one outcome; they would lose. Ever since that Gonzo had left, the team was pretty poor. Gonzo. What a peculiar name. She'd been going to ask him about it, but he'd vanished.

It was probably just as well. She hadn't mentioned to Martin that she had seen rather more of this Gonzo in the flesh than Martin might find appropriate. If Martin had a fault it was a certain lack of easy humour. She had spent quite some time looking at him and had noticed he could be quite self-absorbed at times, lost in his own space, and not happy to be disturbed there. She suspected he would have a temper; which might count as a second fault. It had made her slightly reluctant to accept the fact that she probably counted as his girlfriend now, although there was no reason why she should hesitate at all. Martin had a positive side. He was very keen on her. That much was now obvious, in that he phoned her twice a day and invited her to his functions and put his arm around her and kissed her on the cheek. But it was a very public display. In private, he had made no move to take their relationship to a more intimate level. He was slim of build and obviously taut of muscle, and she would not have minded at all if he had pressed against her. Instead, he remained courteously, almost rigidly, formal and kept her at arm's length physically. If he pulled her closer it was with his generosity. Perhaps her surrender into the role of partner came when she invited him to their house for supper. Martin met her father not in the dining room, but on the bank of the river under the willow tree at the end of the garden, where the old Atco lawnmower lay deep in long grass.

'Delighted to meet you again,' said her father.

'And you, Captain Courtney,' said Martin.

'James, please.' The captain wiped his hands and looked at the lawn and then the Atco. 'Poor thing,' he said. 'It's climate change, I think. In the old days, the old girl would be in the shed by now. But, d'you know, I find myself mowing late into the autumn now. Don't you think?'

Martin confessed he didn't when it came to lawns, but the next day a brand-new Husqvarna sit-on mower was delivered to the Courtney house. Grace had thought her father would never abandon his old Atco, but he pushed it without ado into the shed, and the sit-on replacement had become his dearest companion in the garden. The day she saw him on board, with the blades safely raised and a gin and tonic carefully balanced in his non-steering hand, riding down to the bank of the river, she knew that Martin had been given the nod of approval. It was all slightly mercenary, she had to say, but reality had to be faced, now that things were not going so very well for Godfrey in the City. His bank had found itself exposed. Her brother had survived the first round of redundancies, but a second was expected and nobody, Godfrey had had to admit to his sister, was safe.

Grace told Martin that her father was delighted with the machine as they were walking into City Hall in Cardiff for a black-tie charity dinner. She was wearing a black dress that Martin had bought her.

'You will drive men wild,' he had said as she did a slow twirl before him.

She was just about to say thank you at the top of the marble staircase, before they stepped into the hubbub of the pre-dinner reception, when he turned sharply to see that nobody was following them up the steps and pulled her behind one of the statues. There, for the first time, he kissed her on the mouth. He put his hands on her ribs and squeezed. He then slipped his palms down over her bottom and pressed. It was so unexpected that she almost pulled away, but instead she kissed him back and felt one hand start to go lower. She opened her eyes to see him staring at her with an intensity she took to be desire, but seemed close to ferocity. And then he released her.

'You are beautiful,' he said and smiled. He placed her arm on his and together they made their entrance.

While the Professor churned, his master made the decision for him. It was as if the point had been made. Martin had had his little moment to savour and it was time to return to real life. He ordered the Professor into his office and told him they were withdrawing from the village, and threw a file across the table. The Professor was to assess a new deal on offer. Contaminated land on the site of the old Llanwern steelworks was available for a pittance, allowing Steel-Ag to build their new plant there, with plenty of acreage left over for a second project. The Welsh Rugby Union were inviting Steel-Ag to extend their sponsorship of the rugby academies. There was an incentive in the form of grants for 'greenification' – grass to be sown over this once polluted stretch of the Gwent Levels. The Professor reviewed the plans and could find no fault. He reported enthusiastically to Martin Guest, who made a small one-off supplementary – but farewell – payment to the village club and moved his sponsorship back to the southern end of the region.

'You know that Steel-Ag thing, Professor?' Capper asked one day after the sponsorship ended. 'What's all that about then?'

The Professor was caught on the hop. 'I wouldn't know, Capper... why would I... why do companies come and go?'

'Oh, I don't mean the reasons. We all know up here there's only one fuckin' thing that's ever going to happen, and that's us getting fuckin' shafted. No, I mean Steel-Ag. What sort of a fuckin' name is that?'

The Professor hesitated again, unwilling to say too much, to reveal anything.

'Don't matter, Professor. Just thought you might know.'

'I think it's to do with Ag being silver in the periodic table,' the Professor finally said. 'Steel-Ag, steel to silver. And silver is money. Brass from muck, that sort of thing.'

'Glad you cleared that up, then. Whoever they are, bollocks to the lot of them.'

Gonzo liked the arcades in the centre of Cardiff. He was happy enough where he lived in the Bay, the bottom-most point of the capital, and found it relaxing to sit and watch from his small balcony the tides of people – the politicians and the civil servants, the drinkers and eaters, the walkers and strollers, the media movers and shakers – whose comings and goings had replaced the rise and fall of the water in Cardiff Bay, now at permanent high tide, thanks to the barrage at its entrance. It wasn't always easy, however, for Gonzo to go out and join the crowd. At first, he had been unknown and could walk anywhere, but his rapid rise had made his face well known and if he stepped into the public areas of his neighbourhood he had to stop every few yards to have a photograph taken or to sign an autograph.

'Fuckin' hell, Gonzo,' said Capper as they obligingly stopped every twenty steps on their way through Mermaid Quay one day. 'This is a pain in the arse.'

Capper had said he was going to give Gonzo plenty of time to settle in, allowing him what he called 'a long fuckin' period of mourning.' But two weeks after Gonzo left the village, the hooker appeared one evening at his flat, with a bag packed for the weekend.

'Don't tell me,' Gonzo said. 'You've been banned, haven't you?'

Capper nodded. 'A week, for clouting that old fuckwit, Leighton Farcroft,' he said.

'It's good to see you, don't get me wrong. But you should be up there, Capper, even if you're not playing.'

Capper was about to interrupt, but Gonzo carried on: 'And don't say I should be there, too, because that would make me say: 'Capper, give me break'.'

'I wasn't going to say that. I was going to say it's not easy fighting without you.'

'Go away, Capper. Seriously, you've got to stay with the boys.'

And Capper had left, with his bag unopened, back to the village, back to be part of the inexorable decline of the team. He had left alone his friend on the rise, until after the Argentina game. Late on the following Wednesday, a weary Gonzo opened his flat door to find Capper there.

'No fuckin' bag, no fuckin' ban,' said Capper, walking straight past Gonzo and going to the fridge in the kitchen. 'Just wanted to check. Make sure all this bollocks hasn't gone to your head.'

Reassured by three hours of drinking – Gonzo swore he hadn't touched a drop since he'd been in Cardiff – that his old mucker's feet were still firmly on the ground, Capper had insisted on a tour of the Bay, and it was out there that he discovered that Gonzo was something of a celebrity, no longer able to go out for an uninterrupted stroll.

Where he could find a little privacy was in the arcades in the centre. Gonzo would put on a woollen hat, turn up his collar and march purposefully away from the Bay, towards town. He would skirt around the crowded areas of the waterfront and walk north through the streets of Butetown. If he was recognised there, it prompted only a 'Hello there, Mr Gonzo,' and he could stride on towards town, through the supposed no-man's land of high-rises and low-cost housing. Once in the city centre, he turned into the arcades off the main streets and, with a book in his pocket, would find one of the little cafes tucked away in the covered passageways.

He was settled into Camacho's one day in early December, killing time over a hot drink before training in the late afternoon. In the book he was reading, the Scottish private detective had just walked into big trouble, and Gonzo wondered if he had time to start the next chapter, full, no doubt, of recriminations and complications. He did. More than enough. Time was dragging for someone accustomed to working all day. Ticking off the hours between sessions was costing him a small fortune in paperbacks and cups of tea. Every day he had to fight the temptation to take the car and drive home to the village, but he also knew that Capper had been right and that this was a chance and he needed to give it his unwavering attention. But, hell, it could be dull. He looked up to check the time and his attention was caught by somebody standing on the outside looking in. It was Grace Courtney. So brief was their eye contact that she could have taken the option of walking away. Instead, she turned her gaze back to Gonzo and then walked into Camacho's.

The Professor knew his boss too well to suppose that he was off the hook, but it seemed at least that their working relationship returned to what it had been before the sponsorship. At the club, the Professor smoothed over the departure of the benefactor, telling the committee that Martin Guest was no more able to defy commercial reality than any other investor. Twenty minutes off the M4 was the cut-off point, he told the committee. The village's future, if it had one, was not as a maker of steel.

At work, the Professor was so busy that he had no time to worry. He went back and forth between Cardiff and Newport, charged with speeding up the process of decontamination and the completion of basic infrastructure installations on the Llanwern site, and at the same time advising on how to slow down the building of the new rugby academy. Martin was working on a third angle and he needed some things to happen quickly and others to be delayed. It was a question of juggling the money coming in and going out and the Professor threw himself into the whole intricate process. Martin left him to it and disappeared without telling anyone where he was going. He would be gone for days at a time. The Professor's form picked up and he began to glide over the ground again.

'You've grown your hair,' said Grace over a cup of peppermint tea in Camacho's.

'They said I looked like a Cardiff Ultra,' said Gonzo. Grace looked blank. 'The new breed of Cardiff City fan. Nutters. Either that, or knowing where I'm from, they called me the village idiot.'

'Anyway, it's nice to see you with your clothes on,' said Grace. 'May I?' she asked quickly, turning his book towards her. 'So, this is what you get up to instead.'

'I've got time on my hands,' said Gonzo. 'I'm trying to get my head around this full-time rugby.'

'But congratulations are in order. I've heard all about it.'

'I got away with it. No, seriously, I was within an inch of making a real idiot of myself out there.'

And Gonzo told Grace all about his nerves in the changing room and how, when he was leaving the toilets after being sick he had been mesmerised by a flickering light bulb at the far end of the warm-up area.

'Funny, how I couldn't take my eyes off this flashing

light. I thought somebody was sending me one of those old morse code messages. The only one I know is SOS. Mayday, Mayday. Don't panic. The forwards had to drag me back to reality, into the huddle before we went out.'

'Why do they do that, the huddle thing?' asked Grace.

'A private moment before you face the world. Look each other in the eye. This is it, let's do it for each other. That sort of thing. We did another one when the anthems had finished. I looked up and thought the roof was stuck halfway open. Or halfway shut, it could have been, I suppose. The boys were having their last rant and I was wondering why the roof was stuck. The captain shouted at me and I had to look at him. When I glanced back up before kick-off, it was completely open. Hell, I was in one weird place.'

'But you came through.'

'The team suddenly found their rhythm and I was carried along.'

'But next time will be easier, won't it?'

'If there is a next time. I was picked as a late replacement.'

'Oh, there'll be a next time.'

'Anyway,' said Gonzo, 'How about you? Where are you from?'

Grace told him how she, too, was trying to come to terms with a change in her life. She told him about Martin and what he did, or as much as she knew of his work, because there were a lot of things he did not tell her, which both intrigued her and made her a bit nervous.

'He's away a lot at the moment, working on a deal.'

She didn't tell Gonzo that even when he was around, Martin had reverted to keeping her at a safe distance. Not a stroke, not a caress since the night of the dinner in Cardiff. Not a second of that look. She wondered why the thought of Martin's open eyes had even entered her head. She couldn't help noticing that the eyes of the huge rugby player twinkled with good humour.

'Do you have a temper?' she asked.

'Only when Capper got his window frame measurements wrong. By a foot.'

He asked her about her father, and she was about to ask him why he was called Gonzo, when he looked at the clock and found out that for the first time since he had been in Cardiff, an hour had passed in a flash. He had to dash and they had no time to say anything about meeting again, but the following week she found herself passing Camacho's at the same time, and there he was, reading his book. As he was leaving, in a rush again because the time had flown by even more quickly – she had talked about her father, still mowing the lawn even though the grass had stopped growing, and her brother, still waiting to find out what was going to happen at his bank – he leant down as he was sliding around the back of her chair and gave a her a kiss on the cheek. The third time, planned for only a couple of days later, he filled the hour with tales of the village and real work. He had to hurry again, but not before she had asked him for his mobile number. He scribbled it down and made to leave, lowering his head. She turned hers and he very nearly kissed her on the lips. As he ran out into the arcade, he didn't pull his cap down in time, and a group of three grown men went from being sane window-shoppers outside a menswear outlet to an overexcited pack of puppies who insisted that the great

Gonzo – as they shouted over and over – stop and have a picture taken with them.

Martin was away on his business trips. 'Can't say where at the moment. But have to be here,' he texted Grace. 'Back in three days. Let's do something.'

Two days later, the region had a free afternoon before a game the following day. Grace sent her first text to Gonzo: 'Outside your flat. Look for the steaming car.' And he came down to find her in the Mazda that he had last seen overheating at the Keeper's Pond. He folded himself into the small seat and she drove away from the cities, out of Cardiff and beyond Newport, and up into the most remote corner of Monmouthshire, where the River Monnow forms the border between Wales and England. They had a late snack lunch at the Bell pub in Skenfrith, one couple among three others, all deep in their own conversations. Nobody glanced their way. Afterwards, they walked to the castle, back to the bridge and on along the riverbank. They then turned and strolled back to the pub cark park. Grace excused herself and went inside the Bell. Gonzo stood staring at the bridge and the river, pleased to be out without his hat on and collar up. Grace came back out and took him by the hand and drew him not to the car, but back inside and up the stairs to the room she had just booked.

On the way back to Cardiff, they spoke very little until they were past Usk and heading for Newport. Gonzo reached out and ran the back of his hand down Grace's cheek.

'You know we're in big trouble, don't you?'

She nodded, and he sighed.

'It'll be a test of Capper's theory,' he said.

'What theory is that?'

'That a bloke in love can't play rugby.'

Grace squeezed his hand. 'For the good of your career, and until we work out what's going on and what we're going to do, you'd better make sure you carry on being...' – and here she imitated the men in the arcade – 'the Great Gonzo.'

'Don't. Please, not you.'

'Why Gonzo, though? How did you end up with such a name?'

44

Gwyn stumbled back down the road to Almancillas. Behind him came the lorries, even though it could be seen from Santa Engracia that the bridge was destroyed in the lower town, and that they would have to seek an alternative route into Asturias. They came down until Almancillas was in range of their mortars.

The main column of refugees was visible only as a dust cloud over the road ahead. The last stragglers were hauling themselves and their belongings out of the ravine on the far side. A young boy was holding his hand out towards his grandmother, while trying not to lose control of a large bundle over his shoulder. The knot on the bundle slipped and two cooking pans clattered into the ravine.

The young boy and the grandmother looked down in despair. The old woman slowly started to climb again, but the boy paused and looked back at Almancillas. There, on the other side, he saw a man swaying and falling to his knees, a man as brown as dust but with a bright red stain in his middle.

'Papá,' shouted the boy, the only sound in the valley. A man thirty paces ahead turned and watched his son pull his grandmother up to safety, drop his bundle and then go back down into the ravine. The boy's shout was still echoing when mortar rounds began to fall.

Javier García Ruíz did not have the strength to go back. When the bombers had struck, his family had been at the end of the line, among the youngest, the oldest and the lame. They had not rushed to the destroyed bridge, but had stayed put, clinging to one another, placing the faith of grandmother Pilar in the foreigners who had run past them, back up the hill. They had listened to the distant bursts of rifle-fire, sporadic but intense, and inched their way in line towards the gorge. And now the family at last was on the other side.

But Javier did not leave Gwyn to die. He joined his son, Pedro, in the ravine and together they went back to the other side. The rounds were not raining down, but their accuracy was improving. Father and son picked up the fallen soldier and told him he had to walk. Javier was a waiter, a small man who carried nothing heavier than loaded trays. But halfway up the far side, this tiny, weary father bent his knees, put his shoulder under the swaying Gwyn, lifted him and carried him upward.

They met a relief convoy not far down the valley, a column of lorries, cars and a green grocery van, with 'Thomas Pryce, Wholesalers of Newtown' still visible beneath the white background and red cross that made it an ambulance here in Spain. The convoy had stopped before the human tide coming down the valley. Gwyn, feverish now, managed to brief the commander through an interpreter about the fallen bridge at Almancillas. A medical orderly then took a precious vial of morphine from the supplies and Gwyn sank into a bouncing dreamworld as the convoy turned and went with the flow of the retreat.

Asturias fell quickly and the Republican retreat stretched along the coast towards the Basque Country. Gwyn spent time in a field hospital, but the tent pegs were soon being pulled up and everybody was on the move again as the retreat towards Bilbao accelerated. On the outskirts of the city he was placed in a hospital bed at last.

The cut was so clean that there was no need to operate, other than to tidy up the stump. There was more risk of infection in the wound made by the spike. Nurses sniffed his hand and smiled in encouragement. Gangrene was held at bay. Slowly, the rest of Gwyn's body regained its strength and in the early summer of 1937 he left hospital. He volunteered to join the defence of the city, in Bilbao's Ring of Steel. There had to be something a one-handed man could do. But a soldier who could not hold a rifle was a sign of desperation and possibly bad for morale. Besides, as almost all the defenders of the city said, the Ring of Steel would fall quickly.

When in June it did, Gwyn crept out of the city. The reprisals and settling of scores had already started. In a microcosm of the national civil war, neighbour was turning on neighbour in Bilbao and the city was so traumatised that it was relatively easy for a single outsider to slip into the shadows and leave. Once outside, Gwyn joined up with a small pocket of fighters and ex-fighters heading towards the Aragón front. Gwyn went with them for a few days, but when the able-bodied turned right, away from the Pyrenees, he obeyed their instructions to stay with the group of three incapacitated soldiers, Manolo, Paco and Ajimiro, and guide them to safety over the mountains.

They made good progress at first, but on the third day Gwyn stumbled and hurt his stump against a rock. As they climbed higher, Gwyn began to feel a burning sting in his hand and a fever on his brow. The next day, he could not stand up without assistance and late that afternoon, when they were high enough to have the most magnificent view of the mountains above and mile after mile of Spain below, Gwyn pulled himself out of the slackening grip of his companions, sat heavily against a stone wall and told them to leave him. It was the way of the war and with only the briefest of raised fists, the others were on their way. Gwyn tried to raise his bad hand and failed. His last thought was that even if he had managed to say goodbye to his comrades, his would have been the most powerless salute of the International Brigade, a fist without fingers. He closed his eyes.

He woke up in darkness. He was inside a house. That much he could tell. There was a smell of the coats and dung of animals, mixed with the aroma of straw and herbs. He had no idea how long he had been asleep or unconscious. He was hot and thirsty and his hand was burning and he felt sick, and yet he still felt so tired. He shut his eyes and slept for another two days.

When he awoke again he was outside in the morning sunlight, propped up against an ancient, stubby tree. His hand was exposed, except for a light poultice against the spike mark on his palm. He raised his hand and sniffed. All he could smell was sweet herbs. His hand was not burning. A man of about 60, wiry and dark and creased by the sun, stood watching him. He held out his hand in a pacifying gesture as Gwyn jumped when he saw him.

'*Francés*?' asked the man.

Gwyn shook his head.

'*Inglés*?'

'*Más o menos*,' said Gwyn.

The old man nodded. He had used up half the words he would ever speak to Gwyn. He turned and walked out of sight.

That evening the old man returned. He was leading a donkey that was carrying a pair of panniers. Two large earthenware jars also hung from a rope tied around the donkey's girth. He invited Gwyn with an open palm to mount the donkey. Gwyn stood and took a few steps. He felt strong and he shook his head. The man nodded, turned the donkey and allowed the animal to take the lead. Gwyn fell in behind them and they started walking slowly towards the towering peaks of the Pyrenees.

They stopped occasionally to drink water from the streams that tumbled across their path. Soon after nightfall, they came to a one-roomed stone hut on the edge of the highest meadows. Gwyn was so tired that he could hardly eat the cheese and cured ham that were put before him. He took a swig of wine from one of the jars and was soon asleep. He did not see his guide go out into the open fields and walk among his sheep and goats, tending to them, talking to them.

They climbed all the next day and all through the next night. At some stage, not long after the man stopped the donkey, looked back, pointed and gave Gwyn his last look of Spain – a vast moonlit plain below them, with not a light in sight – the delirious Welshman was folded over the back of the donkey and covered in a coarse blanket, taken from one of the panniers. The man gave the beast a little tap and on it went, upwards for a few more twists and turns and then downwards into France. At dawn the next day, on the edge of the high pastures on the other side of the mountains, Gwyn was eased off the back off the donkey and given more cheese, ham and wine. This time, the old man took the second jar and tapped it against Gwyn's. They drank together. The old man took the two jars, put stoppers back in them and re-tied them to the donkey's back. He reached into the pannier and handed Gwyn a small leather gourd of water. He then drew him into a swift, strong embrace.

'*Soy* Gonzalo,' he said, the last two words he spoke before turning and heading back towards Spain.

45

Our Marnie still wasn't thinking of Gonzo when she caught a train down to Wales at the end of her first term in Manchester. Not for a moment was she thinking about him. She'd told herself she would stay in the north for the whole of the Christmas period, but then she found that everybody who had agreed with her in November about staying and doing a big student Christmas together had gone home to their families as soon as they could in December. She thought it might be good, instead, to catch up with Capper and the Professor. And if there was still a job for her behind the bar at the club over the holidays, then the money would obviously come in handy. But she wasn't thinking about Gonzo as she was passing the menswear shop in the Cardiff arcade and telling herself that the world didn't produce enough cotton to make a shirt big enough to go round his chest and neck, now that he was a pro and all that, and even if there were she certainly wouldn't be able to afford it, not at those prices. Would you just look at them? She wheeled away and stared into Camacho's, and there was Gonzo. And opposite him was Grace, and even before he left the table, squeezing past her chair and kissing her with such a gentleness on the lips that Our Marnie wanted to kick the plate glass in, she knew that she need never waste another thought on Gonzo, because he was lost to her.

She stepped out into the main streets of Cardiff, full of shoppers under the Christmas lights and walked forty paces in one direction before spinning and walking back to where she had started. The Salvation Army brass band was on the march, playing 'O Come All Ye Faithful', and she fell in behind them. They stopped and a young woman in uniform rattled her collection bucket and smiled. Our Marnie reached into her purse and absently dropped some coins into it.

'Thank you,' said the young woman. 'Merry Christmas to you.'

The Professor was striding down St Mary Street when he saw Our Marnie, head down, slowly walking away from the brass band. He did not like to be seen in his working clothes by anyone from the village. They did not know where he lived and what he did for a living and that was how the Professor liked it. He had once seen Buttercup, Fungus and Buddleia on a night out in town and he had darted into an arcade to avoid being seen by them. He knew it was stupid, but he couldn't help it. He thought about crossing the street, but something about the figure in front of him made him hold his course.

'Marnie?'

She looked up, startled.

'Oh, hello Professor,' she said. 'Didn't recognise you... Nice suit.'

'Are you home for Christmas?'

She looked at him blankly.

'Christmas shopping?'

She continued to stare at him without saying a word. But then he saw tears well up in her eyes. He took her arm and steered her into a coffee shop and ordered two large mugs of hot chocolate.

'I don't know what the hell I expected was going to happen,' she said. And now that she had started, it poured out of her. 'I mean, we had a kiss and these bags of crisps exploded and that was the end of it. Damn it, we were laughing. That's all it was, a laugh. And off I went and off he went, and neither of us has said a word since. Not a word. Haven't seen him, haven't spoken to him. But, Professor, I have been thinking about him. And I thought that maybe, you know, if I did see him and he saw me we might start something proper this time. I was even thinking about buying him something nice. For Christmas.'

Two tears fell down her cheeks. She wiped them away with the back of her hand.

'And then I saw them. Him and her. Him and that Grace, the one who came up to the village with that Martin Guest.'

She looked at the Professor.

'A right pair of lovebirds,' she said.

She took a sip of her chocolate and briskly wiped her eyes and mouth with a paper napkin.

'And so that's that then, Professor. The one that got away. No point crying about it now. Too late for all that. On we go.'

He was the one now staring blankly.

'Professor?'

He said nothing and Our Marnie had never seen anyone look so abject.

Grace was in Gonzo's flat when her phone beeped. She ignored it. Gonzo was massaging her back, slowly moving his large hands up the small ridges of her spine, his thumbs spreading out to knead the muscles of her shoulders. She was stretched naked across his bed, slender and tiny under him. She turned over and ran her hands over his stomach.

'Tense,' she said.

'What?'

'Tense your stomach muscles.'

Gonzo grimaced and she punched him. And again and again.

'God, it's like hitting a table,' she said.

They laughed and kissed tenderly. He took her calf and lifted her leg.

'Tense,' he said.

She tightened her thigh and he ran a hand over it.

'Good definition,' he said.

'It's all the exercise,' she replied.

'Untense,' he said, and when she relaxed he kissed the inside of her thigh.

The phone beeped again. This time Grace looked at the two messages.

'I'm back. Table booked for 8 o'clock,' said the first.

'It's Martin,' she said.

'Me again. Confirm dinner?' said the second.

Our Marnie left the Professor in his strange mood, regretting that it must have been her revelation that had unsettled him so, but also thinking that it was surely her problem, not his. She was the one who'd had a shock, and here he was, all seized by melancholy and not able to finish his chocolate. She walked to Cardiff Central Station in time for the next train at five minutes to the hour. She walked up to Platform 2. From the station in Ebbw Vale she could catch a taxi to the village. She could text Capper, the flat would be unlocked and she'd soon be settled in. She'd be home.

But at ten minutes to the hour from Platform 3, a different train was due to depart. And even while Our Marnie was thinking of how she was going to tidy the flat in the club and give the whole place a real feel of Christmas and how it would be part of her new life, she found herself stepping into the train bound for Manchester. Her fresh start became a farewell to Wales, and she would not be back for many a year.

Grace raced home in her old Mazda. Martin was back and guilt seemed to press her foot to the floor. Either that or she needed time to be at home with her father and shut the door and have time to think of what she was going to do next. Martin was back, damn it. What was she going to do? Well, obviously she was going to tell him. Finish with him, because she knew and Gonzo knew that they were in love, and the sooner Martin knew the better. Except, of course, and this was the bit that really worried her, there could never be anything 'better' about any of this because she saw the look in Martin's eye and knew that he would take this badly and that Martin was not the sort of person she wanted to be near when he was ablaze.

She turned into the driveway of her father's house and swung left into the parking area to the side of the house. From there she could see two figures in the bay window of the front room and beyond them, in the large wall mirror, the flickering reflection of the Christmas tree. The two figures moved. At first, Grace thought one of them had to be

Martin, but then she realised that alongside her father was her brother, Godfrey. Grace stepped out of her car and ran to the front door, noticing a brand new Mazda next to her father's old Rover.

'Well, haven't you been doing well?' she said when the front door opened and Godfrey stepped forward to embrace her. 'Welcome home and Happy Christmas.'

Her brother hugged her fondly and then shook his head.

'Nothing to do with me,' he said, looking at the new car. 'I rather think it's yours.'

'The same rather kind chaps who delivered the mower dropped it off this afternoon,' said Captain Courtney, wrapping his daughter in an embrace. 'You smell rather nice, darling.'

Grace had given herself a liberal spray of the perfume Martin had bought her at the same time as he was selecting the little black number for her. She had needed a protective layer, just in case he had come to pick her up from the house, and just in case the scent of Gonzo had come home with her. She clung to her father trying to calm her nerves.

'It's rather impressive, isn't it?' said her father.

'Yes, it is,' whispered Grace, still holding him.

'And I think it means he's rather fond of you, darling.'

'Yes, it does.'

'Are you alright?'

'Not really.'

'That makes two of us, then,' said Godfrey.

Grace unwrapped herself from her father. She looked at her brother and he bowed his head. She took his hands.

'So, it's happened,' she said.

Godfrey nodded.

'Fifteen of us were called in. We said it'd be about the Christmas bonus… but we knew it wasn't.' He sighed, emitting a small cloud of steam into the cold air.

'Let's go in,' said Grace's father.

He poured them a gin and tonic and they sat down by the fire in the front room.

'There's enough of a pay-off to keep me going… to keep us going here… but it's going to be tough in a couple of months' time, I'm afraid. Not unless I find a job pretty soon. And the City's in a sorry state at the moment. We have to brace ourselves for the worst.'

At that moment a pair of headlights swung through the gates.

'That'll be Martin,' said Captain James. 'At least it's not all gloom and doom.'

'Shit,' said Grace.

Godfrey and James looked at each other in surprise. Grace stood up and almost ran for the door that led to the stairs.

'No, look, it's just that I'm not ready. Not at all. Tell him I'll be down in a moment.'

She shot through the door and ran up the stairs, just as Martin, with the briefest of taps on the front door, let himself in.

'You look stunning,' he said twenty minutes later, watching Grace glide down the stairs. He walked to meet her and handed her the keys to the new Mazda. She had made an effort, it was true, if only to buy herself some time to think. What she was going to do? She was not strong. She knew that.

There was something of her mother in her, the unreliable Mary, prone to flight rather than face the consequences of her impetuosity. But she knew on this night that she had to be strong and tell Martin the truth. She had scrubbed at herself in the shower, trying to scrape away every trace of Gonzo. And she had put on not the black number that Martin had bought her, but new black trousers and the blouse that Gonzo had reverentially undone the first time he had touched her. Gonzo Davies. Her Gonzo. She had to be strong and tell Martin that she had met someone else. Somebody else, who wrapped his huge arms around and pressed her against him with a gentleness that made her melt.

'Thank you,' she said. She held up the keys. 'Martin, I… this is ridiculous.'

'Nonsense,' he said brightly. 'Come on, let's take her for a spin.'

'Thank you,' she found herself saying as she opened the car door. 'It's beautiful.'

The new Mazda was smoother and faster than the old one, tighter on the road, softer to sit in. Grace had to be strong. She found herself thinking that if Martin touched her she would have to swerve the new car into the hedge. Instead, he pointed her towards Abergavenny and then told her to take a right off the road to Hereford.

'He's taking me to the Bell at Skenfrith,' thought Grace. 'If he takes me to the Bell I'll have to drive the car into the river.'

Instead, Martin directed her to the Walnut Tree at the base of the Skirrid mountain and carried on talking. He was talking more than he usually did, thought Grace, and willed him to talk and talk and talk. He had just come back from Russia, from the steel city of Cherepovets.

'That's where I've been. The place I couldn't tell you about. Very cloak and dagger.'

He was having a rich terrine as a starter and offered a bite of it on a wafer-thin piece of toast to Grace, who was picking at a goat's cheese salad. She shook her head.

'It's an amazing place,' he said. 'Mile after mile of old Soviet steel-making factories, left to rot. And then, just when you think it's nothing but a giant graveyard of rust, you come across the most modern plant.'

Grace had nearly asked if they could leave the car at the restaurant and take a taxi home. She could then throw herself into a bottle of champagne. The mood seemed celebratory and she could use that to hide the urge to numb herself. But then she thought she had better keep her wits about her. And Martin had been so keen for her to drive, she didn't want to give the impression that she was prepared to abandon the Mazda on its first outing. She forced herself to listen to the world of Russian steel.

'I met this man called Konstantin Mordashov who's part of the steel dynasty up there,' Martin continued. 'He's transformed production, after the sell-off into private ownership. Very interesting man, enormously rich now. And there's something even more interesting about him, Grace.'

'And what's that?' Did that come out a bit dismissively? Grace replayed it in her head and watched Martin carefully. He didn't seem to notice. He was putting the last wafer of toast in his mouth and waited until he had swallowed before replying.

'He wants to buy us.'

'Us?'

'Steel-Ag. Lock, stock and barrel. It seems we make what he doesn't and what we make is soon going to sell very well in Russia. So, he wants to buy us.'

Grace wanted to tell him not to sell. Just to go against him, not agree with him, not have to congratulate him. She forced herself to unclench her hand.

'If the steel – the special steel – you make is going to sell,' she said slowly, not wishing to sound obtuse. 'Why not wait and make the money for yourself?'

'Because the offer right now from Konstantin is as good as it will ever be. And it's very good. Besides, to be honest, I don't care what's going to happen in the world of steel,' said Martin with a carefree gesture that took Grace by surprise.

'You don't?' she said. 'But I thought you did.'

'I did, but now I don't. There, simple. You see, there's something else I want to do.'

Grace knew that this was begging a question, but she shrank from asking it. She was suddenly afraid that he was going to ask her to marry him. She swallowed and stared at the unfinished salad and wished she could down a glass of wine. She took a small sip as the waitress took away the starter plates.

'Go on,' said Martin. 'Ask me.'

'What is it you'd like to do?' she managed to say.

'I'd like… no, I've been asked if I'd like to go into politics. All those hunt balls and all that glad-handing around the county seem to have counted for something, after all. I've been asked if I'd throw my hat into the ring at the next General Election and stand for parliament.'

'And you said yes?'

'I said I'd think about it.'

'And have you?'

'That's what I'm doing. Thinking about it. Talking it over with you.'

The main courses arrived: lamb for Martin, halibut for Grace. Grace could hear the next words. She could see him bending forward and putting his hand over hers. She could see a light coating of lamb fat on his lips as he asked her to marry him.

Martin leant back in his seat and poured himself more red wine. He wiped his mouth with his napkin.

'There's something else I've been thinking about,' he said.

Grace knew it was coming. This was it.

'I had a word with your father, while you were getting ready.'

Grace could not look at him.

'And he told me about Godfrey losing his job.'

It was such a relief that Grace did look up.

'And it strikes me that since I am about to become inordinately wealthy, there's no reason why I shouldn't do something to plug the gap, as it were. Your brother is in no position to help your father now, but I am. Come to think of it, I know one or two people in the City and I'm sure I can put in a good word for Godfrey and have him back up and running in no time.'

Martin took a large swig of wine and put another forkful of meat in his mouth. Grace felt as if she had avoided the mantrap with her left foot but could feel the jaws of another closing on her right.

'And for that matter,' continued Martin, 'I've been thinking about your other brother, Will. Ceramics, right? Well, it just so happens I think we may be able to give him a little boost, too. Invest in an up-and-coming young artist. Put on an exhibition, or whatever it is they do in the art world.'

Grace knew she was beaten. She looked up at Martin and gave him a smile.

'I think that would be very kind of you,' she said softly.

'Anyway, enough of me,' said Martin. 'What have you been up to?'

And Grace had to take the greatest of care because he seemed genuinely interested in all the details of the lies she now told him about how she had been spending her time while he had been away.

Martin had had a notion – not exactly a plan, but perhaps a desire; yes, a desire, he couldn't deny it – to seduce Grace in her new car, however uncomfortable and constricted it might have been. He felt he had earned the right. He felt he had bought the rights. But the moment was far from right, it struck him. And 'struck' was the right word because he felt as if she had smacked him hard. The longer the meal had gone on the clearer it had become that she was sleeping with somebody else. Fornicating with another man. Shagging somebody not Martin. He looked at her as she drove them back to her father's house, and admitted that she was beautiful. But she would not be so very beautiful if he undid her seat belt and grabbed the wheel and drove the shiny new red car into a wall. There, like that one in Llanover. Aim at a tree in Llanfair Kilgeddin. That one. Bang, and the beautiful Grace goes through the windscreen.

'So,' he said quietly. 'This car. Do you like it?'

'I do.'

Duplicitous Grace.

'And my plan, to help your family and go into politics. What do you think?'

'That's exactly what I'm doing.'

'Pardon?'

'I'm thinking.'

And she had the nerve to take her hand off the wheel and pat his. Briefly. And she laughed, as if she were mocking him. She was mocking him. Martin put the patted hand in the pocket of his jacket and found the small box containing the engagement ring and rolled it around in his fingers.

46

Operation Ladysmith in Denbigh began with a diversion that cost four times as much as the police's first, failed attempt to take the Hafod. Two helicopters were dispatched to hover over the Ruthin Road at the other end of town, with searchlights sweeping over the houses and streets of the decoy assault. Ten police cars and vans were sent speeding past the Hafod, sirens blaring, in the direction of the helicopters. The gatekeepers of the estate went from a state of high alert at the first signs of police activity to their customary wariness. A second wave of vehicles went screaming past them. The sentinels relaxed and took no notice when a third wave approached.

This time, however, the police cars turned into the Hafod and stopped. The teenage doorkeepers were trapped at the wheels of their stolen cars. They jumped out and ran. The four entrances were abandoned, gaping holes in the defences of the estate. A fourth wave of police vehicles swept in, vans packed with officers in riot gear. Rear doors were flung open and a sea of uniforms swept towards the middle of the estate, herding the teenagers before them. The helicopters and first two waves of vehicles swung away from the diversionary attack and made their way up to the Hafod. The helicopters hovered low in the sky, a deafening beat above the drama, lighting up the scenes below with their piercing lights.

The vans went to selected addresses, whose front doors had already been flattened. Handcuffed adults by the score were already being led out of the houses, and put into the vans. The odd suspect remained briefly at large, vaulting from garden to garden and looking for an escape route into the countryside. But they were caught in the spotlights of the helicopters, whose throb did not completely drown the barking of the police dogs that were released from smaller vans. One by one, those trying to flee were brought down.

The trouble for the police was that a successful operation in the North became an alarm call to the South. Fully aware of their place in the Welsh Hell, the football fans of Cardiff recognised that they would be next in the hard-line drive to restore order. By slipping away and avoiding the net during Operation Bluebird, the miscreants of the M4 had thumbed their nose at authority, and their turn would come to face justice. Even as the orders were being given to senior officers of the South Wales Police to plan the next strike against those who had defied the law, Ely and Llanrumney began to stir restlessly. A false rumour spread that Calvin Williams, ringleader of the City Ultras, had been taken into custody and given a beating, as revenge for mocking the police.

'The sweetest thing about the Chelsea bun-fight has been watching the pigs chase their tails,' he had, for the record, written, but at the time of his apparent arrest, he was comfortably sitting on his sofa at home.

Eyewitnesses claimed to have seen Doxy Richards, the secretary of the official supporters' club, pulled off the streets in Grangetown and thrown into an unmarked police car. He had one chance to grass up the bun-fighters, or else. So went the word on the street, where it was suspected that Doxy didn't have the bottle to hold out for thirty seconds. It was true that the secretary, who also happened to be a secondary school teacher in Barry, would not have hesitated to co-operate with the police, but at the time of his supposed abduction he was leading a Year 10 Geography field trip in the Preseli Mountains.

It didn't matter. Rumour fuelled rumour and fears grew in the estates that ringed the capital that an invasion was on its way. Which it was, but not in time to prevent a row between a delivery van driver and a pedestrian on the corner of Wheatley Road and Wilson Road in Ely from escalating into a riot. The uninsured van ended up embedded in the boarded-up shop front in a nearby parade, due for demolition. The cost of the damage was minimal, but when the van and the buildings were set alight, the flames served as a beacon and soon there were fires raging in four locations in Ely and three on the other side of the city in Llanrumney.

47

Early in the year following Gonzo's triumphant debut for Wales in November against Argentina, the Professor was summoned to see Martin. There was a lot of steel furniture in the office, and although light poured in through the metal-framed windows, the Professor always thought it was a cold, stark working environment, which did not surprise him at all. The Professor at first had expected the office to overlook the works, in the tradition of the old ironmasters, who liked to look down on what was theirs. But the office faced away from the works, towards nothing more glamorous than a stretch of scrubland before the huge bund that kept the Bristol Channel out.

'There's work to do,' said Martin, staring out at the wasteland.

'There always is,' said the Professor.

'No. This time there is work to do as never before...'

'Before you sell to Konstantin Mordashov.'

It stopped Martin Guest in his tracks. He turned to face the Professor. Behind him seagulls swirled in the sky.

There was a huge landfill site a mile to the east and the gulls formed a constant cloud over it, their cries fighting against the sound of the works at full tilt.

'Well, I'll say one thing. You never cease to amaze me,' said Martin with a straight face. 'This is – was – the most confidential thing I have done. Nobody here knew. Nobody here booked any flights. I made no contact with here from there. Nobody knew where I was. But you, Professor, you knew, didn't you?'

The Professor, poker-faced, held his gaze for as long as he dared and then looked down. Martin turned back to follow a pair of seagulls wheeling over the bund, squabbling over a scrap of food.

'Funny how you always know.'

'You pay me to know things.'

'But not everything. You can know too much. Just make sure you know the limits of your… access to my life.'

Martin continued to stare out of the window for a full minute. And then he turned sharply.

'Right,' he said. 'Let's get to it.'

And for the next hour he was in full business mode, detailing the deal and explaining what needed to be done at the Russian end and at the Welsh end. Who might object and who needed to receive gifts, the covenants that needed to be so watertight that not even an oligarch at his most high-powered would be able to pull a fast one.

'I don't trust them,' said Martin. 'And I trust they're saying exactly the same thing in Cherepovets about me.'

The Professor had filled page after page with notes in a shorthand that only he understood. Even so, Martin pointed to the pad at the end of the hour and said, 'You work from this office. And nothing goes out. Understood?'

The Professor nodded.

'It's all yours,' said Martin, indicating the entire room. 'That's trust, you see, Professor. I'm going back out there and I need you to be right here. You're me, let's say, while I'm away, and I want to be able to speak to me.'

The Professor was aware that this was turning a little weird.

'Trust,' repeated Martin. He stood up at his desk and went to the window.

'I'm going to ask Grace to come with me. A week in the frozen north and then we'll go and have some sun. What d'you think?'

The Professor felt a little trickle of sweat down the middle of his back.

'I'm sure that sounds very nice,' he said.

'Very nice. I'm sure it will be. Yes, very nice.' Martin was still looking at the gulls. 'Two last things. We need to buy some ceramics, Professor. Look up Will Courtney and see what we can acquire that'll give him a little boost. And I tell you what, Professor. You being of a sensitive disposition, you can keep it.'

'That won't …'

Martin held up his hand.

'It's for you. Because you know all this stuff.'

The Professor didn't say anything and Martin let the silence grow.

'The other thing,' he finally said. 'Who owes us a little favour in the City?'

'Well,' said the Professor, relieved to be back to business. 'There's Eckhart at Miller's, Hazell at Cromley's...'

Martin waved a hand.

'You choose. Get one of them to give Godfrey Courtney a job. Nothing too grand. Let's keep him keen, eh?'

The Professor made two more illegible notes on his pad. And waited. Martin still had his back turned.

'That's the Courtney brothers sorted, then. I'm all heart, wouldn't you say?'

And now Martin turned.

'Wouldn't you say?' he repeated.

And the Professor saw the look in his eye and nodded dumbly.

'So, that just leaves the sister then,' said Martin, staring hard at the Professor. 'Grace, who I'm going to invite to come with me on our very nice vacation. So, you tell me, you who know so much... yes, you, Professor...' and he hissed the name. 'Do you know who she's fucking?'

The Professor's mouth opened. And Martin approached his seat and leant down and put his face close to his.

'Well, well,' he whispered and rose. He placed himself behind the Professor's chair, and put his hands on the headrest.

'So,' he said. The spite had gone. He was almost jaunty now. 'You know this thing and you don't want to tell me. Is that it?'

The Professor nodded his head almost imperceptibly.

'Which means that I'm going to know who it is.'

The Professor tried not to move his head.

'And that means we now have to address the matter of

extraction of this information. And I'm going to appear to be… not a very nice person. Isn't that right? Because I'm going to have to threaten you, aren't I? For example, there are things I know, too. Isn't that right? Oh, what could I do to you? Let it be known, perhaps, in the place where you value your name so much…'

The Professor shut his eyes. And took a breath.

'It's Gonzo Davies,' he said.

Martin took his hands off the back of the Professor's chair and walked to his desk.

'There,' he said, spreading his hands over the desk. 'All yours. Think of it as your refuge. I'll be gone and you can stay here. And nobody need ever know what three words you just said to me. And all our secrets will stay exactly that. Secrets.'

Martin reached down and picked up a briefcase. He took his coat off a peg on the wall. He started to walk towards the door and then stopped.

'Here's a last question, Professor? When the deal is done, do you know what I'm going to do?'

The Professor shook his head.

'No? Well, there's a thing. And just as important, do you know what I'm going to do with you?'

Grace saw Gonzo once more. She came to his flat in the Bay, flustered and agitated and out of sorts. She checked behind her as she waited for the buzzer to let her into the block of apartments. She almost fell through the door, such was her anxiety to be off the street.

'I told him I had to buy a few things for going away,' she

said. 'I'm sure he knows. He's been really strange. Really kind.'

She realised these were her opening words and she stopped.

'Sorry,' she said. 'Hello, Gonzo.'

He smiled at her and hugged her. 'Hello, Grace.'

'God, it's hard. I didn't see him for weeks and now he's around the whole time.'

She was off again.

'Sorting this and that out for my father, discussing Godfrey's new job. Brother Will came home for the first time in ages. He said he'd just made his biggest sale yet. I'm sure it was Martin, but he sat there and made out he knew nothing about it. They chatted for hours about ceramics. And now he's asked me to go to Russia with him and then off on holiday. He wants me to go with him, as in with him, full stop. On holiday, into his new life. A politician's wife. His wife, I'm sure that's going to be the next thing. I ask you. What am I going to do?'

Grace was laughing and crying, but mostly crying. Gonzo wiped her salty cheeks.

'Look,' she said softly. She opened her cashmere coat. There was nothing beneath it. 'I did a little striptease in the Mazda.'

'My posh bit of totty,' said Gonzo, sliding his hands inside the coat. 'Listen,' he said. 'I could tell you I could look after your dad. Slip him a few quid. Cash. And I could buy a pot from your Will, and I could get your Godfrey a job, labouring for Capper. That's my world, even if I'm down here living this weird life for the moment. We're about to go into camp before the Six Nations. It's a strange place, Grace, where I'll be fighting for my place. I have to be… selfish about it all. There's no time to do anything but concentrate on the rugby. And that's not fair on you.'

'I could sneak in and see you.'

'And that wouldn't be fair on me. This rugby thing won't last long, so I've got to give it a blast.'

'I could wait for you.'

'You couldn't, Grace. You're a full-on, one hundred per cent… commitment. And anyway, what would you be waiting for? When it's all over, you know what I'll do? I'll be back up the mountain. Back to the village, because that's my real life. And it's not a life for you.'

'So, you're not going to sweep me off my feet and carry me away?'

'Only as far as the bed.'

He picked her up and cradled her.

'What am I going to do with you, Gonzo?' she murmured in his ear.

'You're going to dump me,' he replied.

'No. You're dumping me.'

'Only on this bed, Grace. And I'm not dumping you. I'm letting you down gently.'

Martin wasn't entirely sure why he wanted to take Grace to Russia. To Russia with love hardly applied, not after what she had been up to with her trophy catch, her infatuation, her betrayal. Her fall from grace into the gutter.

He was now disposing of Steel-Ag. He was going to Russia to sell what was his and become rich and be unencumbered for a time by responsibility for others. And he was going with Grace, who was not his. Not entirely his, it seemed. Now there was a paradox. Did he really want to be responsible for her? On the other hand, in his dealings with the local Monmouth Conservative Association, he had been made aware by the party traditionalists that family was important. A wife was really rather an essential part of the package, he was advised, to send out a strong message. From the moment he realised that it wasn't money *per se* that warmed his blood, he had had to accept that he would have to compromise. Martin Guest, a compromiser. Now there was another contradiction. But politics was all about it, he told himself. And the thought of what a career in politics might bring, once the compromises were agreed – now that did bring him up to room temperature. Compromise and control. Politics and power. So, the matter of the wife was in hand, he had told the Association – the petty self-regarding functionaries who were his stable lads, giving him a leg-up. And they had been delighted. Could wedding bells be heard, they wanted to know sweetly, politely, cloyingly? And insistently. A General Election couldn't be far away, they reminded him.

Martin wheeled Grace's large suitcase to the door and handed it to Frank, his driver. Grace was more than a compromise. Grace would require forgiveness. And Martin was not sure he had that in his cold blood.

Martin had made a handful of appointments that were special to him. The Professor, for example, was one – in his own skittish way. On the conventional side, there was Colin

Wright, his Chief Financial Officer, a prudent counsellor and bookkeeper who kept everything proof against stain. Martin had recommended to the Russians that Colin be retained. Frank, the driver, lay between the informally employed Professor and Colin, the company man through and through. Frank was on a basic wage, but earned extras. He was as loyal and discreet as anybody with a rear-view mirror could be. Frank was military, an ex-Commando, and now a chauffeur and a delivery driver: a deliverer of messages, a collector of deliveries. Frank in the car had heard and seen more than even the Professor of Martin at work and, although he could never know as much, he had to be trusted. And he was trustworthy. Frank said that when he retired he wanted to buy a smallholding, for the ponies his wife, Marlene, had always wanted to rear. And he wanted this property to be perched on the edge of a cliff, so that when, or if, Marlene predeceased him, he could walk unhesitatingly off it. Frank came at life – and now death, it seemed – in a straight line. There was a place in Cardiganshire he had his eye on. Martin imagined he had paid Frank enough in bonuses to make its purchase a possibility already. If not, Martin would top up Frank's pot anyway, when the deal with the Russians was sealed.

And then there were the Mewson brothers, Gareth and Daniel. Steel-Ag's interest in sport had been fleeting, little more than a gesture for public relations' sake. But on a tour of inspection of the rugby academy in Llanwern, Martin had asked the director, Rhodri Collins, about recruitment.

'Oh, we get all sorts trying to get in,' said Rhodri. 'Schools and clubs in the city and up the Valleys bombard us with kids who are never going to make it. The best way – the only way – is to have our own scouts. They know what we're looking for. And it may not be just a matter of size. It's often a mental toughness we're after. You've got to be committed to make it. So, we stress that we'll do the recruiting. Doesn't stop 'em trying, mind you... have a look at this.'

Rhodri showed Martin a letter from a John Hatherleigh, principal of Pilgrim Stoke College in Bristol. He was offering the services of a pair of brothers to a rugby academy in Wales, for whose colours they qualified thanks to a maternal grandmother born in Llangammarch Wells.

'We think a change of environment would be of considerable benefit to both Gareth and Daniel,' wrote headteacher Hatherleigh. 'They are outstanding prospects, but have been perhaps adversely conditioned by their upbringing in Bristol.'

'I've got a contact in Pilgrim Stoke,' said Rhodri. 'Derek Parsons. We played together for Abertillery. He's a teacher now at one of Bristol's feeder academies and we live in hope that there's one or two over there who aren't quite what they're looking for, but might be prepared to come over the Severn Bridge to us. He says these lads are a right pair of tearaways. Single mother, tough area – all the usual things. They've been excluded from every school they've been to. And it looks as if the Head of Pilgrim Stoke is trying to dump them on us.'

Martin nodded and read the letter again.

'What happens if you do like the look of someone recommended to you?' he asked.

'Well, we invite them over and put them through some

tests and give them a trial. But nobody's come anywhere near cutting it. These boys may be good on the field, but Bristol say they can't be trusted for a second. It's that mental thing. These lads have got to be disciplined.'

'Do me a favour,' said the sponsor. 'Just so I can see the system at work, would you mind giving them a trial?'

Rhodri was as wary of the influence of sponsors on the playing side of the game as the next coach, but he also knew when an order had been given, veiled as a question. He replied to the principal of Pilgrim Stoke College and said they would be delighted to offer the Mewson brothers a trial.

They were big and a little clumsy in the hand-eye co-ordination tests they were put through. Their strength in relation to their body mass was sub-standard and their aerobic levels were poor. But on the field they stuck together like glue, which wasn't so very easy since Daniel was a hooker and Gareth a back-row forward. They nevertheless imposed themselves on everybody around them, mostly by displaying alarming levels of intimidation. They were even sent to the sin-bin together, for starting a fight in which very few others appeared willing to engage. Rhodri suggested to Martin that they had seen enough. Martin replied that he would like to see the brothers again, and asked Rhodri to make an appointment for the Mewson brothers at his Steel-Ag offices.

They appeared at the appointed hour, awkward in blazers and chinos, with ties pulled tight around the collars of clean but un-ironed shirts. Their hair was smeared tight against their scalps and they were a little damp around the brow. But as a pair they still exuded belligerence. This was an opportunity, they recognised, but they would not be taking too much condescension from another adult trying to put them straight.

'You do not have to speak,' said Martin. 'Just listen.'

He put the 18-year-old Gareth and the 17-year-old Daniel on a retainer and told them that if they put one step out of line, he would have them jailed. The obligation to behave included their rugby. They were on the payroll and that came with responsibility. Did they understand? The brothers nodded, even though Martin had his back to them and was staring out at the seagulls over the Bristol Channel.

'Good,' said Martin, not turning. 'In that case, welcome aboard… and welcome home to Wales.'

Yes, the Mewsons had been good appointments.

48

Gonzo had no time to go into the coffee shops in the arcades of Cardiff. Selection for the Wales squad going into the Six Nations Championship intensified his training routines and consumed his time. When he was not on the rugby field or in the gym, he was sleeping or having sports massages, where cruelly expert fingers and elbows dug the blood of bruises and the acid of overuse out of his muscles. In ten days of training he barely finished eight paragraphs of his latest book. The same pages 12 and 13 stared at him from his pillow every morning. He worked, he rested, he froze in ice baths, he rehydrated, he refuelled and he slept. Round and round went his sporting days with Wales, players and coaches turning slowly in their giant bubble, rolling slowly towards the first day of competition. He was bored senseless.

And then his name was announced in the starting fifteen to face Italy in Rome. He was chosen on merit, not because of injuries to others. Suddenly the tedium of repeated drills and endless physical exercise gave way to levels of concentration and attention to the tiniest detail that left all those previously numbed senses buzzing. Gonzo was now a player in charge of his brief, keen to deliver, to impose himself on his stage. He travelled to Rome, happy to be part of a group that pulled the curtains tight around themselves, not as a tourist with eyes on every attraction.

'You'll have all of eternity to see the Eternal City,' said Conrad Thomas, the New Zealander coach of Wales. 'But not this weekend.'

There was one specific job to do and Gonzo willingly surrendered to the single-minded task. He was nervous only about being too nervous in the changing room, fearful that physical nausea might make him lose the mental mastery of his brief. But from the bus on the way to the Olympic Stadium he allowed himself to look out of the team bubble and he found himself relaxing and taking in the sights and sounds along the way. Most of the other players had music pumping into their ears, but Gonzo enjoyed what he could hear: jeering Italian mingling with wildly supportive Welsh fans, in Rome in their thousands.

He ducked a swipe from his opposite number, Fabio Castellani in the first minute and carried the same player three yards over the advantage line with his opening charge with the ball. For the first time ever, his mind seemed to tot up his contributions: his tackle count, his yards gained, his line-out wins, his passes. It would never happen again, but Gonzo had a clear statistical breakdown of his performance. He won his personal duel and Wales won unspectacularly but comfortably, 26-16. After the game he had ice pressed against his right wrist and left shoulder, and suffered a massage – a stabbing of fingers and the point of an elbow – into his stiff back. The physiotherapist, Knuckles Morgan, told him to go out and stretch his legs, and at ten o'clock in the night after the game, Gonzo and Sam Harris found themselves walking from the Piazza Navona to the Pantheon. There was singing all around them and at one point they thought they were going to be mobbed outside an Irish pub. Instead, the crowd parted.

'Well done, lads,' everyone said. 'Keep it going. Only the start. No, Morgan, fuck off with that camera. And you, Lofty, stop pestering the boys for an autograph. Give 'em a break. Leave 'em alone. Maybe one group shot, eh lads? Well done, Sam. Nice one, Gonzo. Just sign this, boys.'

It took them an hour to break clear.

In the car journey to Heathrow Airport, Grace was attentive, asking about Konstantin Mordashov, teasing Frank about rearing ponies. Martin kept his charm intact, although he still saw only the coquette as she made gentle fun of Frank. On the flight to Moscow she was careful to let Martin sleep and only later, when he took a break from his laptop and the moment seemed right, did she ask him about doing business with the Russians. He was slightly off-hand at first, but she pressed on and asked a few questions about the processes of selling, which became an exercise in Martin explaining the processes of steel-making. At the very moment of exiting the steel industry he had become encyclopaedically fluent in its language. He caught himself talking about hot rolled carbon grades and spherodised annealed nickel alloys and found Grace smiling at him.

'Bloody hell,' he said. 'Where did all that come from? Sorry about that.'

'No, no' said Grace. 'In politics, they'd say you've mastered your brief.'

Martin explained the timetable as he saw it, that after this trip to Russia, if all went well, there would be a visit by Konstantin to Cardiff. He found the talk helped, clarified the time-line. On the flight from Moscow to Cherepovets, Grace slept and when she woke she asked him about her role.

'That's a good question,' said Martin. 'You're here… for me, I suppose. Because I… ' And he ran out of words.

She touched his arm. 'I'm here,' she said. 'That'll do for now. Let's see if I can finish that sentence for you.'

Wales's second game in the Six Nations came a week after the away victory in Rome. Gonzo had not played back-to-back internationals before and his body was struggling to cope with recovery from the first and preparation for the next, against Ireland. He hurt all over and three bits of him in particular gave cause for concern, but everyone wanted to drum home the point that if Italy had been draining, the Irish would be bringing a greater intensity to Cardiff. Gonzo nursed his wrist, his shoulder and tried to ease the stiffness in his back, while Conrad called for more explosive power and more supple body positions.

It was only on the Thursday before the Saturday that the bruising calmed down and he could take a full part in training. The confidence he had felt going into the championship opener had been jarred by the struggle to be fit, and he found his self-assurance sinking into a dark place of doubt. He stayed in it during Friday and in the build-up to the game on Saturday. He did not feel sick or even anxious. He felt low.

During the anthems he opened his eyes and looked up into the second tier of the Millennium Stadium. And he saw Grace, up there, protected against the cold by her cashmere coat and a hat, looking at him and telling him that everything would be fine. He had forced himself not to think about her. He had had no time to think about her. But there she was. He closed his eyes as 'Gwlad, Gwlad,' made his ears ring, and when he opened them again, she was gone. Had never been there. It didn't matter.

The cold in Cherepovets was extreme. Martin and Grace had come prepared, but even so, the sub-zero temperatures assaulted them. They were met at the airport by Vladimir and Igor from the Mordashov Company. These large men were there, it seemed, because they spoke a little English. They did not offer to carry the visitors' luggage, or hold open a door for them. They walked outside, in front of Martin and Grace, and stood in the cold. It was like a little test, to make them wait on the cold side of the Arrivals Terminal.

'Ice hockey,' said Vladimir. 'In Cherepovets, is very good.'

'Good use of a natural resource,' Martin replied, and flapped his arms against the cold.

Vladimir and Igor nodded. Two more minutes passed, and then a large Mercedes pulled out from a parking bay, all of thirty metres away.

'Here is Boris, your driver,' said Igor.

Martin put the suitcases in the boot when it sprang open remotely. A second Mercedes pulled out. Vladimir and Igor climbed into the back, while Martin held the rear door of the first car open for Grace.

'They said nothing at all last time,' said Martin once they were inside.

'They obviously like you,' said Grace, turning to see a third Mercedes join their convoy as it left the airport for their hotel.

'Hello, Boris,' said Martin.

The driver glanced in his mirror, said nothing and looked back at the road ahead.

Ireland locked Wales up in their defensive traps where the game was structured. If Wales tried to build from the formal restarts – the scrum and line-out – Ireland knocked them down, including Gonzo. Especially Gonzo. Green shirts swarmed all over him. The frenzy of the close-quarter contest forced Wales to kick the ball, just what Ireland wanted. They returned it with interest, Cormack O'Reardan, their hefty fly-half, sending the ball spiralling into the air. The rest of Ireland set off in pursuit of the high kicks with a vengeance and in a disciplined line. But the ball was now in open play, and the claustrophobic inches grew. The boot of the Irish playmaker was accurate to within feet of a small target, and the Irish players in pursuit all flew up fast, thinking they could challenge for the ball as a catcher, or thunder into little Dapper Williams on the Welsh wing, as he caught it. But Dapper only needed half a yard to evade the first tackle and Cormack's boot could not be so very accurate every time.

Dapper sidestepped and passed infield to his full-back Huw Martins, who was running at a slight angle back towards the touchline. There was still a healthy line of Irish defenders before him, even if their pursuit had been checked by Dapper's counter attack. They adjusted their line to accommodate Huw's change of angle, and sensed an easy hit as the full back slowed. But the deceleration of the ball-carrier made the surge by Nico Davies, the other wing, seem even faster, especially as he was running at a new angle, back towards the centre of the field. And when he slowed, and when Gonzo ran on to his short pass in a dead straight line and at full pelt, the Irish defence was split and Gonzo stormed forty metres up the middle of the field to score under the posts. They called it in the media outpourings of praise, 'the magic of Welsh improvisation', although the back three of Dapper, Huw and Nico had been practising these changes of direction and velocity all week, and Conrad Thomas had known that if Gonzo could put his body and head back together, he could be the final part of the equation. You could stop Gonzo here and here and here, but you couldn't stop him there. Wales won 18-12.

Grace had expected to be sharing a room with Martin in the huge modern hotel in a business park on the edge of town, but as Miss Courtney she was shown to a vast suite of her own. She had dinner with Martin and they talked about her first impressions of Russia, which amounted to no more than the sentence of conversation with Valdimir and Igor. Martin and Grace's conversation was not much more expansive. Night had fallen early and they seemed locked inside, with an endless, hostile whiteness all around. Martin excused himself, saying he had to prepare for his first meeting the next day, and that was that. Grace slept on her own.

Martin was picked up early the next morning and Grace was left to her own devices in this frozen steel city in northern Russia. She read, she sent emails and texted, building electronic bridges with the outside world. But she felt cut off and isolated. Martin returned, looking tired and serious. He asked her to meet him in the bar.

'It's all in the detail,' he said over an imported Finnish beer. 'It's another test, I'm sure. They've had all the specifications from us, but they keep wanting more. From me. It's all very well for Mordashov. He's been in steel all his life. I'm…'

'You're very good at all this,' said Grace. 'This is what you do.'

'But it feels alien, doesn't it?'

Grace had to nod.

'All very deliberate…' Martin mused. 'A test. Either that, or they're stalling. And that's what worries me. I'm sorry, but I need to contact the office…'

He was standing up to leave when a large body of men swept into the bar. It was the entourage of Konstantin

Mordashov, and behind them came the boss himself. They were all large and square – the bodyguards in their twenties, the personal assistant and the interpreter in their thirties, and the boss in his fifties. Everybody else in the bar knew exactly who had made their entrance and all conversations dipped.

Everything was conducted through the interpreter: the introductions, the ordering of a bottle of vodka and the rounds of toasts. Konstantin was serious, polite and hardly spoke a word to Grace. To Martin he spoke of ice hockey and the team, the Steelers, he sponsored. Four times he raised his glass and they all joined him in saluting Russia, Cherepovets, steel and the Steelers, and downing their shots. And just as abruptly as he had entered, he was gone, he and his men rising as one and sweeping out of the hotel. The interpreter, Oleg, had the last word, asking Martin not to forget the documentation they had requested for the morning.

'What do you think?' asked Martin when the noise level in the bar was back to normal.

Grace's stomach was on fire.

'I think to have a conversation here, you have to know about ice-hockey,' she said. Martin ran a hand along her shoulder on his way to the lift.

The next morning, Martin was picked up and put in the third car of an extended convoy of seven Mercedes. This was Konstantin's car. Grace sighed and prepared for a second day of solitude, but Boris appeared and indicated that she should go with him. Boris was his normal self and car number five in the convoy was silent. Most of the other vehicles on the road were heavy lorries, carrying lumber or steel, and they created a swirl of snow and ice particles on the highway. After about twenty minutes, the convoy began to pass a derelict steelworks, on a scale that Grace had never seen before. A mountain of rusting factory soared over their heads, stretching before them as far as the eye could see. The road was clear, but after a mile, the convoy stopped and remained stationary for five minutes. Boris leant back against the headrest. Grace felt a heat in her stomach. It was not the warm glow from contact made the night before, but an unpleasant after-effect of the vodka. She swallowed. She glanced at the cars ahead and at her driver, who seemed to know that this unexplained wait could go on for some time. She opened the door, making Boris snap his head forward.

'It's ok, Boris. I need some air.'

She walked towards the old works, blowing steam into the freezing air. There was no fence between the road and the steel plant and soon she was in touching distance of the towering structure. She took off her gloves and was reaching into her bag for her small digital camera when a voice made her jump.

'It is not always safe to stand so close to old Soviet industry,' said Konstantin. He was on his own.

'You speak English. Very well.'

'Your driver, Boris, is my teacher. His real name is Billy. He is from Sheffield.'

They both laughed.

'But seriously, it is not safe,' said Konstantin. There is danger from falling debris. And you must put your gloves on in this cold.'

Grace pulled her camera out.

'Ah, the eye of the artist...' he said. 'What you see here is beyond me. To me this is of no interest now.'

'Of no interest now?' said Grace. 'Does that mean there was a time when it was?'

Konstantin paused for a moment and then walked towards a wide opening in the rusted cladding. 'Come,' he said.

'May I?' asked Grace, pointing to her camera.

He shrugged.

'I may surprise you,' said Grace.

'Yes, I think you may,' he said and led her into the plant. 'But put your gloves on between clicks.'

They were inside for half an hour. In the freezing penumbra of the steelworks and against a soundtrack of corrugated sheets high overhead banging in the wind, he told her how he had started at one end of the plant, in the coke works, at the age of fifteen and had worked his way all the way down the line to the other end, where the finished steel came out of the rolling mill. While he talked, he walked and pointed, and Grace took photos, but never pointed the camera directly at his face.

'In the days of communism I was a worker. And now in these days of... free enterprise, I am the owner,' he said at the end. 'You will see my new factory, the improvements. What we made here was of – how do I say it? – fluctuating quality...'

'But...?'

'Yes... you are right. There is a but. I was wrong to say this is of no interest. I have not been in here for many years. This is a place of memories.'

'Can I ask you a question?'

'Of course.'

'Why did the cars stop here?'

Konstantin looked at her for a moment. He shrugged again.

'To see what would happen,' he said.

Wales played their third game in the Six Nations in Paris. They travelled with the confidence born of two wins. Gonzo moved with greater personal ease, his injuries unaffected by the game against Ireland and responding to the free weekend between rounds two and three in the championship. Wales trained expectantly, aware that Conrad the coach was preparing for something special against France. Two years before the World Cup, there were the first stirrings of a new complexity to the Welsh game. The contrasting lines of the back three were being expanded to include all the three-quarters.

'None of this is possible without the dogs snarling,' Conrad had shouted at the forwards in the week after the victory over Ireland. 'So, you lot, the basics come first. First and foremost. Basics, basics.'

But then, in the second week of camp and in the last few days before the French game, he started to demand that the heaviest of the forwards be alert to changes in the direction of the flow. They, too, had to calculate angles of running. Basics gave way to four-pass multiple switches.

'Spaghetti Junction rugby,' Lump-head Morgan, the prop, called it.

The other front-row forwards all agreed, declaring themselves bemused by all this dancing and the reduction in the volume of heavy contact. But after the fourth consecutive training session of nothing but touch rugby, the entire squad was starting to respond to the barked orders from Conrad to cut against the flow, and then change direction with a pass again, and then again. And change speed, and then direction, and then, wait for it, give it to the runner going straight. Gonzo was always the straight man.

The army of Welsh supporters, in bobble-hats or the alternative head-dress of leaks and daffodils, knew nothing of the plan to take on the French at a game of high-risk passing. They arrived in Paris and played a far more traditional game of drinking and singing, travelling in their flocks around the quarters of the capital, falling into the arms of French fans and singing and drinking with their new friends. What they all missed, by virtue of being sound asleep after their carousing, was a breakfast meeting in a small café, run by an old couple from the Auvergne, off the Place des Vosges. It would be said in the media, who quickly dubbed this meeting 'The Pact', that the breakfast took the sting out of the contest. Conrad Thomas and his French counterpart, Marcel Ranchinski, begged to differ. They said they met at the table as two old friends and insomniacs, and that what they both sought was simply a 'moment of clarification over a café au lait.'

'What did you agree?' the press insisted on knowing.

'To give it a rip,' said Conrad.

'So, Billy, it seems we have a little secret, don't we?'

The driver looked at Grace and said nothing as he kept up with the car in front. The convoy sped through the whirls of snow to the new steelworks, gleaming white – a block of solidity the same colour as the swirling storm. There, Konstantin was back in full modern mode, nostalgia hidden beneath brusqueness. Oleg the interpreter was busy because the boss spoke nothing but Russian. But when one of the bodyguards stepped in front of Grace's camera as she lined up a shot of the works, Konstantin held up a thick finger and indicated that she should be allowed to take her snaps.

When the working day was done, Oleg translated an invitation delivered by Anatoly, the personal assistant, for Grace and Martin to have dinner that night at Konstantin's home. Mr Mordashov's wife, Ludmila, would be delighted to prepare a meal for them, relayed Oleg.

As they were heading back to the cars, Konstantin intercepted Martin and Grace.

'My wife and I met at that old factory,' he said in English. 'We shall have workers' food. Potatoes sprinkled with rust.'

If the media were subsequently a bit suspicious of any contrivance in the France-Wales game, the viewing public adored what happened that night. The lead changed hands a dozen times in a match that produced eleven tries. The only two unhappy people were the defence coaches, who said the tackling in the movements leading up to at least six of the tries was below an acceptable standard. Conrad and Marcel agreed with the analysis, but promptly added that by their reckoning that left five tries, scores that were simply beyond the reach of any defensive system.

Gonzo scored two tries and was one player whose tackling could not be faulted. Even he though could only stand and watch as Luc Callais dropped a goal from 45 metres to give France victory in the last minute, 45-43. The sports newspaper, *L'Equipe*, called it the 'Game of the Century' and not many disagreed, even if for Wales it brought to an abrupt halt the quest to win another grand slam in the Six Nations.

'Is that the end of Spaghetti Junction rugby, then?' asked Lump-head as he sat exhausted in the changing room at the end of the game.

'It's only the beginning,' said Conrad.

As Grace was dressing for dinner, there was a knock on her door. She thought it must be Martin, but was surprised to find the most stunning young woman she had ever seen standing before her.

'Hello. I am Natalya. I am a friend of Konstantin's.'

Grace let her into the room. Natalya was carrying a box that she placed on the bed. She frowned, as if trying hard to remember the exact words to say.

'Konstanin says this is a private present. Maybe not for tonight, but to wear when you are at work in the factory.' Natalya paused, to see if this made any sense to Grace.

Grace looked quizzical and Natalya invited her to open the present. Inside the box was a sable fur hat. Grave put it on.

'You look beautiful,' said Natalya sadly. She was in her early twenties and nearly six feet tall. Eyes that suggested she came from the eastern reaches of Russia brimmed with tears. 'Can I ask you a question?' she said.

'Of course, Natalya.'

'Are you going to be Konstantin's next mistress?'

Grace burst out laughing.

'No, Natalya. I am not. I am with somebody else. He is here.'

Natalya's face lit up. She looked at Grace and turned her to face the mirror. Grace stuck her tongue out. Natalya laughed and asked if she could try on the hat. She left her long dark hair loose and pulled the hat on. She looked even more beautiful.

'I will have to please Konstantin to have a hat like this,' she said.

Ludmila Mordashov genuinely did not have a word of English, but thanks to her eighteen-year-old daughter, Tatiana, who spoke it perfectly, Grace was made to feel at home in their hosts' house, a wooden palace in the forest. Konstantin had invited the three women to stay in the living room, where a log-burner blazed away, but Ludmila and Tatiana had taken Grace by an arm each and pulled her into the kitchen. Ludmila was nine inches shorter than Natalya and a few kilos heavier, while Tatiana was in between, with the broad shoulders of a swimmer. She emptied a bottle of full-bodied claret into three large glasses and the three set about preparing dinner to Ludmila's expansive instructions. They emerged an hour later, covered in flour and slightly disorderly, to announce that dinner – anything but potatoes sprinkled in rust – was served.

Only Konstantin seemed sober. Martin was not a big drinker, but on this one night he went with the mood of the house. Tatiana translated for Grace when Ludmila told them what a rogue Konstantin was in his youth. Konstantin translated a completely different version for Martin and they all ended up laughing and raising their glasses to the truth, the non-truth, the past, the present and a big future. Martin leant heavily against Grace in the car and put his hand on her leg.

'Thank you,' he slurred. 'For being here. I needed you.'

He moved his hand and Grace took a deep breath and pressed herself ever so slightly against him. He murmured something. It sounded like, 'I forgive you.' His hand stopped. Grace looked at him. He was fast asleep. She would spend her last night in Russia alone in her suite.

'I'll give you a hand, Miss Grace, putting him to bed,' said Boris. He had his eyes fixed on the road. 'You've done alright, you 'ave.'

49

Gwyn returned to the village just after war was declared on Germany on September 1st 1939. At dawn in Pontypool he climbed down from the lorry that had brought him from Gloucester on the final leg of his journey from Spain to Wales, and began to walk the last dozen miles. After Blaenavon he left the road to cut across the moor and then up the dram road to the top of the mountain. He wanted to see the lie of the land, breathe in the air of home. He wanted to revisit the little scratching in the landscape, where he had last held Lena. Nothing had changed, it seemed. The pit was working and the clanking and banging in the marshalling yard rose through the light mist that still hung over the mountain at mid-day and obscured the view to the south.

'Well, well, bloody well,' said old Mari Lloyd at the door of her lodging house. 'Gwyn bloody Seymour. Thought we'd seen the last of you.'

'Hello, Mrs Lloyd.'

'Still swimming against the tide, eh? Everybody's off to war and you come home.' Mari pushed the door fully open and turned painfully on her arthritic hip. 'You'd better come in.'

The house was a little weary, but spotless. In the hallway, where there used to be a whole row of miners' boots, now there were only two pairs. Mari poured strong tea, dipped a spoon into the sugar bowl, thought about it, tapped half the amount back and stirred it into Gwyn's cup.

'They say there'll be rationing soon enough,' she said.

'I'd forgotten what a cup of village tea tastes like,' said Gwyn. He sat for a moment, sipping from the cup he held in his left hand.

'Spain, was it?' asked Mari.

Gwyn nodded.

'They hunted high and low for you, you know. The police. Running away like that put you right in the frame.' Mari put her cup in its saucer. 'Maybe you don't know.'

'Know what?'

'Why they wanted you. What is it now, three years ago? Why they were after you.'

'They were just after me. Could have been for any one of a hundred reasons.'

'No, Gwyn Seymour. You were wanted for murder.'

Mari told Gwyn about the discovery of the body of Alfie Trott, and how Gwyn was the number one suspect, at least in the eyes of the police.

'Of course, people in the village knew better, even if you were a bit wild. We had a bit of fun, I don't mind telling you, sending the coppers down a few blind alleys. Anyway, after a while, the trail went cold. You were gone and the police were getting nowhere. A couple of years passed. And then the countdown starts to this war and, at last, they start turning up the heat on those blackshirts. And they round up them two brothers, the Crabbs. Remember? Ugly pair on a motorbike. Inseparable. Well, inseparable until the police split them up. That made a difference. Before you know it, they're singing like canaries. This is all new to you, isn't it?'

Gwyn had a flashback of the brothers at the Keeper's Pond, the roar of their Triumph. He nodded.

'Well, it gets even better,' Mari went on. 'They spill the beans and confess to the murder of this Alfie Trott, who, it turns out, worked for the Cranshaws. Aye, Richard bloody Cranshaw. Well, that was the rumour. They covered it up, of course, and Cranshaw did the honourable thing and joined up as soon as he could. No questioning his loyalty. But his wife… seems she's the fascist in the family. Last we heard from Dai the Beat – before he joined up, too – was that she's going to be rounded up and packed off to the Isle of Man.'

Gwyn saw Richard Cranshaw pointing his finger at him. 'A consequence,' he heard the mine owner say.

'They strung the Crabbs up in Swansea jail, three months ago,' said Mari.

Gwyn saw their heads flashing between the mounds as they set off in pursuit of Alfie Trott. It could have been Gwyn who'd ended up dead at their hands. Mari poured him a second cup of tea and spooned in a full ration of sugar.

'So, you're back. And you want a room.'

Gwyn nodded.

'And let me guess. You've no money, right?'

Gwyn shook his head.

'No job?'

Gwyn looked down.

'And no bloody fingers.'

She took his right hand and examined it.

'Was it worth it, Gwyn Seymour?'

There was work at the mine, even for a one-handed invalid. Mining was not yet included in the list of reserved occupations and there was a steady trickle out of the village to join up, leaving spaces to fill. Gwyn was given a job above ground in the manager's office, filling in the ledgers, updating the records. His early attempts to write with a pen held between the thumb and the palm of his right hand left an indecipherable mess on the pages. He forced himself to use his left hand. After hours and hours of practice, his script was slow, but his pages were clear.

'So, you've crossed to the other side, Gwyn boy,' was the barb among the miners. 'All that light in your office, all those books – you're in the perfect position now to tell 'em how they can screw us.'

It was a joke and Gwyn went along with it, but it was an undeniable truth that he was no longer part of the underground brotherhood. He no longer shared the mood of his community. The mine and the village, like the country at large, were energised by the war effort. Even the Reverend Arthur Davies had marched off, to train as a chaplain in the Royal Navy. Everybody was caught up in the preparation for conflict, all except the ex-miner who had already fought and lost his battles. Gwyn felt isolated in his home and fell prey to an increasing sense of solitude. He soon paid Mari what he owed her in rent. His landlady's money worries were eased; Gwyn sank lower.

If there was another unhappy person in the village it was Gwen Davies, the vicar's wife. Round and rosy in the days when she debated international affairs with Gwyn, in the three years he had been away she had grown weary of being patronised and patted by her husband. She had grown rounder when Arthur was at home and now that he was gone, she was growing more flushed, partial to sherry by the schooner and then in fleets of schooners, and even to a nip of communion wine. The pounds fell off her as she forsook bread to go with her wine. Gwen was falling measure by measure for the demon drink. Gwyn sometimes went past the vicarage and noticed that the once immaculate rose beds were untended. The lawn was unkempt and weeds spilled through the iron railing. He never saw the vicar's wife.

The weeks and months passed and nothing came to the village. Coal left it, and so did more men. Gwyn became busier and busier on the management side, organising a shrinking workforce to keep the output as high as possible.

He was very good at his increasingly responsible job, but it hardly made him the most popular person at the mine. His spirits could not improve, especially since the surrounding mood was far less optimistic now. The war was not going well. In the early summer of 1940 the Phoney War gave way to the German invasion of France and the British Expeditionary Force began its retreat to Dunkirk. At the end of May, the Reverend Arthur Davies left his training base in Dartmouth, as instructed, travelled by bus and train to Hythe in Kent, and in complete contravention of his orders, jumped aboard a fishing boat called *Excalibur* and joined the armada of little ships that crossed the Channel to help bring the broken army home. Three times the vicar went back and forth, pulling soldiers out of the water and ferrying them home.

Two days later, he managed to send word through the church that he was back safely. Gwen received the information late in the afternoon from the ancient Canon Digby Davies, who phoned her from Ebbw Vale. She put the receiver down with a vague sense of disappointment. To lose Arthur at sea, heroically, would have freed her from his condescension and pats. She pulled the last bottle of sherry from the cupboard beneath the sink. It was empty. She cursed and then remembered where there was a last stock of wine.

Gwyn had finished work and was heading for the reading room at the Institute. Dunkirk had been on everybody's mind all day and he felt he should try to work out to what extent the evacuation was the miracle that church leaders and politicians were calling it, or a military catastrophe. As he walked through the streets of the village, however, he felt the lure of his old centre of self-improvement fade. What was the point? He sensed the dark clouds gathering in his head, a depression that would soon obscure everything. Why even bother? He stopped walking, almost willing the shroud to envelope him. It wasn't quite there yet. The spike had yet to be hammered into his mind. He found himself outside the church and for no reason that he would ever be able to provide, he walked deliberately up to its door and went inside. He sat in a pew and waited for the swing of the cleaver, the blow that would drop him into the pit.

'Goodness me, it's Red Gwyn,' said Gwen. 'And what brings you to the house of the Lord?'

She sat down beside him and noticed his hand. He noticed the fumes on her breath, the slightly creased look to her blouse and long summer skirt.

'Hello, Mrs Davies,' he said quietly. 'What a pair we make.'

'Gwyn and Gwen. It's absurd.'

For a moment they sat there and said nothing. Gwyn looked at the stained glass window above the altar without really seeing it, and then turned to look Mrs Davies in her ruddy face. She reached out, took his right hand and studied the stump. And Gwyn started to tell her the story he had told nobody else, about his journey from the moment he left the village to the moment he returned. And the tears that he had never shed in Spain or France began to fall. And as they did, Gwen Davies stood up and went to the door of the church and turned the large key in the lock. She returned to the pew, took Gwyn's hand again and let him finish his story and his crying, all thoughts of drinking the last of the communion wine in the vestry now gone. When Gwyn's tale was told, they sat in silence again. She then placed his mutilated hand on her left breast. And when Gwyn did not remove it, she stood, and in the coolness of St Cadoc's she hitched up her creased floral skirt, straddled him and seduced him back to life.

50

For a few weeks after the trip to Cherepovets, Martin put Grace first. He still had work duties to assign to the Professor and to Colin, but the deal was as good as done and Martin could concentrate on the next stage of his life. He did not drink again to excess on their extended holiday, wishing to remain sharp of wit in his wooing of her and not reveal anything of the nature that he regarded as his weaker side. Or the truer side, or was it the stronger side? He couldn't tell. All he knew was that at this particular juncture, he needed to put Grace first, and once the decision was taken, only on a single occasion did he feel the heat of the flame from the other side.

It happened when they were in Amsterdam, a city neither of them had visited before. The Siberian wind that had frozen them in the far north had pursued them south and they were wrapping up against it, dressing for Holland as they had for

Russia. Martin had expected Grace to put her list of visitor destinations to him, from the Van Gogh Museum to the Anne Frank House, but on the first morning of their arrival at the Hotel Pulitzer she had suggested they simply walk and explore.

'What do you think?' she asked, putting a box on their double bed. 'Konstantin gave it to me.' She pulled out her sable hat.

And Martin heard a little whisper in his head: 'Whore.'

He pushed the thought back and down, not brutally enough to crush it, but pressing it until he felt a little internal click of the ratchet, the catch of the mechanism that would hold the word at bay, conceal the image of Grace's betrayal.

'It suits you perfectly,' he said.

They walked and they talked and that night they ate in a restaurant by the Keizersgracht canal. Grace tried to drink as little as Martin, but she needed to fortify herself and was working her way through most of a bottle of Sancerre.

'I've been thinking about your life in politics,' she said. 'Do you mind if I ask you a bit more about it?'

'You can grill me as much as you like. Once you've been through the Monmouth Conservative Association vetting process you have no fingernails left to pull out. You cannot hurt me.'

'OK. Why the Conservatives?'

'Because I am a Conservative – by natural inclination and by conviction. I do not have a liberal bone in my body and I am not of the working class.'

'But how conservative a Conservative are you?'

'I am a traditional Tory.' Martin looked around the

restaurant. 'I like Europe, but do not want to be part of its political union. I believe in the United Kingdom, a strong country that trades and grows without interference. Without being nannied. I believe in small government.'

'But not as small as the one in Wales. You live there. Why not go into Welsh politics?'

Martin nearly choked.

'You can hurt me after all, madam chairman,' he said. 'Two things. One, the Conservatives will never run Wales. And I do not want to be a politician in opposition. Two, the Welsh Assembly Government is useless. They cannot run a bath. Devolution was a… misfortune. Wales would be better managed from outside. I want to be part of real politics. And that means the UK government in Westminster.'

'So, you don't want to be part of a federal Europe, run from Brussels, but you do want Wales to be part of a federal Britain, run from London.'

'Very good, Grace. You can write my speeches.'

'I was sort of joking.'

'Politics can be such fun, can't it?'

Grace looked at the bottle. She thought Martin might disapprove of her consumption, but he reached across and poured himself a thimbleful and the rest into her glass.

'Cheers,' he said.

'*Gezondheid*,' she replied.

'Alarmingly European,' he said.

They clinked glasses.

'This grilling you had,' said Grace. 'They must have asked you something that made you squirm a little.'

'They asked if I had a wife.'

'Ah, the little wifey question…'

'Yes, that one.'

'How tricky. Did you hold out your hand and say, 'Take a nail', or did you say that on some issues you weren't such a traditional Tory, after all?'

'No. I said I was working flat-out to rectify the shortcoming in my life.'

That night, in their shared suite on the top floor of the Pulitzer Hotel, they made love. Not with abandon or at any great length, but satisfactorily. Traditionally, thought Grace.

The next morning she awoke to find him gone. She thought for a moment it was for good – that he had somehow made an official record of the bedding of his woman to prove his credentials to the Monmouth Association. Within ten minutes, however, the door opened and Martin was back. He was holding a bunch of flowers.

'Too early, even in Holland, for tulips,' he said. 'But I managed to find some red roses.'

'Probably shipped in from the colonies,' said Grace. 'Ours, of course.'

'Excellent, Grace. We'll make a high Tory of you, yet.'

Wales tried to play with the same extravagance in Scotland as they had in Paris, the trouble being that the rain fell as a cold curtain across Murrayfield, shrinking the gap between the fast and the slow, negating the contrasts in angles and distance that could set a defence on its heels. Besides, Scotland had studied the recordings of the Welsh performance against France and had spotted trends within the supposedly indecipherable bursts from the back. They slowed as a line and let the initial runners weave and dance and concentrated on gang-tackling the player who mattered most, the straight-running Gonzo.

He began the game in the best condition of his life, every bruise and contusion forced from his muscles by days of penetrating, painful massage. He had suffered on the table, but felt fresh and reconditioned on the field before the fourth encounter of the Six Nations. Every time he surged on to the ball, however, he was felled by a minimum of two defenders, including Callum Browne and Stuart Craig, opponents with whom he had locked horns before. On this occasion, they did not attempt to rile him verbally, but saved their breath for stopping him physically. Caught out in the open, with blue shirts buzzing into the gaps where he hoped to find a supporting player in red, Gonzo was unable to slip passes out of the tackle. He had to take the ball to ground and the Welsh attacks splashed to a halt in the mud of Scotland.

The home team displayed no adventure in attack, saving all their energy, it seemed, for their defence. They would not yield a try and were hell-bent on not even giving Wales the consolation of a penalty attempt. Silently and with obsessive discipline, Scotland threw themselves at the legs and chests of Welsh players in possession of the ball, jumped back to their feet and rejoined the defensive system, denying their opponents a single sniff of the Scottish goal line. If they could hold Wales at zero, crumbs at the other end might be enough for a Scottish victory, their second of the Six Nations.

Scotland rarely entered the Welsh half, even in the second period when the wind and rain blew at their backs, but whenever they crept into kicking range they came away with three points. With fifteen minutes remaining Scotland led 12-0. At that point, Gonzo called a meeting of his increasingly frustrated and flustered teammates and ordered a return to 'Spuds, not spaghetti.' They scored an unconverted try from a driving maul, a collective effort finished by Lump-head Morgan, who then played his part in the final push of the day, a heave against a scrum six metres from the Scottish line. The scrum began to slide in the Murrayfield morass, the only time the conditions would conspire against the home team. Scotland's goal line was going to be crossed for the second time and they took the decision to infringe, the front row buckling deliberately. The scrum nose-dived to a halt, but the referee was heading for the posts, awarding Wales a penalty try that was easily converted. Wales escaped with a 12-12 draw.

Disappointment at the end of the grand slam dream in Paris was compounded now by the shock of no longer being in the running for the title. The draw was greeted with sullen disapproval on the day by the Welsh fans in Edinburgh and with harsh criticism from the media in the days that followed. Once the cadaver of the defeat and the draw had been dissected and the post-mortem verdict delivered – it was declared that Wales had twice been victims of an attack of the vapours – thoughts turned to the last game of the Six Nations. Wales had seven days to put their grand folly behind them. Changes would have to be made. Gonzo, tackled out of the game for sixty-five minutes, was vulnerable. The coach, Conrad Thomas, would have to preach common sense. Or like his number 8, he might as well start packing his bags. The 'game of the century' had quickly turned to gloom. Everybody feared the team was too deeply infected with a cavalier spirit, forgetting the ten minutes, commissioned by Gonzo, that had saved them against Scotland. England, winners of all their matches, including a grinding defeat of France in the fourth round – the English had rejected the invitation to 'give it a rip' – would be Wales's final opponents. England were now going for the grand slam and would travel to Cardiff, it was generally concluded, with little to fear.

Cold Amsterdam gave way to a fortnight of Indian Ocean sunshine at the Desroches Island resort in the Seychelles. It seemed to Grace that this was a paradise for honeymooners or for couples celebrating their engagement, and that she was kept one question away from joining them in their delight. She waited for Martin to propose, and she waited. He spent an hour in the gym every morning, his workout crisp and precise. Otherwise, he sat by the pool or lay on the beach and seemed content to watch the world, including Grace, engage in physical activity that did not appeal to him. She began to swim, unenthusiastically at first, but with increasing confidence and ferocity. She then supplemented this exercise by running at dawn, lapping the island on cycle paths. She was toned and tanned and feeling good about everything, except her role in Martin's life. She tried one night to take the initiative in bed but found him sleepily unresponsive.

As if he sensed the growing suspicion in her that they were two singles in an island resort made for a shared holiday, he led her to bed the next day after lunch and devoted the entire afternoon to giving her pleasure. She sensed he wasn't particularly aroused himself, but he massaged and caressed her with an intensity that she had to admit did the trick. Afterwards she draped herself over him and felt the gentle breeze through the open window cooling her. When she awoke, he was gone, the question of marriage as unasked as ever.

51

The Carmarthen Young Farmers were aware that since they were the third point of the Devil's Trident, the last prong of the Welsh Hell, the peacefulness to which they had returned after the incident in Guildhall Square might be shaken if, as seemed to be the case, there arose the political will for retribution. They were not sure what alarmed them more, the crackdown in Denbigh or the renewed insurrection in Cardiff. Both scenarios were prejudicial to their desire for a resumption of normal rural life.

It struck them that to leave town might suit all parties. Lie low elsewhere. They knew the march from the north had settled in Builth and they knew the road from west to mid-Wales as well as any. Travelling to the Royal Welsh Show in the summer was part of the rural fabric in which they wished to wrap themselves once more. The cause was just, they declared ardently in the Plume of Feathers, for they all cared deeply about the Welsh language. The destination was perfect, a home from home for agricultural refugees, and the timing could not have been more opportune. Two days after Operation Ladysmith in Denbigh, and three days into the Aprilfest in Builth Wells, a convoy of temporary asylum seekers set off up the A40 for Llandeilo, then Llandovery and beyond to Builth. On the road, they were the first to report the police activity, but soon messages and phone calls from all points were telling of an encirclement of the town.

The meetings between the management of BBC Wales, the leaders of the march and the academics had led to one conclusion – that the decision to reduce output in the Welsh language could only be reversed by politicians. They reached that finding in no time at all, but since they were all old friends, they decided to make the most of their time together and tarry in Builth. They continued to meet in the BBC pavilion on the showground, stretching their ruminations beyond the issue of the language and into the broader pastures of the events shaking Wales. The Welsh Hell, the phrase that Meirion Owen Jones had helped to coin, seemed an odd companion to this protest march. Was there a connection? The presence of the Trelawnyd choir seemed to suggest there was, as did the arrival of the Carmarthen farmers. The whole idea of the march was to reach Cardiff, where hell had been reignited.

But the people discussing these matters were not revolutionaries, they told themselves. They sought to analyse the road ahead. They sent out an invitation to the Secretary of State for Wales to meet them, and also to the Welsh Assembly Government. From the Senedd in Cardiff came a positive response and an offer of a meeting in Cardiff Bay. From London came a frosty reply, a simple no.

For three days the meetings went on, and at the end of each day the Sages – a name given to the elders pondering the ways and the woes of Wales by the throng on the other side – crossed the river. Their fifteen-strong stroll over the bridge became something of a ritual. A mock roar went up as they entered the rugby field, although on the evening of the third day, a more serious assembly formed around them to see if they could verify the rumours that the police were descending on Builth.

Doctor Meirion Owen Jones was ushered forward by the other Sages. He climbed on a table in front of Hazel's snack bar.

'We are in the middle of... something,' he shouted. Brian stepped forward and thrust a loud hailer into his hand. 'Literally in the middle, here in Builth. But the middle of what – apart from Wales? Things are happening behind us and ahead of us. And we are in the middle. Are the police coming for us? Why would they do that?'

The crowd was growing all the time, locals and protestors coming to hear the address of the Sage.

'Cardiff,' Meirion continued, 'is where we are still going. And if on our travels – our peaceful march – we become part of a greater... turbulence, then so be it. But we go in peace.'

He paused and surveyed the crowd.

'I suggest we wait,' he said. 'What are we in the middle of? When all is said and done, we're in the middle of a beer festival.'

A huge roar went up.

'Not so long ago I mocked the notion of revolution on a full bladder. Well, tonight let's fill it up and tomorrow we'll see what will be.'

The advice to wait and see what was coming the way of Builth was not quite what the news crews accompanying the protest march wanted. The pause in the town had gone on long enough, and to justify their continued presence in mid-Wales they needed the Welsh Hell to be a bit more hellish. Three days of drinking at a beer festival provided neither pictures nor sound of a nation about to tear itself to pieces.

They were soon on the move. A police car, dawdling its way towards the scene of a minor break-in at a social club in Pillgwenlly – Pill, as it was known across Newport – had come under attack. All police cars approached this central part of the city with care, and on this occasion with every reason, because at the far end of Commercial Road they were in range of fifty stone-throwing youngsters. The car was last seen flying past the Waterloo pub and a dozen cameras, held by locals who just happened to have been tipped off about a filming opportunity coming their way. There was a scramble to share the images with newsrooms across the country. The most popular footage was transferred from an iPhone that revealed the speeding police car in the foreground – complete with a brick bouncing off its roof – and behind it, Newport's signature landmark, the Transporter Bridge, before everything was suddenly blotted out by a face, hidden in a balaclava, thrusting itself into the lens.

'See you at the Westgate,' the face shouted.

It made no sense until somebody pointed out that this was the hotel in the city centre, attacked by the Chartists in 1839. Newport was back in the news and in a matter of hours, Gwent Police were as busy as forces up and down Wales, trebling their patrols. Up and down Commercial Road they prowled, but not straying too far off it to venture into the heart of Pill.

In Swansea it was the fire service that ran into trouble. A pair of tenders on their way to put out a small fire in an abandoned chapel in the Townhill area of the city, found their way blocked by homemade barricades at either end of Powys Avenue.

'Take ten, guys,' said a young woman to the firefighters. She made no attempt to hide her face. 'It's an empty shell. Let the flames rise.'

The fire fighters tried to persuade the builders of the barricade that they were obliged to put out the blaze, but the woman held her ground.

'You don't get it,' she shouted as the flames grew behind her. 'This is revolution, guys, and Swansea's going to burn brighter than Cardiff.'

After the stone-throwing in Pill came fire in the city. Newport had its own version, pyres on the banks of the Usk, from Caerleon down to the point where the river ran into the Bristol Channel. The fire-setters used wood, rather than cars or buildings, to burn. There seemed to be an endless supply of driftwood and other combustible detritus along the river, and the attraction of simple bonfires was that they could be built quickly in places the emergency services could not easily reach. There was no grand conflagration in the city, but instead there formed a whole chain of smaller blazes that wound with the Usk in the still of a spring night. Smoke from this meandering river of fire settled as a haze over the city, a dome of grey that could be seen in Cardiff. Newport was burning, too.

52

Martin and Grace returned to Cardiff three days before the Wales-England game. Martin ignored the event, plunging himself instead into the final details of the sale of Steel-Ag to Konstantin Mordashov, who was due to arrive on the Friday. He also more or less dismissed Grace the moment they landed in Cardiff Wales Airport from Amsterdam Schipol, saying that he would see her when his schedule allowed. Stunned for a moment, Grace turned away to see her father waiting in Arrivals, holding out his arms. She was about to fall into them when Martin reappeared.

'Sorry,' he said. 'That sounded bad. I'll see you as soon as I can, if that's all right.'

He kissed her on the mouth and gave her a big hug. He shook Captain James warmly by the hand and asked after Godfrey and Will and the house and the garden. And only then did he leave them. James Courtney took his daughter's two hands in his and ran a thumb over her ring finger and raised an eyebrow. She laughed, and shook her head. On the way back to Monmouthshire, she told him all about Russia, Holland and the Seychelles and when they were home she showed him the photographs she had taken. As she revealed the shots of Cherepovets, her stream of chatter slowed and the captain found himself sitting in silence as she began to sift carefully through her images of the frozen north.

After the Scotland game, serious training for the showdown with England began on the Tuesday. The Welsh players were sore and anxious, unsure if the defeat and the draw in the last two rounds would force a rethink in selection and strategy. Gonzo was called in to see Conrad the day before the announcement of the team.

'Sit down,' said the coach.

Here it comes, thought Gonzo. Conrad leant back and put his two hands together as if in prayer.

'I hope you're not listening to any of the bullshit in the media,' he said. 'Because if you are, you'll be thinking I'm about to tell you you're off the team.' The coach looked hard at his number 8. 'Or that I'm resigning because I've lost the plot.'

Gonzo was thinking that he only had five caps to his name and that this was awkward.

'Uncomfortable, isn't it?' said Conrad.

Gonzo nodded.

'Well, I'm not resigning and you're not dropped.'

They sat there for a few seconds in silence.

'But we do have a problem, don't we?' continued the New Zealander.

'Only if you believe what you read in the media,' said Gonzo.

'Touché, mate.'

'It's all about predictability, isn't it?' said Gonzo, leaning forward.

'Go on.'

'What we started against Ireland developed into something against France, even if the circumstances were a bit…'

'Artificial,' said Conrad.

'And there's no way England are going to come to Cardiff and agree to a game like that. They'll be thinking they can read us like Scotland did. That we've become predictable and that they can stop us.'

'So what do we do?'

Gonzo looked at his coach and knew that Conrad already had the answers.

'Well,' he said, 'I think there are three options.'

'Go on.'

'First, we say it's our home stadium, where we can influence the conditions by closing the roof. Then we can play however we like, and there's no way we can be stopped as easily as we were in the rain at Murrayfield.'

'Option two?'

'We accept that basics come first. The last ten minutes against Scotland become the opening half hour against England. We do the hard work up front. Nothing pretty, and only when we've taken the sting out of them do we dare open up.'

'So, we've got a fairly predictable option one, and a totally predictable option two.'

Gonzo nodded. 'Or there's option three,' he said.

'Which is?'

'Well,' said Gonzo. 'I suppose option three is where I'm the sacrificial lamb.'

'The tethered goat.'

'Thanks, coach.'

'You're welcome. I reckon it'll work.'

The meeting at Steel-Ag was a strangely hesitant affair. It was to put the final signatures to the deed of sale, but there was tension in the room. Martin kept to the company of Colin Wright on one side of the office, while Konstantin remained in a huddle with a pair of Russian lawyers, sheltered by a trio of burly sidekicks. Konstantin had briefly lit up when Grace appeared and they had talked about his wife and daughter. She had not mentioned the hat, and he soon excused himself and returned to the company of his fellow countrymen. Grace knew that caterers were standing by with trolleys of food and drink, but it seemed they were a long way from the start of any toasts. She wanted to ask Martin if anything was the matter, but he was clearly on edge. It was all very awkward. She went into the outside office and picked up a large package, protected in bubble-wrap and wrapping paper. She carried it back into Martin's office.

'I have a little present for you,' she said to Konstantin.

He frowned and looked at the lawyers, who looked equally irritated. But he took the gift and pulled off the layers. Inside was the framed blow-up of a photo Grace had taken inside the old factory at Cherepovets. It showed Konstantin staring up at the dereliction in the factory where he had once worked. Ice in the foreground and rust in the background framed his strong head, and his face was partly obscured by a cloud of his own breath in the frozen air. There was a reverie in his expression. He was not smiling but, above all, he looked a kind man.

'I tried not to point the camera at you,' said Grace. 'But it sort of found you.'

Konstantin was still frowning as he examined the photo. The seconds passed, but suddenly his expression softened and he roared with laughter. He held up the photo for the Russians to see and they all started to clap. He kissed the photo, put it down, held out his arms to Grace and gave her a hug, picking her up off the floor. When he lowered her, he paused for a second before summoning everybody in the room to gather round the photo.

'So,' he said, 'This is how you see me. Well, please let me tell you how I see you.' He looked directly at Martin. 'You see, we have a story about a dog, a half-wolf, that lives in the forest. But one winter, when the weather is at its coldest, he has to come out from the woods and into the village. He knows there is good food here, but he also knows there are traps laid. The villagers must protect their food. The dog is very clever. He approaches carefully at night and goes through the streets, his nose telling him where to go, his instincts guiding him through the dangers. Finally he comes to the barn he is looking for. Fresh chicken. Maybe a goose. And he is so excited at the smell and so confident that he has avoided all the traps that he relaxes. And he does not see the last one of all, a tiny mousetrap. And it snaps him on the nose. Not so hard that he cannot take the food, but hard enough that as he is eating the best meal of his life, he can feel the pain and taste his own blood.'

He looked down at the photo of himself and shook his head.

'It is true that I came here with a mousetrap. What do you call them? Snagging points... I like snagging points. Snap. To hurt you on the nose. I am the big bad Russian, after all.'

He looked up at Grace.

'But I am exposed.'

He tapped the glass of the photo.

'How could this man think of such a thing?'

He snapped his fingers and held his hand out to his lawyers.

'Come, let's sign.'

In a matter of minutes the sale was completed and the trolleys were wheeled in and the champagne was flowing. Martin stood close to Grace and she felt his arm around her, a public gesture of affection. She felt his hand squeeze her hip, pulling her towards him. She let herself be drawn to him.

'And now that I am a Welshman,' roared Konstantin, 'I must embrace the culture of my new country. *Iechyd da*, no?' The glasses were raised and everyone apart from the Russian minders drank. 'So, my dear Martin, this rugby... I am very interested. Wales against England, I read many things about it. Is it possible to go to the game tomorrow?'

'Of course,' said Martin impassively. 'What a good idea.' He had already released Grace when he stepped forward to shake Konstantin's hand one last time.

53

Gwyn and Gwen's spirits soared. It was as if some anchor chain, holding their happiness down, had been severed and they were now released. There and then, Gwen renounced alcohol and stepped back into the open air. Within two days, the front lawn of the vicarage was restored to manicured perfection and she took once again to kneeling on her cushion, tending her roses. Gwyn would stroll past the front of the vicarage on his way to the mine, running a finger along the railing and would wink at her. She would greet him with a cool 'Good morning,' but when he slipped through the side door of her home at dusk she would throw herself into his arms.

If Gwen renounced the drink, Gwyn looked to his body and declared himself soft and out of condition. Within days, he began a regime of striding out over the mountains. He did not make a conscious decision to stay away from the old paths he had taken with Lena, or even the track to the Keeper's Pond, but he found himself exploring new routes, that carried him further afield. Mere days after what he called his conversion in the church, and as he still tingled with the thought of seeing Gwen next, he found himself so drawn to exercise that he dropped his pen on his ledger and left the office. He abandoned work and began walking, towards Blaenavon, keeping above the town but steering clear of the Keeper's Pond, then turning on to the ridge south of the Blorenge, the gently declining spine that led towards Pontypool. It was a beautiful day and Monmouthshire to his left and the moorland and valleys to his right shimmered in the haze.

In front of him on the ridge lay the Folly, an octagonal tower forty feet high, built by the Pontypool ironmaster, John Hanbury, in the eighteenth century. It had been the scene of a mighty beacon in 1935 to celebrate the Silver Jubilee of King George V, a commemorative event Gwyn had studiously ignored. Since then, the Folly had fallen into disrepair, but in the summer of 1940 it still stood high on the skyline, so prominent that it was feared it would serve as a navigational aid to the Luftwaffe on any bombing raids on the Royal Ordnance Factory at Glascoed, buried in the hills a few miles to the east. The War Office had accordingly ordered that the Folly tower be destroyed. And so it was on this fine day that a party of army engineers was about to raze the local landmark. The sappers checked to the south, west and east – the accesses most used by walkers to the tower – and glanced only perfunctorily to the northern wilderness, just before Gwyn strode into view. He marched on, unimpeded. The command was given and the high explosives were detonated. Six small fragments of masonry, with the accuracy of a firing squad, struck Gwyn, killing him instantly.

It was never explained how the victim came to be at the Folly tower rather than at work. The police noted the testimony of a few witnesses in the village, especially his landlady, that the essentially lugubrious Gwyn Seymour had been in some sort of state of ecstasy for a few days, but in the light of the lack of care taken by the demolition team at the scene of the tragedy, the War Office encouraged the investigators to probe only superficially, and Gwyn was laid to rest as an unfortunate casualty of the war effort. The secret of his affair with Gwen never escaped the vicarage.

The Reverend Arthur Davies returned home on leave four months later, something of a casualty of war in his own right. He had been reprimanded and commended at the same time for his part in the Dunkirk evacuation, and he came back to the village as something of a hero, the fisher of men from perilous waters. But somewhere in the midst of the burning, boiling waters into which he had watched as many screaming soldiers sink as he managed to pull to safety, Arthur had suffered a crisis of faith. What God could allow any of this to happen? When he came home to his vicarage in the village he fell to his knees in the rose garden and clung to his Gwen, and could not release her.

Gwen had returned to the sherry when Gwyn died, but had abruptly stopped again when she found she was pregnant. By the time her husband came home, she was firm of mind, robust of constitution and slightly round of belly. She managed to prise herself out of the lock of Arthur's arms and wiped away his tears with the back of her thick gardening glove. She looked down at her new swelling and his eyes followed hers.

With his head bowed, he asked her: 'Do you wish to leave me?'

She lifted his chin, looked him in the eye and shook her head. To her amazement, her husband cupped her face in his hands and kissed her squarely on the lips.

'It is a little miracle,' he whispered and never mentioned the matter of his child's conception again.

Five months later, Gwen gave birth to a son and named him John, after Arthur's father, and Henry, after this father's father. As she was registering the birth, she added at the last moment a second middle name, Gonzalo, plucked from her memories of the day Gwyn told her of his time in Spain. It was a G to remind her of her lover, an exotic addition on the birth certificate that Arthur never saw. He returned home – on leave again – shortly after John Henry arrived. Gwen decided that Gonzalo was best left as an undeclared supplementary, especially since Arthur obviously doted on the child. If the lack of a biological link betrayed itself, it was only when the father of the clergy broke an obvious convention by not baptising the infant. Otherwise, Arthur invested compassion and love in his wife and the child he unhesitatingly called his son. For a few days in the late summer of 1941, Arthur and Gwen and John led a family life far from the turmoil of war.

And then Arthur was granted passage aboard the refitted battleship, HMS *Prince of Wales*, bound from Greenock for Singapore. He landed safely at the distant outpost of empire and said goodbye to the ship's chaplain, Wilfrid Parker, a New Zealander who had patiently rebuilt his travelling companion's faith during their passage to the Far East. Eight days later, the *Prince of Wales* was attacked by Japanese aircraft off the coast of Malaya and was struck by four torpedoes and a 1,100-pound bomb. Tending to wounded seamen at the bottom of a shaft, the chaplain heard the order to seal a hatch over their heads, but refused to leave the men. The battleship sank and the chaplain was one of the 327 who went down with her.

Arthur barely had time to register the loss of his mentor – his seafaring shepherd – before Singapore fell to the Imperial Japanese Army and he spent the next three years as a prisoner of war in Changi Prison. Strangely enough, in his bleakest hours, it was the thought of his wife and son – his unfaithful Gwen and his illegitimate John – that kept his spirits alive. When he eventually returned home he could not stop himself from patting Gwen, only this time it was because of a permanent shaking in his emaciated arms and hands.

54

At the same time as Martin was signing his steelmaking over to Konstantin, Gonzo and the rest of the Welsh team were going through their last session, the captain's run, at their training camp in the Vale of Glamorgan. For the final game of the championship, against England, Conrad had made not a single alteration to his team and replacements, and the media had arrived in force to probe this obstinacy in the face of their calls for change. Convention had it that the television cameras and reporters were allowed to stay for the first fifteen minutes – for the stretching and warm-up exercises that revealed nothing – before being ejected unceremoniously by Mal No Comment Davies, the media manager of the Welsh Rugby Union. On this occasion, however, they were still filming and jotting down their notes when the team began to rehearse more seriously. Counter-attacking, it was noted on the sidelines, was the first priority and the patterns still looked the same: a lot of zigzagging before Gonzo Davies drove straight up the middle.

'Good,' shouted Conrad at the players. He then noticed the cameras. 'No Comment, get rid of those bloody people.'

It was the day of the game, Wales against England at the Millennium Stadium. Martin had been given the best seats in the house. He was a valued sponsor and the Welsh Rugby Union saw the potential of Konstantin as an even more generous benefactor. Grace joined them in a hospitality box above the halfway line and they were wined and dined in style. Konstantin had ordered his minders to stay away and had dived into the occasion, walking in wonder through the streets of Cardiff, absorbing the pre-match atmosphere. He stopped to buy a Welsh scarf and wrapped it around him. He laughed at the excesses of those dressed from head to toe in red, but made a serious note about the mood of the crowd spilling out of Cardiff Central Station.

'These people in white,' he observed. 'They think they are going to win.'

An hour before kick-off he asked if he might leave the hospitality box and go outside to savour the scenes again. Grace and he stood in the middle of Westgate Street, feeling the throng surge around them. Martin stayed within. He sat and watched the stadium fill, outwardly detached, inwardly wishing great harm on Gonzo Davies.

Word had reached the England camp from the reporters that had overstayed their welcome at the Vale of Glamorgan that Wales were still intent on running the ball back at every opportunity, with Gonzo Davies the final receiver after all the fancy angles and passing of the ball-handlers before him. England had the best defence in the championship, watertight against structured attacks and now reinforced to deal with Wales's improvised counter-offensives. They sat in their changing room and repeated the mantra: Stop Gonzo Davies; Win the Grand Slam.

In the Welsh changing room Gonzo felt the bile rising in his throat. Everything depended on him handling what lay ahead with calmness and precision, but here he was, giving in to those nerves that had rendered him useless on the day of his first appearance for Wales. He sat in his kit and felt sick, unable to concentrate. He was shaking.

He took a deep breath and shut his eyes. He lifted himself out of his trembling skin, seeing himself below, a player caught between regurgitating the incantations of battle and keeping down the contents of his stomach. Gonzo floated away, drifting on gauze away from this bedlam into some part of the stadium where he could think clearly. He went down lines of men in corridors, all with flared nostrils and wild eyes, leaving them behind until the stamp of all their feet, the pawing of the ground before the charge, faded. He found peace in a yellow sea of spare stewards' jackets. And the sea parted, and out stepped Grace. And Gonzo opened her coat and ran his liniment-soaked hands over her bare skin.

Gonzo opened his eyes. He was on the field, standing in a line beneath the closed roof of the Millennium Stadium.

The crowd was halfway through the anthem: '... *Dros ryddid collasant eu gwaed...*' He was staring straight at Grace, who was up there in the middle of the president's box. It couldn't be her. It was her. Grace in her brown coat, staring back at him.

55

In accordance with guidelines that had been hastily rewritten to deal with the 'quasi-emergency' in Wales, the Dyfed Powys Police encircled the protestors in Builth and waited for the order to move in, or, better still, for an act of criminality to be committed. If somebody did something wrong, the police would have a simple reason to break up the party. The few police that had escorted the march through Wales reported, however, that there might have been the odd waft of marijuana on the breeze – ever since the hippies from the western woods joined – but in the main it had been an entirely undemanding assignment. It came as something of a surprise to this escort service, given the events in the South, that their colleagues had congregated here in such numbers. And in such battle gear. The visible front line consisted of standard marked police cars, but behind and out of sight lay vans packed with enough manpower and equipment to quell a riot. The only thing missing was the riot. What was equally worrying was that there seemed to be a delegation of well-respected members of the Welsh establishment approaching the senior officers over the bridge. And for every one of these legates there seemed to be a television camera. The officers were not entirely sure they were in full control of what they had been led to believe was a situation. They tried not to fidget as the Sages made their way across the bridge over the River Wye.

As Meirion Owen Jones neared the bridge's parapet, Cosmos Phillips, orange-haired elder of the hippies of the western woods, who thought he might have been invited to join the bardic assembly of the Sages, especially since he had wrapped himself in a Welsh flag for the voyage, popped up out of nowhere.

'Head Sage, man, take this,' he said and handed Meirion a white flag on a freshly cut piece of hazel. 'Just in case they've got snipers in the showground.'

'Cosmos Phillips,' growled Meirion, without diverting his eyes from the road ahead and the police. 'We were at school together. If you want to help, give me your shirt.'

'I'm with you, brother,' said Cosmos and pulled off his Welsh flag, revealing a bare and surprisingly toned torso beneath a mat of greying chest hair. He flexed his biceps for Danish television and dropped out of sight. Meirion tied the slightly stained dragon to the hazel and, trying not to wrinkle his nose as he held the flag of Wales aloft, he led the way to his parley with the police.

When he was twenty paces from the far bank – close enough to hear the crackle of static on the police radios – there was movement up and down the blue line in front of him. Officers came forward and went back. Arms were raised, pointing this way and that. And then the police began to retreat, leaving the senior officer for a brief moment on his own. The officer stared at Meirion and then touched the peak of his cap. He turned on his heel and within a minute all the police officers and all their cars and all the vans parked against the hedgerows all around the town were gone.

Only PC Derwena Davies from Aberystwyth was left. She had escorted the march into Builth, but had then gone off duty and missed the Aprilfest. Now she was back on, and it was her duty to escort the march out of town.

'Change of plan, it appears, Dr Jones,' she said to Meirion. 'Seems you've got the green light to carry on.'

'Were they going to stop us, my dear?' asked the academic.

'I couldn't possibly comment, sir. But I think Plan B now comes into effect.'

'Which is?'

'As I said, to let you march.'

'Then shall we?' Meirion offered his arm and possibly against regulations and certainly against the intentions of the original plan A, to break up the Builth gathering, Meirion and Derwena walked back over the Wye to tell the marchers that it was time to be on the road. The television news crews reported that all was quiet, but the shot of the policewoman smiling broadly on the arm of the academic did appear in the *Sun* above the caption: 'Welsh Hell? Don't make me laugh.'

56

The first time England had possession they kicked as far downfield as they could and invited Wales to run back at them. Dapper Williams and Huw Martins and Nico Davies obligingly launched into their preamble of running at varying angles and speeds, before the ball was given to Gonzo. He was hit so hard by four tacklers that his gumshield flew into the air, its spinning arc caught in super slow motion by one of the twenty-four television cameras that witnessed Wales's supposedly most dangerous runner coming off spectacularly second best in the first collision of the encounter. Gonzo was driven back three yards and when he hit the ground, three more white shirts arrived to tread all over his ankles and thighs and try to rip the ball off him. He clung on to it and the referee awarded a penalty against him. George Swain, deadly with his left boot, landed the kick at goal and England led 3-0.

In mid-flight and in full retreat during the tackle, Gonzo had managed to make the minute adjustment, even in the four-man grip of his assailants, that gave him a relatively safe landing. The stamping of his ankles was a little more worrying, but he knew that no deep-seated damage had been done. He limped back towards the posts and heard the hush of a Welsh crowd that had had its worst fears confirmed. This was going to be gruesome.

England were so keen to kick the ball to the Welsh back three that they let their tight-head prop, James Hopward, take on the duty. It didn't matter if it wasn't the most elegant dispatch of the ball into the air, because all that mattered was that Wales were being invited again to try to run back at the English defence. Dapper and Huw and Nico began their routine and Gonzo took up his position in the middle. England lined up the same four tacklers and they hit him again, even harder. The only thing was that Gonzo, instead of catching the ball, had patted it back inside to Lump-head Morgan, who ran thirty metres before passing to Dapper for the try that brought the Millennium Stadium back to life. Gonzo was gingerly rising to his feet when Lump-head came striding back in celebration.

'Spaghetti Junction,' roared the prop. 'I fuckin' loves it.'

Two minutes later, England kicked again and Gonzo was smashed by his markers. This time he had been a decoy runner and Dapper gave a long pass to Gren Jenkins, the second row, who ran thirty metres, as many as he had accumulated in the previous four matches, to score. Gonzo, lying beneath a tangle of bodies, wearily watched his teammates celebrate. Now he really was starting to feel the effects of the punishment and he took half a minute to haul some air into his lungs. As he straightened and walked back to join his team he heard the crowd. They had exploded at the try, but now they began to clap, their hands acknowledging the role of Gonzo, united in their appreciation of the tethered goat. In the presidential box, Konstantin applauded too and wondered why Grace, on his left, and Martin, on his right, did not join in.

England stopped kicking to Wales, but the damage had been done and they never managed to close the gap. The game ended with Gonzo driving for the line from three metres out. In his way stood three of his four original

211

tacklers. Now it was their turn to be weary. Their dream of winning the grand slam was over. They threw themselves unflinchingly at their target, but without the venom of their opening assaults. Gonzo felt a head bounce off his hip and carried on running. He felt another tackler slip down from his chest and he strode on, carrying the third over the line. Wales 27 England 9. Gonzo's finest hour.

57

It seemed the *Sun's* caption had it right. The march south from Builth Wells was difficult. The granting of permission to advance took the sting out of the protest and since the anger that had caused Caernarfon to rise up and walk had already been diluted by four days on the beer at the Aprilfest, there was a fear that the march would melt away before it reached the Brecon Beacons. The hearses of Rhyl had turned around in Builth, their presence at a beer festival having been deemed slightly inappropriate. The Rhyl tractors stayed for a couple of days, more at ease in the setting, but they too had turned and headed north. Without the mechanical accompaniment, something of the character seemed to go out of the pilgrimage. Children in Llyswen did a head-count, and posted 187. Business was slowing at Hazel's.

All was calm on either side of Cardiff. Swansea and Newport had flared up and now settled down again. The police in the three cities were kept on their toes, taunted from the shadows. When they turned, nobody was there, but at least the skies of South Wales remained free of smoke.

58

Martin excused himself at the final whistle and went inside the hospitality box to use his mobile phone. He rang Gareth Mewson. From his seat, Konstantin was still drinking in the atmosphere. Gonzo was doing a lap of the field with the rest of the team. He stopped in front of the president's box and looked up at Grace.

'That player,' said Konstantin. 'The good one. Gonzo Davies. It is as if he is looking at us. At you. Do you know him?'

Konstantin began to clap as Gonzo held his ground. Grace checked where Martin was. He had his back turned to the pitch.

'Not any more,' she said.

'He is very good,' said Konstantin.

'Yes, he is,' said Grace and began to clap too.

'I have a job for you,' said Martin to Gareth Mewson.

59

Three weeks later, Gonzo played in a regional Welsh derby. He was still sore of rib and stiff of back, but Murray Collins had asked him to make himself available.

'These bloody all-Welsh games,' sighed the coach. 'You all turn into cavemen.'

The fixture fell in the last few weeks of the season, but the trend towards more expansive rugby on dry surfaces was interrupted by a burst of spring showers on the day of the game. Gonzo didn't really mind. He was playing against Gareth Mewson. Once, it had seemed they would be teammates, but the deal had fallen through and Gareth had begun to do the rounds of the other regions, his short-term contracts rarely extended. He was big but slow. If there was a threat from a Mewson, it came from Danny, Gareth's brother, who had been warned by the referee as early as the first minute for reckless use of the shoulder.

It was an uninspiring game. Gonzo's team led comfortably and he was starting to think, with twenty minutes to go, that he might be taken off. He ordered himself to snap out of it, and went looking for work. He took a pass from Sam Harris and moved it on smartly. The two-metre pass was already in the hands of the receiver when Gareth Mewson hit him and drove him sideways into a pile of bodies. These fallen players should have softened the landing. Besides, as he was flying through the air, Gonzo made the slight readjustment, the additional insurance that would ensure he did not come down dangerously. But something was wrong. Gareth continued to hold him tightly and they came down hard.

Gonzo grunted as he hit the ground. He tried to wriggle free but Gareth increased the strength of his grip, forcing Gonzo's face into the ground. In these micro-seconds Gonzo worked out that something unusual was happening, but through the thicket of legs and arms into which he had been propelled, well away from the ball that was now disappearing across the field, he did not see the boot coming down on the back of his head. He only felt the shock of the impact and then the studs raking down his skull. He instinctively jerked his head away and was able to look up. But Gareth still held him tight. Danny Mewson's boot came down a second time, harder. And everything inside the head of Gonzo Davies was turned off.

60

Gonzo regained consciousness in the ambulance taking him to the University of Wales Hospital in Cardiff. He was bleeding heavily from the L-shaped wound to the back of his head, and it took quite a time to insert the thirty stitches that reattached the flap of skin. By the time the medical team had finished wrapping him in a bandage, Gonzo was aware of a loss of feeling around his right eye socket, below the site of the second stamp. An x-ray revealed a blowout fracture of the orbital floor. He stayed in hospital for observation.

Other investigations were taking place. Gareth was immediately cited for the late challenge and Danny for use of the boot. The media played hard on the fraternal connection

– the mad Mewsons, bad brothers – but nobody was aware of any collaboration in the past to commit such an act of foul play, and it was nowhere suggested that there was any premeditated intent to do harm to Gonzo. Gareth apologised to the disciplinary board and in public to Gonzo. He did not visit him in hospital, and neither did Danny, who offered no apology – no word of any sort.

Grace knew about the injury. There was no avoiding it in Wales. The country's star player made the British press and opened a fresh debate about how rugby still could not shake off its reputation for offering a haven to psychopaths. At their disciplinary panel, Gareth was banned for one match, Danny for 50 weeks, his sentence increased when his poor disciplinary record was taken into consideration. He accepted his sentence in silence and chose never to play rugby again.

On the inside pages of her father's *Times*, Grace read that Gonzo was making steady progress and was expected to make a full recovery. She wondered if she might visit him in hospital, but she remembered his last words to her: 'You must stay away, Grace. Please.'

She obeyed the instruction and devoted herself to Martin, who seemed to have shaken off his reserve and was in positively ebullient form. The sale of Steel-Ag had been completed and Martin had made a leap from well-off to genuinely rich. He treated Grace with a new respect now. She thought it must be gratitude for the opportune timing of her gift to Konstantin. Martin respected her because Gonzo was out of his system.

In March, the Member of Parliament for Monmouth, George Hampshire, Conservative, declared that he would not be standing at the next General Election. Retirement beckoned for the MP who had become known in the course of his one and only parliament as one of the most genial and unproductive members of the House of Commons. Martin Guest, already on the Conservatives' approved list, was endorsed by the outgoing Member, which may not have counted as a blessing, given that the Party was looking for somebody with greater zeal than George, whose life in retirement would scarcely be any easier than his life in politics. By way of more legitimate backing, Martin was the favourite of the local association and was duly selected as the Conservative candidate for the Monmouth constituency. Three days after his adoption, he proposed to Grace and she accepted.

Gonzo's scalp wound was healing well, but when he awoke in hospital from a deep, troubled sleep three days after the incident, he had double vision. The doctors asked if he felt discomfort in his right eye, to which he replied no – but that might be because he could not feel anything at all. His area of numbness, if anything, had expanded. The doctors told him they suspected a displacement of his eyeball. They might have to operate, they advised him, but they would wait for the swelling to subside first. Gonzo lay in bed, the back of his head pulsing healthily, while the front was cold and desensitised. He shut his eyes.

Martin and Grace were to be married before the General Election that had just been called. The race was on to make their wedding both personally and politically special. It was a grand affair. The Courtney home had seen better days, but the marquee ordered by Martin – and that now covered every square inch of the captain's manicured side lawn, apart from the gentle slope leading down to the river Usk – was opulent. The company was impressive, too. A clutch of Tory grandees had accepted the invitation from the new candidate, for the Party was looking to gain favourable coverage from the marriage of their golden couple.

Even the weather smiled on the occasion, a freak day of warmth at the end of March. The gas heaters in the marquee had been set to maximum at dawn, but Martin's wedding planner had them turned off before the reception in the afternoon. The flaps at the river end of the tent were removed and the Usk flowed past, smooth and sparkling in the spring sunshine.

'Lovely spot,' said the grandest of the grandees, Lord Jerricoh, standing on the top of the riverbank and looking up at the Blorenge. He took a sip from his schooner of driest sherry. 'Know much about this chap?'

'Not a lot,' said Sir Bernard Chiltern, stopping a waiter and swapping his small glass for a flute of champagne. 'Lovely bride, I must say. Damned fetching.'

The doctors hoped Gonzo's eye would heal spontaneously, but after ten days the double vision was still there, and they decided to operate. A brief media update announced that the procedure had gone well, but there would now be a hiatus.

Until the bandages were removed, nobody would be able to tell if the operation had been one hundred per cent successful. Gonzo lay in bed and felt sensation gradually return to the area around his eye. It was while he was appreciating the slightest touch of a fingertip to his cheek that he felt the start of a much more intense sensation behind his eyes. A dull ache was escalating quickly into a stabbing pain so brutal that he nearly passed out. Painkillers were administered and Gonzo was sent for another scan. No intracranial haemorrhage could be found, but the patient faced more time in his hospital bed.

It was while he was behind bandages that Gonzo first had his dream about the River Monnow. There was no Grace at the bridge at Skenfrith, no echo of the afternoon they had spent in the bedroom of the Bell there. No love – just an explosion and decapitation by flying glass. After that came characters he recognised. As his head rolled to face the depths of the river, out of the blackness loomed Martin Guest. When it continued gently to spin in the water, he went from one bank to the sky and on through ninety degrees to be looking at the other bank, where Danny Mewson stood in tendrils of mist. As Gonzo's one eye began to roll beneath the water, Danny reached out with a branch and jabbed him in the other.

The days went by and there was no repeat of the headache, but when the bandages were removed, Gonzo was still suffering from double vision.

Grace and Martin had a weekend honeymoon in a luxury hotel in the Cotswolds. There was no time for anything more extended. Besides, as Grace pointed out, perhaps they needed a break from going on holiday. There was another good reason to choose Gloucestershire. They were invited to dinner at the home of the man who was seeking a second term as Prime Minister. It was a splendid affair, packed with celebrities, but also an intimate gathering, an embrace of his inner circle and trusted friends before they stepped out to face the public and to campaign for a new term in office. Martin was honoured to be included and he recognised that he owed a lot to Grace. He also left the Prime Minister's home sensing there was nothing to fear from these people, that he could more than match them. He left the dinner party more committed to his new career as a politician than he had ever been to his career as a businessman, and heaven knew that Martin had been boundless in his ambitions to succeed in stage one of his life.

Gonzo was released from hospital on a Tuesday mid-morning. He had been there so long that he had ceased to be a story, and whereas photographers had swarmed at the bedside of the Welsh Player of the Six Nations for a first shot of his freshly stitched head and swollen eye, now he left the University Hospital of Wales with only Capper to greet him.

For the moment there was nothing further to be done about the double vision. There had been some improvement with surgery, but his sight was still affected. The specialists had debated whether leaving the eye open might encourage realignment, but Gonzo found the swimming images before him induced nausea, and the doctors were worried that any strain might provoke another of the migraines, whose diagnosis they had not yet managed to pinpoint. Gonzo remained a bit of a mystery to them and they reminded him that they would need to monitor his recovery closely. The nurses warned him more bluntly that he couldn't afford to mess around.

'Ah, the traditional pirate look,' said nurse Daisy Williams, sliding the elasticated band of a black eye patch over Gonzo's head, taking care to avoid the scar at the back, still livid beneath the stubble of the area that had been shaved. 'Seriously,' she added, holding his head in two hands, 'You've got to take care of yourself. There's something going on in here they don't like.'

He was not allowed to drive and Capper had volunteered to take half a day off work at Jones the Other Builder's in order to take him back to the village. Gonzo's flat in the Bay was already occupied by an Australian player, Mark Ferdley, shipped in from the Perpignan reserves in France and put on a short-term contract. There was room in the apartment for Gonzo, but he told the region he'd prefer to convalesce at home. He was sure they would understand. They did, and assured him they were working on a settlement with the insurers, should – they were sure Gonzo would understand – the worse come to the worse. Gonzo did.

'Looks all right to me,' said Capper, lifting up the patch and peering into Gonzo's right eye.

'It's looking out of it that's the problem,' said Gonzo.

61

The Rev Arthur survived for ten years after the end of the Second World War. For five of these he even managed to keep working at St Cadoc's. But the vicar and his church were in terminal decline and it was with relief that Gwen handed the doors of the church and the vicarage over to the bishop's agent and drove her husband and son to a small terraced house in Beaufort Street. Arthur wanted to stay in the village. He said the mountain air was good for him, even though it was well known that Beaufort Street was at the wrong height and caught more smoke and smuts from the chimney of the mine's engine house than any other street in the village. Arthur lived long enough to see the nationalisation of the coal industry and the building of the pithead baths, but not long enough to see the conversion to diesel in the engine house.

He may not have noticed even had he lived to see it. He spent his Beaufort Street years on the mountain, planning his ascents as carefully as he walked them, choosing only the gentlest of inclines to the moorland. Gwen had pushed John Henry (Gonzalo) Davies in his pram around the village, but Arthur now led his son slowly by the hand to higher open spaces.

'To be nearer to God, John Henry Davies,' he said. 'Or at least a little further away from the hellish work down there,' he added as they looked back down on the village far below.

When John was nine, they climbed to the top of the mountain one final time. They could see the Bristol Channel to the south, a silver horizontal shimmer at the end of a corridor of vertical plumes of smoke. Arthur was breathing hard, his chest wheezing and rattling at the same time. He leant over his walking stick, both hands on its grip. John waited patiently at his side until Arthur raised a shaking finger and pointed it at the water in the distance.

'They say it's good to see the world, my son. Well, there it is.'

'It's a long way away,' said John, wiry like his biological father, tall after his mother's family.

'That's just the start of it,' said Arthur.

'And shiny.'

'Not in my experience.'

'Will I see it?'

'You will decide for yourself. But I just wanted you to know that it's there.'

And with that they went slowly back down the shallow incline, John now leading Arthur. Within a few weeks the son stood holding his mother's hand as Arthur was lowered into the graveyard at St Cadoc's, the last person to be buried there before the church closed.

62

It came as something of a shock to all at Conservative Party Headquarters when their new candidate in Monmouth was beaten into second place by Labour. For some voters in the constituency, George Hampshire had been incorrigibly idle and Martin arrived a little too late to mend the harm done. For others, old George had been just the ticket for Monmouth, hardly a radical hotspot, and they distrusted so much slick passion on the stump and so many fresh ideas from his successor.

Perhaps it wasn't George or Martin's fault at all. Perhaps it was simply time for a change. Monmouth was anything but a constituency prone to wild fluctuations, but it had long been a marginal seat and almost by rote it was to be Labour's turn. Mike Edwards-Jones duly overturned the Conservative advantage of 1,201 at the previous Election and won after a recount by 588 votes.

'You're bound to be down,' said Lord Jericoh, dispatched from London to have a reassuring word in the candidate's ear. 'But fear not. We had a good night in England and as you know our overall majority in the House of Commons has grown. Quite frankly, the PM can't believe it. So, keep your spirits up. There's plenty of dead wood in our ranks, plenty of by-elections to be fought soon enough. Your time will come, Guest.'

Martin made all the right noises in public, but he shrank into himself at home, where he spent too much time, as Grace recognised. He claimed to have found a project to keep himself busy, the renovation of the Courtney house, but having told Grace that this was something they would do together, he lost interest quickly and left her to take all the decisions. Or he would suddenly appear from his study and demand changes that were costly and, to Grace's mind, unnecessary. She told him so at first, confident that she could soothe him and win him round, but she sensed a gradual drop in his core temperature.

Gonzo moved back in with Capper, into the very first house they had renovated in the village. He made an effort to pull himself from his bed in the mornings.

'What do you get up to in that bathroom?' he asked. 'No man could stay in bed and listen to you in there. I've enough trouble with this eye, without doing damage to my ears and nose.'

'It's the sound and smell of a healthy diet,' said Capper. 'My bowels are a temple.'

Once Capper was gone from the house, Gonzo went back upstairs and spent too many daylight hours, he knew, in the smaller of the two tiny bedrooms, with the curtains drawn and the eyepatch removed. He found semi darkness the most comfortable light, the only problem being that this penumbra soon took a hold on his spirits. Gonzo began to sink. He fought against it and forced himself one day to leave the house and walk to the moors and breathe in fresh air. But fifty paces from the front door he felt the ache of a migraine and retreated to his shadows.

One lunchtime, while Grace was away in Cardiff, making her final selection of carpets and curtains, Martin was in his makeshift study, a bedroom on the first floor hastily converted while work was completed downstairs. For once, all was relatively hushed in the house. The banging and drilling of the past few weeks had given way to the quieter work of the plasterers and decorators. In the distance Radio 1 was playing and he could hear Baz the painter whistling. Martin was listening to a debate on Radio 4's lunchtime news about the housing shortage. Making an inadequate contribution was an experienced but poorly briefed government minister. It ended with a splutter of interruptions and accusations by the Opposition spokesperson of government ineptitude. The overwhelmed minister's bluster was exposed.

'Why don't you just die?' muttered Martin.

He turned off the radio and walked to the French window, opened it and stepped out on to the narrow balcony that ran in front of the three bedrooms on this side of the house. Down below, Captain Courtney was going up and down on his lawnmower, his mechanical pride and joy. He raised a hand when he saw Martin. Martin did not respond. Ten minutes later he was still there, as the mower went to turn at the river end of the lawn. Suddenly the captain seemed to slump and his machine slewed off its perfectly formed stripes. It nearly toppled into the river, but the captain somehow managed to regain control. He stopped the mower once it was back on track and facing the house. The driver took a deep breath and opened the throttle, only for his foot to slip off the pedal ten yards later. The lawnmower stopped at an angle across the stripes and the captain slumped again in his seat.

Martin stood watching him and did not move. The captain weakly raised his head and stared at his son-in-law. The last thought Captain James Courtney ever had was that his darling Grace hadn't managed to work out Martin Guest after all.

63

Gwen lived to a ripe old age. She never thought she would stand being on her own in the village. She had always imagined that she would go back down to the Vale of Glamorgan, where South Wales rolled gently from the valleys of the coalfield to the sea. But she never moved off the mountain, settling into the cleaner air of Beaufort Street when the conversion to diesel at the engine house finally came, and into widowhood. She stayed sober and serene for the rest of her days and lived long enough to see the closure of the pit and a decade later, the birth of a grandson.

Before that, she devoted herself to raising her son. John grew up in the village, contented and tranquil. Born into the vicarage, in the village's eyes he was not expected to follow the path to the mine. The sons of miners followed their fathers underground, but the son of the Reverend Arthur had licence to go wherever his destiny lay. Not into his father's parish church, however, because as a portent of what lay ahead, and not long after Arthur was laid to rest in his grave, his replacement confessed to the bishop that he had failed to arrest the decline in his congregations, and St Cadoc's closed as a place of worship.

The chapel in James Street lasted for another two decades, but not long after the mine was finally declared economically unviable, the last minister admitted spiritual bankruptcy in the village and departed, shutting the door behind him. Jones the Other Builder made a calculation, followed by a cheeky two-for-one offer on the church and chapel, which to his surprise was ecumenically accepted. But the plans he hatched to make a killing through the conversion of two houses of God into a dozen apartments remained on hold and Dick Jones worried that he had misread the signs of upward mobility in the village.

'Aye, for sure,' said his old drinking mates at the Colliers' Arms when he moaned about the untouched church and the chapel still sitting on his books. 'Yuppies move in mysterious ways.'

John Davies would not have gone into his father's church even if it had remained open. He had inherited not only Gwyn Seymour's wiry frame, but he discovered – after growing up without ever uttering, it seemed to his friends and teachers at school, any imprecation or displaying any flash of temper – a restless spirit. Perhaps he remembered the view from the top of the incline of the world beyond the village and decided he would like to see it. He applied to university, excelled in his exams at school and left for Birmingham. And when he finished his degree in History he opted to train as a teacher. A year later, he took up a position at Trent College in Derbyshire, and three years after that, left to teach at St George's School in Hong Kong.

Gwen thought she would never see him again, but every five years an airline ticket arrived in the post and she would take the many hops by plane that carried her from her home in South Wales to the little bit of Britain in South China. Six times she flew through the time zones to be with her son, and not once did he come home to the village. She never received a seventh ticket. Instead, John sent her a letter saying that he had qualified for early retirement and was coming back.

He bought a house in Straight Row and at the age of 50 and unmarried, moved home.

Gwen was in her 80s by now, but still had all her mental faculties and was certainly sharp enough of wit to wonder if the name of the street her son had chosen to live in accorded with what she believed was termed nowadays his sexual orientation. She had never met – and he had never spoken of – a woman in his life. On his return he threw himself into community projects, which made them sound, thought Gwen, like shared tasks. She soon realised that they were jobs for the good of the community, but performed by one person – that individual being her John. He took it upon himself, for example, to keep the Miners' Institute going, or at least its Reading Room, by persuading the council not to let another village institution go the way of the church and the chapel. He swept and decorated and stoked up the old boiler once a week and bought daily newspapers with his own money for villagers to read on a Thursday. They came in a steady trickle and the building was saved.

His next project was the Recreation Ground down among the waste tips. What Lena and her fellow volunteers had started to clear and level in pre-war days had been neglected ever since and lay unrecognisable as a place where sport and leisure activities might be enjoyed. John Davies nevertheless stood in the brambles in front of the bulldozers sent to level the waste tips – they were on the verge of collapse a dozen years after the closure of the pit – and ordered the contractors to mind the playing field. They thought they were in the presence of a madman, but John would not be budged and produced the blueprints he had found while clearing out the

Institute and again persuaded the council to think of rebirth in the village, rather than burial.

The council could not promise to re-create the facilities of the original plan, but they did order the bulldozers to leave a flat area on the edge of the site, and went as far as to skim off the brambles and spread a load of top soil – still black, but fertile enough to support grass. The rugby field was born, a postage stamp of green, once the seed John sowed took root, in the grey wilderness around the pithead. Just when the council thought they had conceded enough to their scourge, he came back for more, asking for assistance in building a stand, complete with changing facilities. The council pointed out that the village did not even have a team, whereupon John went to the timber merchants in Brynmawr, put up a set of rough posts, organised the local primary school to play a game on the new ground and persuaded the local *Clarion* newspaper to take a photo, that appeared the following Thursday. Three weeks later a motley crew of adults, some more enthusiastic than others, took to the field and a second picture appeared in the paper.

John campaigned for grants from the National Playing Fields Association, the Welsh Development Agency, the European Regional Development Fund, and applied, on the very first day it was launched, for assistance from the new National Lottery. Slowly but surely, the village rugby club grew. These were still the days when property in the village was almost being given away – when the streetlights would go out in West Street and not go back on – and a single terraced house there was bought for a song. The new club had a clubhouse.

When he went to Llanfoist Street in the village to arrange the first game on the new playing field, John met Carmen Alvarado Jones, a teacher who was equally passionate about saving another local institution – her school on the street – from closure. Carmen's family was from Spanish Row, the nickname given to Alphonso Street in Penywern above Merthyr Tydfil, built to house immigrant Spanish miners in the 1900s. The family had spread a few yards into Dowlais, but were reluctant to go any further from the starting point of their new life in Wales. Carmen, teaching in her school less than twenty miles from home, was as farflung as anybody in the family had gone in almost a century. She was fifth generation Welsh, one hundred per cent Spanish, irredeemably single according to her colleagues in Llanfoist Street, and twenty years younger than John. In a whirlwind of the most unlikely romance they began to see each other and it was much to Gwen's surprise that her bachelor son told her after just five months of knowing Carmen, that he had proposed to her, and that she had accepted.

At this point, Gwen sat the pair down in her front room in Beaufort Street and told them about how John Henry Davies was on his birth certificate John Henry Gonzalo Davies and how he came to be so called. It was John's turn to be surprised. And then overwhelmed, because in the next sentence, Carmen was telling Gwen that not only was she going to be a mother-in-law, but also a grandmother. Six months later, Carmen gave birth to a son and they named him Gonzalo. Carmen insisted on pronouncing it the Castillian way, with the *ceceo* of the 'z', but when her son came to her class on Llanfoist Street she soon found she could save neither its

231

sound nor its length. Gonzalo was soon known to everyone – his mother and grandmother apart – as Gonzo.

64

The months passed and Gonzo stayed indoors. One rugby season ended, a summer passed, and a new one began. Capper told him that the village team was worse than ever – that on the third Saturday, for example, they had turned up with thirteen players and that on training nights they were down to half a dozen.

'Might help if you, like, came down and... you know...' tried the hooker.

But Gonzo stayed away. The insurance money never appeared and, with his failure to keep his appointments noted on his hospital records, never would. There was no evidence in those records – no shadow, no lesion – to explain the migraines to which the claimant alleged he was susceptible. There was, moreover, just as little to show in the micro-measurements of everything in and around the former patient's orbits to make the insurance company feel obliged to pay out for double-vision that existed – and here the assessor kept his wry smile to himself – only in the eye of the beholder.

Lord Jericoh intimated that by-elections were looming in London. Martin left Monmouthshire for a flat he bought in Chelsea. Grace stayed in Wales, mourning the loss of her father, but determined to complete the work he had appreciated so much, the restoration of the Courtney family home. She visited Martin regularly, oblivious to what he had done – or not done – at the time of the fatal heart attack. She loved the old house, now restored to its discreet splendour on the side of the Usk. She liked the new flat in Chelsea. She liked London. She was pleased that Martin was moving on. She was beginning to emerge from her grief.

'I've been chatting to your brothers,' said Martin one evening.

'Will and Godfrey?'

'And they agree with me.'

Grace knew that whatever was coming next was not going to be to her advantage. It was Martin's way to tease and then deliver a cruel punchline.

'You're supposed to say: 'Agree with what?'' he said.

'I know.'

'And?'

'I know I'm not going to like whatever it is.'

'How do you know?'

'Because I know you, Martin.'

'That obvious, eh?' he said and put a hand on hers.

'Tell me I'm wrong, then,' said Grace and put her hand over his.

'Well, let's face it, Will could do with some capital and now your Godfrey's a teacher he's hardly enjoying the salad days of old.'

'So, you want to sell the house.'

Martin was surprised.

'There's another person who reads my mind,' he said. 'I

truly must be too transparent.' He raised a smile and then it disappeared. 'They could do with the money, Grace.'

'But I don't need it. We don't need it, Martin,' she said. 'And it's my home, not theirs.'

'It belongs to all three of you now...'

'You can't do this to me...'

'Listen to me,' he said. 'I'm done with Wales. My future – our future – is here.'

That night in the huge bed in their luxury home he tried to coax her into agreement, and when in the soft light she finally said she'd think about it, he made love to her, gently at first but with an increasingly strident rhythm. When it was done and Martin had turned off his dimmable bedside light, Grace lay in the dark, sore and cold.

65

Gwen died while Gonzo was still at junior school. John and Carmen stayed in the village to see him leave secondary school in Brynmawr and set up his business with Capper, an enterprise the parents viewed with some suspicion, but helped none the less with some of the money they had set aside from the sale of Gwen's house in Beaufort Street. Carmen retired from teaching and out of the blue inherited from a distant relative half a house in the old part of Cuenca. Prompted by John, she used the remainder of the Beaufort Street fund to buy the other half of this property in Spain from a cousin she had never met, and having been born and raised in Wales, she left for the country of her ancestors. A week later, her husband, shrinking with age and his fingers curled by arthritis, joined her and they sat out their days in the sun.

John followed his son and his village from afar. When he passed away in his sleep, Gonzo was yet to be discovered and the club was drifting along under the chaotic management of Piggybank Parsons and his committee, the collective that had replaced John at the helm. A memorial service was held in the club, a sing-along around the piano, a knees-up that John Henry Gonzalo Davies RIP would have loved.

66

One Thursday morning, after Capper had filled the bathroom with gas and left for work at Jones the Other Builder's, Gonzo stood up from the kitchen table, tidied the wreckage of Capper's breakfast and made for the stairs. He passed the long, thin mirror at the bottom of the staircase and stopped. He eased off his eyepatch and looked at himself – himselves. Two overlapping reflections came back at him, both loosening around the middle, both fuller of face. Gonzo sighed and headed up the stairs, but only to pull outdoor clothes out of his drawer and find shoes he had not worn for weeks. He slid them on, pulled his patch back into place and opened the curtains. He made his bed, another first for weeks, went back down the stairs and without pausing opened the front door and started walking towards the centre of the village.

He reached the Institute and went into the Reading Room. He sat down and took twenty slow breaths. His head did not hurt. He waited a full fifteen minutes, staring out of the window, before he noticed how overheated the room was. He slowly rose and tried to open the sash window, only to find the cords on both sides had snapped. He tried the next window, but this was jammed shut. He put an edition of the National Coal Board's 1956 Annual Report between the sill and the lower sash of the first window, returned to his seat and picked up a copy of that morning's *Western Mail*. He studiously ignored the back pages. In fact he had barely started on the front-page headline – about missed targets in Welsh hospital waiting lists and school exam results – when he felt a familiar nagging ache in his head. He closed his eyes and gently placed his forehead against the newspaper on the table.

He dreamt that his head rolled and rolled downstream, gathering pace in brown flood waters of the Monnow, slowing in deep pools of the River Wye, but always travelling south. He found himself passing from the ribbon of the border between Wales and Engand into the vastness of the Severn Estuary, pushed down by the falling fresh water, pushed back by the tides of the Bristol Channel. He was decaying, flesh falling in strips, but was still sufficiently intact to be a food source. As he slowly yo-yoed his way towards the open sea – bumping down the Gwent Levels, passing Newport – flocks of seagulls began to circle overhead. They began to swoop down on him, pecking at what flesh remained. Two white gulls, the biggest, saw off all other challengers for these scraps, and began to fight for the prize. They dug in with their bills and took such a hold that they lifted his head into the air and Gonzo found himself no longer waterborne but soaring above his homeland.

He awoke with a start. His headache, to his surprise, had gone. The room was cold. He shut the window and tested the warmth of the radiator. There was barely any heat there. He folded the *Western Mail* and put it back on the shelf and walked cautiously home. When he checked in the mirror his forehead was black with newsprint.

'Well, well,' said Capper from the kitchen. 'Rip Van Fuckin' Winkle stirs.'

Grace, still reluctant to sell the house in Wales, wouldn't leave it. Perhaps, Martin thought, she feared it would be snatched from her. It had crossed his mind, he had to admit. He couldn't avoid a fantasy that would save him a lot of time and effort. He saw a fire, tall and cleansing, and the wretched place burning, falling to the ground. He kept such thoughts to himself.

Not before time, he deemed, a second chance presented itself. Lord Jericoh had promised him a crack at a by-election, and Croydon South was 'on the market', as the grandee told him. He suggested that the prospective candidate stay out of the unseemly scrap for selection, but Martin decamped to London and prowled the Chelsea flat restlessly. Grace came with him, playing her part, preferring to stay in the background but also prepared to be visible on the arm of her husband. They made a splendid couple, as photogenic as ever, and while Grace was by his side, Martin organised a burglary at the house in Monmouthshire. And then, for good measure, he arranged a second, complete with extensive vandalism of the furniture, fittings and personal belongings. He thought the finishing touch, excrement smeared over their bedroom wall, was inspired. He would tell the electorate of Croydon South, where the issue of law and order was always topical, that he too was a victim of senseless crime.

After the second break-in, Grace agreed to sell up. They didn't receive the asking price, but a couple from Newport – he was in lithium batteries – increased their initial offer twice, and the Estate Agents in Usk recommended acceptance. All parties, apart from Grace, were happy and the deal went through quickly, which was more than happened to Martin, who was not selected to stand in the Croydon South by-election.

Will was going to leave London to open a craft shop in an old forge in Whitebrook, between Monmouth and Tintern. Before her brother left, Grace used to go and see him in Shoreditch. It became a family ritual, Grace coming in from Chelsea, Godfrey from Essex, to meet Will in the middle. The family was soon extended, with a group of Will's friends – artists, potters, painters – joining them and coming back for more. Included in the gang was a photographer called Tom. The gatherings grew into whole evenings of hilarity, and at the end of a particularly riotous Mexican meal, Tom took her by the hand and said he wanted to see her again. Grace had been trying to bring some life back into the Chelsea flat, but Martin remained obstinately distant after his rejection in Croydon. She enjoyed every moment of this precious release from his surly silence. She was being asked out, and she wanted to see this Tom again, this laughing, positive, penniless photographer. She told him it was out of the question.

Gonzo returned to the Reading Room in the Institute the following Thursday, this time armed with his old toolbox. He spent an hour cursing his inability to gauge distance through one eye, but ordered himself to be patient. By mid-morning he had the sash windows dismantled. He stopped for lunch, replaced the sash cords, planed some wood off the frames, reassembled them and spent ten whole minutes sliding them up and down smoothly. He then slept, his head resting on a leather-bound volume of Dyrkin's *Diary of Monmouthshire*, published in 1876. When he woke up, the radiators were stone cold. He went into the basement and wrote 'Do Not Feed' on a piece of cardboard and placed it against the door of the coal-fired boiler.

The following Monday he checked his bank statements on-line and then walked up to Garth Street, where Capper was purportedly pricing up a small loft-insulation job. He had to knock three times before a flustered Mrs Hapwood opened the door.

'Morning, Bethan,' said Gonzo.

'Well, look who it isn't,' said Bethan. 'Gonzo Davies, back from the dead.'

'Is he in?'

The married Bethan Hapwood thought about telling a lie, decided it was not worth the bother, nodded and stepped back to let Gonzo in. Capper was in the front room, pulling on a pair of boxer shorts, a slice of toast between his teeth.

'Thought we'd had breakfast,' said Gonzo. 'Can you spare me five?'

'Can't you see I'm busy?' replied Capper, his mouth still full. He finished pulling on his boots and they walked to the front door.

'I'll, um... I'll let you have that quote, then,' said Capper.

'Don't worry, Capper love,' said Bethan. 'There's always another way to keep warm in this house. I'll tell Denzil you were too expensive.'

Capper nodded and followed Gonzo down Garth Street. Gonzo waited until they were round the corner and into Brenin Terrace, before digging an elbow into Capper's ribs. They laughed their way down to the Institute. Gonzo opened up with the key that the janitor, Dan Jones – Dan the Jan – had given him. They went into the basement and Gonzo pointed at the ancient boiler.

'Mend it,' he ordered.

'What's in it for me?' replied Capper.

'Mend it.'

They spent six hours working on the boiler and had it running smoothly by the end of the day. That night over a takeaway cottage pie from the café, Gonzo told Capper that he had enough money in the bank, thanks to what he had saved as a regional player and the Six Nations bonus for playing for Wales, to buy a little property – for them, as a partnership. Capper phoned Jones the Builder and told him that he'd like to leave, and Dick Jones told him that it would be a relief because, in all honesty, he didn't have much on at the moment. It was as easy as that. Dick became Jones the Other Builder, and Gonzo and Capper were back in business.

They bought the cottage on the moor for a tiny sum, but before they started work there, were offered a derelict mid-terrace house in Blaina Street for even less. They set to work on the second property, Capper the workhorse, but also the nanny, as he put it, to Gonzo, forcing him to stick to light work, to be a cautious overseer, a planner of projects ahead.

There was a general exodus of the Courtney family from London, which struck Grace as bizarre because they no longer had a home to welcome them back to Wales. She also found it wounding that while Martin had persuaded the Courtneys to sell the house on the Usk, he had managed to retain his flat in Cardiff Bay. What was more, she was now expected to return there and join her husband on his latest campaign trail. The years had passed, and impatiently he had waited before another by-election opportunity came his way, in Swansea West. Lord Jericoh was sending him back to Wales, but at least this time he was adopted as the Tory candidate. Grace went with him.

Martin said all the right things, made his points on the doortstep concisely, and was given a sympathetic hearing. He lost the by-election narrowly. Lord Jericoh told him it was the view in the party that if he were to continue with his political ambitions, perhaps he ought to stand for the Welsh Assembly. Martin said he would consider the option, but his mind was already made up. His political flirtation was over. The Party thanked him for all his hard work. Martin went home to his Cardiff apartment and stood in his study at the full-length double windows that commanded majestic views over the Bay, from Penarth at the entrance across the water to the docks, and then left to the signature buildings, the Welsh Assembly Senedd and the Millennium Centre. For two hours he stood there, not moving.

67

More years passed and the profile at the top of the valley slowly changed, from moribund pit village to quaintly desirable – in an isolated sort of way – commuter community. Gonzo and Capper in their small way helped to make the village attractive to incomers, refurbishing old properties to a high standard and either letting or selling them – it depended on Gonzo's feeling 'on the day', as he put it – at prices below the cost of similar houses in the valley to the south, and a lot lower than properties below the escarpment to the north and east, in rolling Monmouthshire. The village's new inhabitants lowered the average age, but these were people used to life on the go, and just as they drove long distances to work every day, so they drove to Abergavenny to shop, or to Cardiff for their social life.

They occupied houses in their gentrified pair of streets above the valley floor, but beneath them nothing changed and the heart of the village felt little of their spending power. It was only the older locals who frequented The Colliers' Arms, the shops and the café around the square. The church and the chapel were closed and while Jones the Other Builder had plans to convert them into flats, he was waiting for the narrow band of affluence to spread beyond Edgar Street and

Straight Row. Just as Gonzo and Capper had mothballed the cottage, so Dick Jones sat on the old centres of worship, let them decay and prayed they would not bankrupt him.

The Institute stayed open because Gonzo kept it alive, a shrine to his father, a reading room, a hideaway for sleep. And what Gonzo did for this place of self-improvement in the years after his injury, Capper did for the rugby club. It was a two-site operation: maintaining the clubhouse, high on the slope above the village, at the end of West Street; and down on the bleak wasteland around the old mine, he looked after the ground, with its wooden stand, changing rooms beneath the seats, and its playing area. Capper was a one-man club: groundsman, barman, player, coach – with the Professor as his overwrought assistant – and kit-washer. But even the irrepressible Capper accepted that the days of the rugby club were numbered. Each Saturday it was a struggle to put out a team. Training nights had shrunk to one a week, and even on this single Thursday, only between six and ten players turned up.

Gonzo stayed away from both the field and the clubhouse. It was as if injury had triggered a revulsion for his sport. He neither went up to the clubhouse nor down to the ground. He stayed away and the village rugby club sank ever closer to oblivion.

One morning, when he was taking measurements in the kitchen of a house in Straight Row, there was a clatter at the front door. Capper was trying to force a bundle of long battens through the entrance and round an angle, before going upstairs to the bedroom where he was putting in a dry lining. The front end of the battens was caught in the stair balusters and the more he huffed and puffed, the more they jammed into the gaps beneath the banister.

'Easy, easy,' said Gonzo, coming to give him a hand.

'Fuckin' things,' muttered Capper.

'Pull gently.'

Capper went backwards and Gonzo eased the battening out of their trap.

Gonzo bent down to inspect the woodwork for any marks.

'It's fine,' he said.

'What's that?'

'I said it's fine.'

Capper took this as a signal to bring his load in again. Gonzo was straightening up from his crouched position when the end of a protruding batten caught him in the right eye. It wasn't a hard blow, but his head jerked back and he sat down hard on the stairs. Capper dropped his cargo, rushed in, saw blood and went to pull the patch from Gonzo's eye. Gonzo held up a hand.

'It's fine,' he said.

'You keep saying that.'

'No, it is.'

Gonzo wiped a smear of red away from a nick to his cheekbone. His eye was watering and he pulled off the eye patch. He could feel the lid swelling and held his closed eye against his shirtsleeve. Capper went into the kitchen and came back with a wet cloth and it took the place of the sleeve. For a couple of minutes they did not move.

'Right. Let's get on,' said Gonzo.

'Are you sure?'

'It's fine.'

'Stop saying that.'

Gonzo stood up and carefully opened his eye as best he could.

'Fuck me,' he said.

Capper expected him to be going down with a headache, but instead Gonzo lifted his head to the light.

'There's only one of you,' he said.

'I'll say.'

'A bit blurry, but just one bald old bastard.'

Capper looked closely at the cut and the swelling and the film of water.

'Don't look so good to me,' he said.

'You're not the one looking out of it.'

Gonzo picked up his eye-patch and put it in his pocket.

'Right, where were we?' he said. 'Let's get back at it.'

Godfrey Courtney followed his younger brother Will back to Wales – but not immediately. He had given up banking and gone into teaching. He stayed in his school in Essex for five years, enjoying his release from the stresses of making money in the City, invigorated by the process of making what went on inside the Square Mile, whose towers he could still see in the distance, comprehensible to his A-level students of Economics. He was so at ease in his new life that he thought he would never feel the tug of ambition, but one morning as he was sitting in the staff room he saw a job notice, inviting applications for the post of Head of Economics at Christ College Brecon, and Godfrey suddenly saw not the marshes of the Thames Estuary, but caught an irresistible glimpse of the Beacons and the Usk. He found himself dusting off his CV, filling out a form and travelling to Wales to be interviewed.

When he was offerd the job he accepted without hesitation and spent the last few weeks of his final summer term – having steered his students with typical thoroughness into their exams – planning his farewells. The school valedictory party was a serious affair, for Godfrey was seen as a sober chap. But as his goodbye to London he summoned Will back to Shoreditch and told him to rustle up the Bohemians. His younger brother assembled his crowd of artists, painters and potters – and Tom the photographer, who texted Grace and told her to bring her portfolio with her, the collection Will had told him about.

Grace had no intention of showing her portfolio to Tom. But as she was about to leave the Chelsea home for Godfrey's farewell party – Martin had told her he'd stay in Cardiff – she found herself opening the middle drawer of a tall wooden filing cabinet and pulling out her album of favourite photographs. She had them on a memory stick and on her phone, but she still liked to run her hand over photographic paper. She told herself she was being ridiculous, but put the album in a plastic shopping bag and headed for Shoreditch.

After a four-hour meal, Godfrey gave a little speech – a failed banker, he called himself, among so many world-class bohemians – and while he spoke of friendship and good times, Tom held out his hand to Grace.

'Right, let's see it,' he whispered.

Without saying anything, Grace gave him the album and while the artists prepared one last, spiteful cocktail for the willing Godfrey, he examined her prints.

'These are special,' he said. 'I think we should work together.'

'You wanted to see me again, and now you want us to work together,' said Grace. She shook her head. 'You are a terrible man.'

'I mean it,' said Tom. 'You are very talented.'

'I can't, Tom,' she said.

An hour later, the party broke up. Tom approached Grace as she was outside, hailing a taxi.

'This is my last attempt,' he said.

She laughed. 'Go on, then.'

'I want you to sit for me. Pose. You're…'

'Stop,' she said.

'It was worth a try,' he said and shrugged. 'Email me the photos, anyway, will you?'

Grace nodded, stepped forward and kissed him briefly on the mouth. 'Goodbye, Tom,' she said and stepped into her cab.

From the shadows of a shop doorway twenty metres away, Martin watched without moving.

68

Gonzo did not throw himself back into rugby. He waited weeks, until he was sure his eyeball was locked back into place, and that the headaches had gone for good. And then he turned up one day to watch an end-of-season home game. The village were trounced. The season ended and two months passed, and then one Sunday morning in July he came down to breakfast in an old vest and shorts, and told Capper they were going for a run.

'I was thinking of packing it in,' said Capper. 'We're too old for all this nonsense. The club's fucked.'

'No, we're not,' said Gonzo. 'And it's not. We're going to give it our best shot. Roll back the years.'

An hour and a half later, Capper carried Gonzo back into the house and lay him on the floor of the front room. Gonzo did not move for the rest of the day. It took him three weeks to rediscover any sort of fitness, but by then, the homemade weights had been dusted off and word had spread that Gonzo was back. The Twins came out of retirement, Mystic pledged to carry on, while Useless and the Professor set about recruiting new players and helpers. The Professor, remembering the days when the old committee tried to run the bar, set in motion a new rota system, where the players did a stint at the beer taps, and dared to dream that one day the club would recover its place as a hub of the village, busy enough to merit a full-time steward.

Useless went to Coleg Gwent in Ebbw Vale and found a group of youngsters who were about to pack in rugby, frustrated at being overlooked by the academies and not big enough – or simply not good enough – to entertain the notion of a job with the professional regions. In ones and a two and a final three, the Children joined the club, and it rose from the dead. Few promises were made about where this influx of youthful energy might take the village, for its renascent rugby remained entangled in the grass roots of Wales. But the team improved season upon season, and when Gonzo was in his mid-30s, he found himself leading his players on a run in the Babcock Cup.

Grace was invited to exhibit her photos at a small gallery in Penarth. She had sent Tom her pictures and he had promoted her work. She sold four pictures on the first day and was asked by an emissary of the owner of Cardiff City Football Club to create a matchday gallery for him. She could shoot whatever she liked, inside or outside the stadium. She chose the theme of 'Expectation' and produced a series of eight portraits, all shot before a home game. Among her favourites was an old woman, laden down with shopping bags, in a sea of fans parting to let her through. It sat alongside the face of an away fan walking at the head of a column, heavily flanked by a defocused police escort. Grace had caught the young striker, Scott Plesch, leaning down to kiss his girlriend through the side window of their sports car. She had her hands on the steering wheel. He had his eyes on her, his kitbag in his left hand, and was reaching out with his right to sign an autograph for a young boy whose club scarf, wrapped around his face, only half obscured his broad grin. The series of photographs was hung in the boardroom.

Martin had to find something new, too. He could not bear to be near Grace when she was making plans for her next shoot, her next exhibition. He despised her photography, her plaything. He thought about renting office space in Cardiff for her, or him, but did not trust her to be out of his sight on a daily basis. So, he stayed nearby, converting the Bay flat's third bedroom into a studio-office for her and making the study into his own little den. And there they set up their workspaces: Grace absorbed in hers, Martin less able to concentrate in his. Behind his unworried façade churned the thoughts of the failure, the cuckold.

The successful Martin did his research into leisure and tourism in Wales and took a stake in a luxury hotel, a converted small manor house, near Aberaeron. The jilted husband hacked into Grace's phone and once he knew where she was, dared join up with the other self. This Martin became part owner of a restaurant with rooms in Forest Coal Pit in the Black Mountains, where local beef and lamb proved to be very popular. His interest in meat grew and he followed the chain from the livestock market outside Raglan up to the new super-abattoir in Merthyr, putting his mind to work on increasing capacity and selling to a flourishing domestic and overseas market, hungry for quality Welsh produce. The former manufacturer of the finest, hardest steel became an expert in the softest, most succulent cuts. He spent a little too much time, should anyone have counted his watching hours, spellbound before the processes of slaughter on an industrial scale. It was true. He was mesmerised by the legs of one beast after another buckling under the stungun, by their inversion and desanguination, by the swift carving of the carcasses. He became an investor when the company sought funds to expand.

Martin could never double his fortune, but over the years he steadily increased their wealth. *His* wealth. Grace had her own business. She was good, he was assured by people who assumed he would be proud of her artistic eye and technical expertise with her camera. Very good. She was so acclaimed that he thought of buying a reviewer to trash her work. He let it go and instead took her to dinner at the FCP, the Forest Coal Pit restaurant. She went reluctantly, hoping he would not be looking for a physical reward for their public togetherness. He left her alone.

Martin preferred to be on his own. He had begun to collect mobile phones and tablets, and found a channel for his bile Below The Line, blogging, trolling, smearing and insulting, lashing anonymously at just about everyone his dancing fingers found on the internet. And then he grew weary of his own faceless tirades, and found solace instead in the interchanges between real people, with real ideas about converting mere words of wreckage and destruction into action. Gleeflully – and from the comfort of his luxury apartment in Cardiff Bay – Martin joined the wreckers who were leading the police a merry dance in the Welsh Hell.

A few weeks later, Grace informed him – she didn't ask him, he noted, but casually told him – that she was going to see Tom in London to discuss an exhibition in Greenwich.

'Would you like to come with me?' she asked.

Very clever, thought Martin. He shook his head.

251

'There are French buyers coming over,' he replied. 'Wouldn't you prefer to be selling tender veal with me?' he asked.

'It's very tempting,' she said, still able to play his little game. 'And who knows, one day I could do a carcass shoot for you. One for the bedroom wall.'

Martin smiled and thought about wiping the sarcastic little smile off her face. Stungun the whore. See her legs give way and with one smooth sweep of a slaughterhouse blade open her carotid.

'What's Greenwich about?' he asked pleasantly.

'I'm part of an exhibition. The theme is the Thames.'

'Its entire course, or through London?'

'London.'

'How very metropolitan,' he said and turned back to his plans to extend the hotel in Ceredigion. It was the end of their longest conversation of the year.

She came home on the last train. Her tracker knew where she had been, although Martin told himself she could still have been anywhere. He acknowledged her cunning.

Grace had been nowhere. She was exhausted. Tom had been professionally demanding, pressing her for ideas, showing off a little in front of the bubbling publicist he was obviously seeing.

'Does she sit for you?' Grace had asked as she left them to it in Greenwich.

She was surprised to find Martin in her bed. He had not been there for many months. She resigned herself to giving herself to him.

He wanted to smell the other man on her. He let Grace climb into bed.

'Hello,' she said. 'This is a surprise.'

He turned to her and pulled her sharply under him. And he held her arms hard and took her. Painfully and cruelly. And when she thought it was over, he took her again, because that was what the whore she had always been deserved. And again. Whore.

He awoke early the next morning on his own in the bloodstained bed. Martin reached for one of his phones and tried to track his wife down. It seemed she was still in the bedroom with him. Her phone lay on the carpet, but Grace was gone.

69

In all the weeks of the Hell in their land, the Welsh Assembly Government had raged impotently. There had been an incandescent all-party reaction among the Assembly Members to the events in Carmarthen, Rhyl and Newport. A majority of the AMs had voiced their support for the march out of Caernarfon and a few had even joined it for a few stages. The fire-raising in Ely in Cardiff, and Townhill in Swansea and along the banks of the Usk in Newport had provoked emergency debates in the Senedd. The First Minister of Wales and the Presiding Officer were implored to do all they could to bring pressure to bear on Westminster. The response from the UK government was to remind Wales that the current situation was entirely home-grown, perhaps a symptom of the flaws in the devolutionary process, a consequence of letting inexperienced enthusiasts anywhere near the serious process of running a country. The Assembly Government was bluntly told to tend to matters for which it was responsible. Who did these Members think they were, wagging their finger at London when all around them the hospitals and schools they ran were failing? Wales reacted apoplectically to the put-down and the Senedd set committees to work on drawing up a roadmap to greater autonomy. London scoffed and Cardiff seethed.

Grace swayed by the gate. Her long brown hair, greasy and lank, hung to her thin shoulders that shook beneath her brown coat. She had driven the last few miles in a daze. She fell into the arms of Gonzo only because her legs gave way as he ran towards her.

There was nothing in the cottage. Not a door or a window; not a floor or a ceiling. Grace would not go anywhere else. There was a small gas stove for making a cup of tea, but that was as far as the kitchen facilities went. The mains electricity was off and the water supply yet to be connected. There was a generator for the power tools, but nothing, apart from the drills and saws and planers, to plug into it.

'It's perfect,' she murmured.

She came to life only when Gonzo said he should take her to hospital. She refused point blank. 'He'll find out,' she said firmly. 'And he mustn't. Promise me.'

Gonzo sat down and she curled up against him. Capper asked if her car was locked. She shook her head. He found the keys but checked first inside their van. He found only the blanket that had been the favourite of his old dog, Priestland. He sniffed it and threw it back inside. He ran down the track and found the car where Grace had left it, one wheel in a ditch. He drove it back to the cottage. Inside her bag was nothing to keep her anywhere near warm enough in a cottage open to the elements on the mountain in early spring. He jumped into the van and drove off, returning an hour later with a mattress, two old armchairs, a duvet, blankets and two cushions, sheets of plywood and chipboard, a gas heater, paraffin lamps, a set of candles, a large plastic container full of water, a gas-fired boiler, two cylinders of butane and an old tin bath. They put Grace on the mattress, still in her coat, and covered her with the duvet and a blanket. Within two hours, Gonzo and he had knocked up a stud wall, blocked up the windows in the front room and bedroom above, made a front door of sorts, and lit the heater and the candles.

'Very romantic,' said Capper. 'Fuckin' en suite, I'd say. And on that note, I'll be gone.'

Grace stirred. 'Capper,' she said.

'Aye?'

'Not a word. Please.'

'As if,' he said. 'Not sure I believe it myself.'

'And, Capper...'

'Aye?'

'Thank you.'

70

Our Marnie was back in the steward's flat. She hadn't been sure whom to contact in the village, but in the end had tried the Professor's old mobile number and was amazed when it rang and he answered. She could hardly speak at first but eventually told him that her life was a mess and she was a mess and she needed to sort it and herself out. She sounded him out about coming home. He said – with a certain degree of typically professorial caution – that the time was perhaps not inappropriate. He talked to everybody at the club and it was unanimously agreed that the flat, unused all these years, should have the dust sheets pulled away and be reactivated as the place where the new steward, the permanent appointment at last, should reside.

She threw herself into scrubbing and wiping and polishing the flat back into shape. Every stroke was a furious attempt to eradicate the years she had been away. She had run and run, from job to job, from man to man, and from country to country. Everything, everyone and everywhere had been a disaster. And it had all started with what she and the Professor had done all those years ago.

She set about the last job, cleaning and polishing the full-length mirror in the bedroom. The flat was ready and sparkling. She stood and admired her home. 'That's one thing back into shape,' she said to her reflection. 'Shame about the other.'

Our Marnie had spread a little in her unhappiness. Not too much; just enough to keep the lines on her face filled, she told herself. But she was padded. She could hear her father, dead these five years from the drink in Dublin: 'You've got an arse on you, all right, Marnie.'

Grace lay in the bathtub and felt cleansed. She went under the hot water for a last rinse of her hair and could hear the muffled beat of the generator. She felt herself almost floating. The generator stopped. She came up for air.

'Gonzo?' she called. 'Gonzo, are you there?'

She was about to call again, louder this time, but he replied, quietly: 'I'm here. Outside.'

'Can you come in, please?'

'Are you sure?'

'Gonzo, come in.'

A sheet of chipboard moved and he slipped into the room, dimly lit by a pair of candles. But he had let in some daylight and before he could pull the makeshift door to, he saw the dark marks on her arm. He looked at her and slowly she pulled her arms clear of the water and he saw all the bruises.

Twelve days before the Babcock Cup semi-final, everybody in the club turned up for training. The old guard was there: Mystic, Useless, Twin Tub and Twin Town, Capper and the Professor. The *Plant* were there: Daisy, Buttercup, Daff, Tulip, Moss, Buddleia, Blossom and Fungus. And this younger section, on their college campuses, had managed to mobilise the entire cast of the club's registered extras – all eight of them. Some of these reserves were regulars in the role of sitting on the bench, while others rarely appeared. All of them had been snubbed at some point in their juvenile rugby careers by the selection process for the nation's elite, and all wanted to be part of the big day, when the village had a crack at another group deemed to be their superiors, the academy players of Stalag Two.

Everybody was there except Gonzo. And only Capper knew why. The training session started in a riot of enthusiasm, but when the number 8 failed to appear, the concentration levels began to waver and the team all started to talk among themselves. The drills turned sloppy and all the urgency went out of the running. The rain began to fall.

'Jesus fuckin' Christ,' shouted Capper. 'We are not a fuckin' one-man team.' But they all knew they were.

71

One thing the Senedd had been able to influence with the limited fruits of devolution was the future of the Welsh urban landscape. What to do with the towns of Wales was a question that had spread beyond the industrial valleys. Old coal towns there had to change, but so too did old rural market towns. The Assembly Government had recognised that to renovate the towns of the South Wales coalfield would 'require funds that might sink the European Central Bank', as the First Minister put it, but the need to do something was pressing and a decision was made, in the end almost by lottery, to select one place to be a test-case for renovation. Brecon had been chosen, a once handsome market town on the banks of the River Usk, the starting point of the

Monmouthshire-Brecon Canal and, most pertinently, a signpost to a brighter tourist-driven future, the gateway to the splendours of the Beacons.

The town centre was in the process of being revamped, with flat conversions, new bars and restaurants drawing residents and visitors back into the streets where retail outlets had perished. 'The Beacons' on Wheat Street had been nominated Welsh boutique hotel of the year, while the 'Pigalle' restaurant on the wharf of the canal basin had recently been awarded a second Michelin star. The Brecon Jazz Festival had been reshaped into a summer strum, a season of music that boosted the local economy to the tune of several million pounds a year. Visitor numbers in all months were rising. Market research showed that people were prepared to travel from far and wide to enjoy the experiment in regeneration. Accordingly, into the master plan – the Brecon Blueprint – was written an upgrade of the main road to the town from both the north and south, the A470. For years, this connection between north and south Wales had symbolised a severely restricted Welsh solidarity. How could Wales ever be a united country when its top wasn't connected properly to its bottom?

'Between head and arse we have the A470,' said Assembly Member for Merioneth, Iolo ap Gerallt. 'No wonder we do not stand together. We have no spine.'

Brecon stood on the A470 and the road would be rebuilt there first. Six lanes would stretch up into mid-Wales and down into the Beacons, until the northern and southern ends of Wales were joined by the new M470. But to expand tarmac on this scale – especially through a national park –

required commitment and, above all, funds from the UK government, and the news reached the fast diminishing band of marchers heading from Builth Wells to Brecon that the Wales Office in London had just announced that the road-building programme had been suspended.

'It would appear that despite all our endeavours to bring the A470 up to a standard fit for purpose for the next thirty years, there is a reluctance in Wales to move on it at anything faster than a walking pace,' said the Secretary of State for Wales in the House of Commons.

Those in the chamber who had heard of the protest march laughed and waved their order papers. The abandoned project didn't create much of a stir elsewhere in London. On the march itself, the news of another cut to a service in Wales put a fresh spring in the step of Doctor Meirion Owen Jones, and since he was at the head of the marchers, the rest followed. It meant that PC Derwena had to stride out, too, making her puff a little on the road to Brecon. For the moment it was the only sign of strain among the police.

Ahead, in Brecon, the reaction was very different. The procession on the road had accelerated; in Brecon, the town was brought to a halt. The media sensed a story at last.

'That would be foolish,' said the mayor, Beti Evans, when the *Western Mail* asked her if there was any danger, in her view, of Brecon following the example of the cities of the South and venting their anger through fire and trouble on the streets. 'So much has been built here for the good of Brecon. Why should we want to ruin all the hard work?'

Her town found a different way to express its disgust.

Brecon welcomed the marchers, refreshed them and joined them. The original language issue now had Neglect as a travelling companion. The Pigalle laid on a complimentary breakfast, serving eggs benedict on the wharf, until they were overwhelmed by the numbers and had to ask Hazel, never likely to earn a single Michelin star, to come to the rescue. The children of the village of Libanus, four miles south, counted 245 as the march went through on the A470, now a cause as well as the road to the South.

Capper and the Professor sat in the clubhouse after training. Everybody else had sloped off home, and the plates of bread, cheese and raw onion, normally consumed in a flash, lay untouched on the tables. Our Marnie stood behind the bar and watched the two senior players, picking up the odd word as they leant towards each other.

'You know, don't you?' said the Professor quietly. Capper nodded. 'And I suspect you're going to tell me.'

'Look, Professor, it's been on my mind all fuckin' day. Fuck me, it was almost a relief when he didn't turn up. Saves the lads seeing what may have fuckin' happened to him. I've always said it and I'm going to tell you, Professor.'

'Stop right there,' said the Professor sharply. 'I don't want to know.' He looked in panic towards Our Marnie.

'Boys in love can't run through a paper fuckin' bag,' said Capper.

'I mean it, Capper. Don't say any…'

But Capper blurted it out and the Professor and Our Marnie heard every word.

On the other side of the Brecon Beacons lay Merthyr Tydfil, very different from Brecon. Nobody in the old iron town suggested that a sense of civic pride in anything recently restored should be an obstacle to kicking up a storm. Most townspeople took a certain pride in Merthyr's history of industrial militancy. On the other hand, the town had been in decline for so long that the news that the A470 would not be turned into the M470 caused no real outrage.

'Just a kick in the ribs of a corpse,' said one of the town councillors, Ted Thomas.

Councillor Ted nevertheless raised himself from his chair in the front room of his house on Sycamore Road in Gurnos, took himself off down to the High Street and kept vigil in front of the Old Town Hall, whose restoration had been his pride and joy. He knew all the tales about Merthyr in an age before electricity, glowing at night from the furnaces of the four great ironworks: Dowlais, Penydarren, Plymouth and Cyfarthfa. He didn't want the town to glow again from his Town Hall going up in flames.

Councillor Ted's instincts hadn't let him down. He had simply chosen the wrong building. There was no outrage in Merthyr, but the town's sense of mischief had been tickled. A few hundred yards away, up in a more battered part of Pontmorlais, lay the shell of the old YMCA, a vast Victorian building that had been decaying, lifeless, for years. It teemed now, as youngsters scuttled in and out of its broken windows and doors, coming and going through holes in the security fence, ferrying in enough combustible material to melt iron. A match flickered and up went the YMCA in a matter of minutes.

High in the Beacons, at the cusp of the high pass through the mountains, where Hazel and Brian sold sausages to the marchers who had been on the go all day, heads turned to the south and saw that the night sky had turned orange.

Meirion walked up and down the line, assessing fatigue levels, sensing the buzz of excitement that came with the glow in the distance.

'Let's march on,' was whispered to him.

He gathered the four Sages still on the march and they discussed the options. The night was cold and it wasn't difficult to persuade even the most venerable to carry on through the night. They had a target now, and not long after dawn the next day the marchers crossed the Heads of the Valleys road and entered South Wales. They turned off the A470, crossed the River Taff and marched up Merthyr High Street. They passed the Old Town Hall, collecting Ted Thomas on the way, and climbed towards the smouldering ruin of the YMCA.

'Good morning to you all,' said Meirion through his loud-hailer, standing on top of a van, parked in front of the last of the fire tenders at the scene. 'We made it through the night. And thank you, Merthyr.'

The marchers filled the road leading back down the hill. They were pressing forward, straining to hear and be close to the remains of the fire. 'For all of us, the angry of Caernarfon, the sorrowful of Rhyl and the neglected of Brecon... for the farmers of Carmarthen and, yes, the tree-huggers of the western woods...' He paused as Cosmos's band raised a cheer. 'For all of us, wherever we have come from, for whatever reason, this is a moment. We are different in many ways, but we must decide whether we can make the next step together.' He pointed at the YMCA. 'This is a gateway of fire. There will be danger ahead. Do we march on?'

A roar went up and Meirion laid out the plan: to rest first, because the next day they would be in Cardiff.

Capper was at a loose end, fretting about the Babcock Cup semi-final. It was the middle of the morning and he needed to be working to take his mind off the rugby. But the cottage was a no-go area, what with him and her reducing each other to putty by candlelight. Capper needed to see Gonzo and take him out for a run in the great outdoors, to be reassured that the best player in the team was in a fit state of mind to play in the biggest fixture of the other boys' careers. It was all right for him. He'd played in all sorts of bigger games than this, but for everyone else this was as big as it was ever going to be. He knew that was being unfair on Gonzo, but even his best mate would have to admit the timing of love's sweet return couldn't be worse. Damn it, he needed to see him and just make sure everything was going to be OK. And there was something else nagging away at Capper. He wished he hadn't told Our Marnie and the Professor about Grace. Not because he didn't trust them, but it was just one of those things that you found yourself doing even when you'd made a promise that you wouldn't, and the last thing Capper wanted to do was tempt any sort of fate, especially since there seemed to be plenty of other people tickling old fate in the ribs.

Not knowing quite what he could say to Our Marnie without her taking the hump and accusing him of not trusting her to keep a secret, he found himself parking the van outside the rugby club. He couldn't go to the cottage, so he may as well do something. He'd have a look at that stain of Wales on the end wall. Our Marnie opened the door and Capper had to admit that she looked great with a few extra pounds on her. She let him up to the first floor and he crept into the narrow loft space above the clubhouse lounge and traced the damp up the wall to the roofline. He reversed and went outside to place a ladder against the gable end of the clubhouse. When he reached the top, he found a couple of ridge tiles had split. That would explain the ingress of water, Capper said to himself, rolling the 'r' of one of his favourite words.

'The fuckin' ingress of water,' he repeated, aloud this time.

'Whatever you say,' said Our Marnie at the bottom of the ladder.

Capper nearly fell off.

'Jesus, Our Marnie.'

'I've made you a coffee,' she said.

'Be right there,' said Capper. 'Then I'll go and get a couple of ridge tiles.' But as he was climbing down the ladder he noticed a crack in the render and when he picked at it, a chunk fell away, and a larger crack in the stonework was revealed.

'And this will explain why the fuckin' ridge tiles are bust,' he said. He picked his way down the wall, with the cement render peeling away under his fingertips.

'Oh fuck,' said Capper. 'We've got an ingress of water up there because the fuckin' clubhouse is coming apart down here. Subsidence, our Marnie. Fuckin' subsidence.'

The marchers rested in Merthyr town centre, prepared to doze wherever they could and fortify themselves with hot drinks for the long day that would follow their long night. Merthyr opened its doors to the pilgrims. First, the arm of an unseen keeper at the entrance of the Old Town Hall pulled in one handful of strangers, and then another. All the old chapels opened up, offering shelter to the weary. Three hours later, the grateful walkers drifted down, as if lured in their semi-conscious state by gravity, to the bottom of town and reassembled outside the gates of the old Hoover factory. Merthyr Vale opened up before them, inviting them south, the ongoing downhill run to the capital. Above them, to their right, ran the A470, now a dual carriageway. They could have taken the sweeping slip road up to it and made a statement against the skyline: 'The march resumes. Twenty miles to go.' Instead, almost as a last-second change of mind, Meirion ignored the main exit for Cardiff on the roundabout and led his column to the next one, the A5054, the signposts steering them towards Pentrebach and Troedyrhiw.

Meirion knew what he was doing, because the third village they came to on the old coal road along the bottom of the valley was Aberfan. The column slowed as one as it neared the name sign and came to a complete halt in the heart of the community. The arrival of the march had brought the villagers out in force, but as the incomers paused, so the clapping and cheering of those welcoming them died. It was as if this surge into the village suddenly reminded the inhabitants of what else had come their way, the avalanche of waste that, one bleak October day in 1966, had engulfed them. For five full minutes Aberfan, stood frozen in time, remembering.

Our Marnie handed Capper his coffee. They were sitting in the flat. Capper was trying to explain that it wasn't uncommon for buildings in any village built on top of underground workings to be prone to a little slippage here and there, and that underpinning such threatened properties sounded expensive, but didn't always have to be so. Our Marnie wasn't listening.

'Are you gay, Capper?' she asked.

Capper stopped talking.

'Don't think so,' he replied equably. 'Nobody's ever noticed, but I seem to have been out with a few of your kind over the years. Just haven't found the right one, as they say, for a long-term commitment.'

'But you know who is, don't you?'

'Who's what?'

'Gay.'

'Aye, I reckon.'

'And should he say he is?'

'Up to him, isn't it?'

'But what would you say would happen if he did?'

'The way things are going at the moment, I'd say it'd be the least of our fuckin' worries.'

Our Marnie put her hand on his. 'You're a good man, Capper Harris.'

Gonzo arrived late at training, but at least he was there. He had not wanted to leave Grace on her own, but she had pushed him out of the house.

'They're relying on you,' she said. 'This is the biggest game of their lives and they need you. I'll be fine.'

'I'll be back as soon as I can. And don't answer the chipboard to anyone.'

She smiled. She did feel better, warmer. She felt loved. 'Go and show them you can run through a paper bag.'

Training went more or less satisfactorily. Capper had something on his mind and the Professor was all over the shop, but the others knuckled down and concentrated on accuracy and precision in their drills. The *Plant* were normally worried when they dropped the odd ball or threw an occasional wayward pass, because Gonzo placed a real emphasis on doing the simple things well in training, so that they were second nature in the heat of a real game, and he usually nagged them incessantly to work on their skills. But he scolded nobody here and seemed to be spending most of this fine Thursday evening staring across the moorland. Halfway through the session, he suddenly turned, put two fingers in his mouth and whistled loudly.

'Come around, lads,' he said. 'Sit down in a circle. That's it, nice and still now.' Gonzo pointed at the waste ground between the field and the village. 'Look at us. Look where we are. A shitheap in the arse-end of nowhere.'

The team smiled.

'I don't suppose all of you can remember the days when we had a sponsor here.'

The children shook their heads.

'A sponsor, just imagine. But we did. Isn't that right, Mystic? Remember, the Twins?'

Other heads nodded.

'Steel-Ag. They came and then they left. They went south and put their money into something else. The Steel-

Ag Academy. Only for the best. And they had such a good time, these best in Wales, that when one of them was caught running away... remember, Useless? Little Pretzel Davies – couldn't take it any more. When they asked him what it was like, he said: 'It's like being in a prisoner of war camp.' That's why Steel-Ag became Stalag. Stalag One in Cardiff, Stalag Two in Newport. Down in the west they had to be a bit different, didn't they? So they changed theirs to the Gulags.'

'I always wondered...' said one of the children.

'Aye, way before your time, Buttercup. They didn't stay long with these academies, either, that Steel-Ag. Gone in a flash and all they left behind was the nickname, Stalag.'

Gonzo stepped out of the circle and took a few steps. Nobody else moved.

'And you know what?' he asked. 'They work. The academies work. They take the best talent and turn them into the best players. We all go down to the Millennium Stadium and all the players we see playing for Wales have been through the system. Make no mistake – and forget what Pretzel Davies once said – they're good. We got lucky in the last round and caught them unawares. It won't happen again.'

'Some fuckin' pep talk,' muttered Capper.

'But it's right, Capper,' continued Gonzo. 'They're the best raw talent, they've got the best skills, the best facilities, the best physiques. They are going to be the best.'

'Do we bother turning up, then?' said Capper.

Gonzo paused and stepped back into the circle.

'D'you remember why these brilliant kids play in the Babcock Cup? Why they invented this competition in the first place? Because if there was one thing missing in the rugby education of these stars in the making, it was having their head shoved up their arse by some old twat like you, Capper.'

A cheer went up.

'If you wear Gucci shoes you can forget what grass feels like under your feet. Look around us. This is a shit-heap, but it's our shit-heap. Our wilderness. Let's see if those kids can walk on our grass.'

At the end of the training session, the Professor checked that everybody was going back to the clubhouse. Daisy, Tulip and Moss of the *Plant* said they weren't planning to, and Gonzo was hoping to go back to Grace as quickly as possible. But he caught the look of desperation in the Professor's eye and told everyone to fall in. He needed to have a word with Capper, anyway, because something was obviously playing on the hooker's mind, and there were only so many minds they could afford to have distracted so close to the big day.

Capper, it appeared, was worried about the clubhouse, which came as a relief to Gonzo, who felt that his friend could deal with anything to do with bricks and mortar. Human dramas might be another matter. Gonzo allowed himself to be pulled to the far end of the clubhouse, while everybody else trooped inside.

'So, come on, Capper, what's…' he started. Then he saw the crack going from top to bottom of the gable end. 'Oh, shit.'

Round the corner, a procession was still going into the clubhouse, and not merely of players. It was as if some secret message had done the rounds of the village, declaring that everybody on this midweek night needed to be there. The Widowers were there and Meg and Annie were clip-clopping on their heels along the pavement. Dario was not far behind. Capper and Gonzo followed them all. As the rest of the gathering arranged themselves around the tables they occupied on match days, they examined the stain of Wales on the wall. The Professor stood up and called for attention.

'I wasn't expecting such a crowd,' he said, 'And I suppose that just makes it a little harder for me. But I'm going to say it anyway.'

He looked at Our Marnie. She smiled at him encouragingly from behind the bar.

'No, it's not easy. Not after all this time. Especially, I suppose, because I've been here for such a long time now. This place has always been very important to me and I never wanted to spoil anything. I mean, we go back a long way...'

Capper was still looking at the damp patch. The Professor had paused.

'It's OK, Professor,' Capper said quietly without turning. 'We know.'

'You know?'

'We know,' said Gonzo.

'You know?'

'Always have done,' said Mystic.

'That I'm gay?'

'We know,' said Useless.

Gonzo went up to the Professor and shook his hand and then clapped him on the back. Capper gave him a hug. One by one, the players all went up to the wing and shook his hand. Then the Widowers did the same, followed by Dario and finally Meg and Annie, who hugged him and kissed him full on the lips.

'Bit of a waste, love, but there you go,' said Meg.

Ten minutes later the club was empty, except for the Professor who was standing by the piano, and Our Marnie. She came down from the bar and slipped an arm through his.

'How d'you feel?' she asked.

'Amazing,' said the Professor.

Capper arrived at the clubhouse early the next morning. Gonzo was still, no doubt, wrapped in the arms of Grace and good for nothing, which left his mate in a quandary because somebody had to take responsibility, what with the semi-final coming up and the clubhouse falling down. Hitched to the back of the van was the company trailer.

'Company trailer, my arse,' said Capper to himself. 'Fourth fuckin' hand load of temperamental scrap.'

On the flat bed of the trailer sat the mini-digger.

'Now you, my little beauty, are the company dog's bollocks,' he said aloud. 'Down you come.' He looked up at the roof of the club. Up and down. To sort out the up you had to go down. Semi coming up; clubhouse coming down. To fix the roof you had to dig. He pulled up the two limbs of the ramp and lay them down to the ground. Up and down.

He was just about to start reversing the digger off the trailer when Our Marnie appeared, wearing, as far as Capper could see through the mud-spattered side window, not much more than a short dressing gown.

'Oi,' he said above the sound of the engine. 'Put some

clothes on, will you? Some people round here are trying to concentrate.'

She said something back to him, but it was lost in the noise.

'What's that?' he said, poking his head through the window. 'Jesus, Our Marnie, you'll catch your death.'

'I was going to get dressed, but then I decided not to.'

'Suit yourself.' He noticed she was wearing wellington boots. 'Very fetching.'

Our Marnie did not reply. Capper looked her up and down one last time, shook his head and restarted the engine of the digger.

'It's time to move on,' said Our Marnie.

'What's that?' Capper sighed and cut the engine again.

'I said it's time to move on.'

'Well, if you get out the way I'll do exactly that.'

'No, I mean it's time to move on.'

'Whatever you say.'

'There's something else you've got to have a look at. In the flat.'

'What, is it serious?'

Our Marnie nodded her head, turned and went back into the club.

Capper shook his head.

'One fuckin' thing at a time,' he muttered to himself and restarted the engine. But then he sighed again and turned the key. There was not a sound in the street or on the moor.

'Sorry, my baby,' he said, patting the side of the cabin. 'I'll be back.'

He went into the club and saw that Our Marnie had left her boots at the bottom of the stairs. He took his working boots off and put them next to hers. Up the stairs he went.

'Right,' he said. 'Where's the problem?'

'In here,' said Our Marnie.

'Are you decent?' asked Capper from outside the bedroom door.

'No,' came the reply. 'So get your big bald head in here and get your clothes off.'

Capper opened the door. And just before the Babcock Cup semi-final, he fell in love.

72

The call came as no surprise. Not a day had gone by in all the years since Martin Guest left Steel-Ag when the Professor thought he was safe. He had never had, let alone enjoyed, a moment of release, of freedom. Not even in the recesses of his fantasy life in sport, that refuge from the frustrations – the numbing boredom, the responsibilities, the cares of the working week – had the Professor ever thought that Martin Guest was out of his life. On his wing, scared of being caught and crushed by opponents that would wish him physical harm, and yet energised, electrified by such fear, knowing that it could make him elusive and fast and uncatchable, the Professor knew that Martin Guest would always catch him. And now he had. This was the moment. And it wasn't some showdown dripping in menace, wracked by tension, the two of them in an empty street at noon, or on some desolate plain. The Professor was in the cafeteria at the Senedd, deep in the small print of the Welsh Assembly Government's Rural Development Plan, with his vibrating phone revealing the number he dreaded. Well, he was as ready as he ever would be, because he had never enjoyed a moment of peace, until now.

'Hello, Professor,' said Martin brightly. 'It's me.'

'I know,' said the Professor. Not one moment. Until now. He was ready.

'Of course, you do. It's why I value you still...' said his old master.

The Professor was tempted to end the call. Press the red button and stamp on the mobile phone. He felt the sinking feeling of the institutionally manipulated being bent out of shape yet again.

'Don't think about putting the phone down on me,' said Martin, with an edge that peeled back the years.

The Professor said nothing. This was it.

'I've told them, you know.'

'My, my,' said Martin. 'Well, that was unusually brave of you. Outing yourself after all this time. That must have caused a stir among the cavemen.'

'It didn't actually.'

'How very enlightened. You must have felt a bit foolish, then. Keeping that secret all those years, and no need for any of it.'

'It means I don't have to...'

'Yes, it means you don't have to tell me anything ever

again,' said Martin reasonably. 'Well, in that case, I wish you good luck with your life, Professor.'

Neither of them continued. Neither ended the call.

'Just one thing,' said Martin finally. 'In this confession of yours, this declaration of your true self, did you by any chance happen to mention that it was you that told me about… about the tryst?'

The Professor couldn't speak.

'No, I thought not. So, they may know that you are what you are, but what they may not know is that it was you that ended the village hero's glorious career. And if that's the case, then you can tell me one more thing after all. And take the greatest care, Professor, because it'll be a different matter when – if – the Troglodytes find out it was you that brought down the great Gonzo. That would be a seal of trust broken, wouldn't it?'

'I'm not afraid of you.'

'Yes, you are, Professor. So, tell me…' Martin paused and then counted to three. 'Tell me… is she back?' And he counted to three again, more slowly. 'Is she?'

The Professor had known. Of course, he had known the question was coming. And not a word came to him.

'Thank you, Professor. Your silence tells me everything I need to know. Another little matter to sort out. I think you can assume – and you can tell this to whomever you please – that there will be consequences.'

73

Gareth and Danny Mewson had served their master well, but at the end of their playing days came the question of what would become of them. The stamping incident gave Danny a toxic reputation. He left rugby, unemployed and with no qualifications. Mr Guest had taken him off the Steel-Ag payroll when he secured his professional deal, and with his former employer no longer in his life, Danny feared for what lay in wait for him in the world beyond sport. In this state of uncertainty he felt the pull of the old days in Bristol. Part of him had never stopped longing for nights in the underworld, but he was spared when payments from Mr Guest suddenly resumed, and Danny was able to resist the temptation to let his feral self reclaim him. He had made a pledge of his own, back on the day Mr Guest gave Gareth and him their chance, and he had kept his nose, if not exactly clean, then dedicated to follow the scent of his master.

Gareth had needed no help at all. He was a classic case, a model reformed character. He had obeyed his master's instructions to the letter and when, like his brother, he was released from his playing contract, for being a little too slow and one-paced in an age of rapidly advancing fitness levels, he transferred seamlessly into coaching. The boy who had remained beyond the reach of instruction for so many years in Bristol became a patient, gifted educator in sport. He swept through the courses that took him out of playing and into developing skills in others. He had not managed to make himself a honed athlete, but he encouraged devotion to physical sleekness in those he trained.

Even though he was earmarked for success, he still had to cut his teeth in the lower reaches, and the money on offer in the semi-professional leagues was limited. He was therefore pleasantly surprised to find his meagre income supplemented by Mr Guest. He recognised with gratitude that he had not been forgotten and he knew, too, that one day he would be called upon to serve once again. Not that he needed the cushion of the retainer for long. He coached Llanharan to promotion in successive seasons and became forwards' coach at Pontypridd. From there he was fast-tracked into the regional set-up, where he paused only briefly before he was given his breakthrough. The academies were being overhauled and fresh, innovative coaches were being put in charge. He didn't land the top job of director of rugby, but was appointed head coach. He wasn't the overall strategist and manager and head of recruitment, but he was the figure in a track-suit who had hands-on control over the best young talent in the region. This was the most influential role in the game, a chance to mould young minds, to enlighten them and broaden their view of the world and their sport. He wanted them to play with a spirit of adventure, never with fear. Gareth Mewson was the coach of Stalag 2, about to play the village in the semi-final of the Babcock Cup.

Danny was phoned first. He recognised the voice immediately. This was the same master who had commanded him all those years ago to do some really weird things – like those burglaries. He had been asked to go back to the Bristol days, except the target was in Monmouthshire. Mr Guest's own house. If Danny had been confused he hadn't show it.

He was there to follow orders. He took care with the first break-in and enjoyed the rush of adrenaline of being back in business. But when he was told to upgrade the damage on the second occasion he entered the property, he nearly gasped with pleasure. The risks involved – of going back so soon to a place he'd already turned over, with licence to be wanton with his destruction of a family home – had given Danny a thrill he hadn't known since the day he put Gonzo Davies away.

If he had been ordered to stand down at that moment he would have been grateful. It would have done him for life. But he was under starter's orders again. Mr Guest wanted more. He was given a phone number that he had to remember, not write down. That was all. He dialled it now. Frank the driver answered immediately and told him to be at a certain bus stop on Newport Road in Cardiff, the next morning at half past four.

Danny was on time and climbed into the van that rolled up to the kerb.

'It's a reconnaissance mission,' said Frank. 'So we are going to be careful… because you might get a bit excited by what you see on this one… who you see.'

'Who's that then?

'It's your old mate, Gonzo fucking Davies.'

Little Dario saw the van coming. He had been up for hours, unable to sleep. This was not, however, a case of a lifelong fan in the grip of heightened anticipation of the big day ahead, but a measured response to the little alarm going off inside Dario's head. Gonzo had missed a training session, the

Professor had made his statement in the club and nobody had seen Capper for two days. Something was up and Dario, starting at an hour so early that the sky to the east had only just started to lighten, was keeping watch.

He didn't have to wait long. From his observation post, the remains of a hut on the lowest dram road on the mountain, Dario watched the van approach the village from the south. He took a pair of binoculars out of his bag and watched in close-up as it went past the turning for the track that led to the cottage, but as soon as it slowed on the approaches to the village, Dario knew that it was going to do a U-turn. He speed-dialled Gonzo and the phone was answered immediately. Somebody else was not sleeping.

'White van coming your way. ETA three minutes,' said Dario in a clear, unhurried voice. From the cottage Gonzo appeared and then waved a second, much smaller, figure out. They ran towards the open moorland. Dario watched them reach the natural tussocks that grew out of the boggy ground. From there, they could make it unseen to the cropped grassy bumps of the old waste mounds that ran in an irregular line almost as far as the village.

Dario checked the light and reached into his bag again. He watched as the van made its way back to the turning. It stopped and turned again, going back to a gateway on a rise in the road, a point from which the cottage could be seen in the distance. There the van stayed. And watching it for every second of the many hours was Dario. At lunchtime the van moved again, going back to the turning down the rutted track. This time, it took the turning and pulled up outside the cottage. The driver and passenger slid open their front doors and stepped down. Slowly they walked to the front of the cottage. The driver put his ear to the door, while the passenger circled the property. When he had completed the short circuit, the passenger gave the chipboard front door a push and it fell open. They both went inside. Five minutes later, and without a sound having reached Dario, they reappeared. The driver spoke into his phone. They climbed back into the van and drove back down the track. Only when it was a speck did Dario gently put down the camera he'd been using. He noticed that the hand that had held the long lens rock-steady was now trembling.

Gonzo and Grace approached the village across the moor. Gonzo was heading for the gate at the end of West Street and once they were there, he made a distracted note of the familiar mini-digger and the van and the trailer, parked haphazardly by the end of the clubhouse. He was more interested in finding the spare front door key, left by way of tradition under the last outcrop of rock on the wilderness side of the gate. His fingers found it at last and he steered Grace quickly inside the clubhouse. Up the staircase to the flat there was a trail of boots and clothes, and Gonzo's heart skipped a beat. Had the unwanted visitors been here first? He motioned to Grace to stay in the lounge and quietly went upstairs. Our Marnie's door was ajar. He crept inside, expecting to find the whole place trashed. But everything was in place, except for a few more clothes strewn across the carpet. He heard a grunt and a snore – sounds he knew all too well. He tiptoed to the bedroom door and peeked inside. Our Marnie and Capper were locked in each other's arms, half in and half out of the duvet, both sound asleep. He shut the door and went into the kitchen, thinking that this was going to put a certain theory to the test. He flicked on the kettle and went downstairs to fetch Grace.

'Funny old start to the morning,' he whispered to her over a cup of tea. 'Can't say which bit of it worries me most.'

When Frank and Danny returned empty-handed from Gonzo's cottage, Martin next phoned Gareth Mewson. He spoke more freely to the other brother. He explained what he wanted. It flew in the face of everything the coach instilled in his players, threatened the good name of the academy and could well cost Gareth his job. He said yes immediately.

Our Marnie was shooing Capper and Gonzo out of the flat, ordering them to move the machinery from the end of the clubhouse.

'You can't have all that stuff lying around,' she said. She was still wearing Capper's T-shirt, that she had hastily pulled on when she realised there was somebody in the kitchen.

'We should do something about that wall,' said Capper, in his boxer shorts. 'I suppose.' It was the last thing he wanted to do. He wanted to go back to bed with Our Marnie.

'Out, the pair of you,' she said. 'Shift it, if for no other reason than the van and the digger say, 'Hello, we're here.' You don't have to ask too many questions in the village to find out they're yours. Is that what you want?'

Gonzo waited for Capper to collect his clothes, minus the T-shirt, from the floor and stairs. They left the flat and soon there was the sound of the mini-digger starting and being loaded on the trailer. The van drove away down West Street. Our Marnie sat Grace down in the kitchen and made more tea.

'Right,' she said. 'He wants you to stay here, doesn't he?' Grace nodded. 'That's no problem. Except, first, I'm going to have to tell you something... a story, I suppose. And it's not easy for me.'

Grace reached out a hand, but Our Marnie pushed it away.

'No, you'd better hear it first.'

She took a deep breath and told Grace about what she had felt for Gonzo all those years ago and how she had seen him and Grace in the café in the arcade and how she had known in an instant that what she had dreamed of could never be because she had just seen something that she didn't think she would ever be able to inspire in the man she couldn't love now and how in her jealousy she had told the Professor and how she had always feared – no, how she had known – that she was responsible for what happened next.

74

It was the day of the Babcock Cup semi-final and scores of locals gathered at the rugby club on the morning of the game. It was, according to the Widowers, who were among the first to arrive, the largest single gathering at the clubhouse since the mine shut. They ordered their halves of weak beer and wondered if this Cup fever might prove a little too much for a team that, with the exception of Gonzo in his wonder days before injury, had never had to cope with such excitement in their sporting lives. The match-day squad had gathered for a morning meeting, thinking they would be able to sprawl about in the lounge and kill a couple of hours there. But they were squeezed into a corner by the crush and eventually retreated to the café in the middle of the village. Outside the clubhouse, they had to force their way through a press of supporters at the door and down a corridor of wellwishers lining West Street and cheering them wildly all the way.

Gonzo mingled with the *Plant*, calming them, telling them not to reach a state of frenzy too soon. The youngsters looked at him blankly, removed their headphones and said, 'Say again', before retreating into their music with a rolling of their eyes at all the fuss.

Only Daisy replied to Gonzo's pointless soothing. 'No disrespect, Gonzo,' he said. 'But if you've got to have a word, you might want it with the old fool up there.'

Gonzo looked up at the window of Our Marnie's flat on the upper floor of the clubhouse. Capper and Our Marnie were standing there, watching the team. Capper had his arms wrapped around her and seemed in no rush to leave. Gonzo gestured to him to put Our Marnie down and join the team. And to Our Marnie to put Capper down and go and help Grace, who had refused to stay in hiding and was now pulling pints behind the bar. To be fair to Our Marnie, it was clear she was trying to extricate herself from Capper's embrace. Gonzo could sense the hooker's heavy sigh and reluctance as he planted a final kiss on her mouth and stepped away from the window. Gonzo waited for him and half-dragged him out of the congestion, through the streets to the café in the deserted centre of the village.

The march continued downhill on the old Cardiff Road, from Aberfan to Quaker's Yard and Cilfynydd. Respectful silence gave way to song as the marchers walked past Pontypridd towards Treforest. '*Mae Hen Wlad Fy Nhadau*' began in the town where the anthem was written and turned to 'Why, Why, Why, Delilah…?' as they passed the birthplace of Tom Jones, the strides of the massed choir lengthening and their pace quickening. In Tongwynlais, however, they stopped in front of the banner that put their numbers at 286, a figure that would have been bigger had the local children included the twenty police officers in their squad cars that now followed the procession.

Meirion was conscious of the increasing police presence behind him. He had to decide how to enter the capital. It didn't take him long. Without his mechanised support vehicles – the hearses and tractors that had turned back in Builth – there was no need to stick to the road. Meirion purposefully led his followers down to the Taff Trail and they set off along the riverside path that would take them all the way to Cardiff Bay. It was a Saturday and Meirion was aware that the National Assembly would not be in session. His plan was to occupy a space in front of the Senedd, to create a camp and prepare for a demonstration on the steps of the building when it opened for work on Monday.

For a few minutes they had the off-road Trail to themselves. Hazel was the only bit of the motorised convoy that was not thrown by the detour. She pointed the Nissan and snack bar in the direction of the city centre, confident in her instincts and the feeding routines of the protestors. Others were less certain. The television crews hopped in and out of their satellite vans, trying to work out whether to follow on foot or stay with Hazel. The police had to seek advice on how they should proceed. Half the officers were ordered to follow the march, but this was quickly countermanded by a fresh instruction. Three constables were assigned to the march and the rest were deployed to new positions as part of an emergency defensive system in the centre of the city. The squad cars departed in a blast of sirens and lights, and were soon tearing past Hazel at 70 mph. The satellite trucks dithered no more, but set off in hot pursuit of the new story, whatever it was.

It took Martin all of fifteen text messages to activate the mobs of Newport and Swansea and set them on their way to Cardiff. Thirteen untraceable little pieces of goading and taunting went east, daring the mindless of Newport to put their discontent on the road, carry their fight to Cardiff. A day out in the capital, but not for shopping. Up the revolution. The puppet-master watched the ripple effect of his pebbles, the geometric spread of the word through Duffryn, Bettws, Pill and Ringland, the rising lust for trouble.

Swansea had required two simple trigger words, 'Havana Jacks'. The uprising there had been set up well in advance. Swansea had been on stand-by, to be mobilised – summoned – by nothing more than the press of a button by an unseen hand. Martin waited for one of the scores of mobile phones in front of him to respond. A screen lit up and he read the request for the confirmation codeword. He keyed in 'White Army' and pressed Send.

It took a few more texts to stir the capital into action. Nobody would dare invade it. No way. Newport and Swansea didn't have the bottle. Martin had to leak the invasion to the police, and then alert the complacent defenders that the police were for once ahead of the local grapevine and were implementing a long-planned city-wide response, which included a round-up of all those who had wriggled through the net of Operation Bluebird. It had the desired effect. Cardiff was roused.

The academy brought few supporters with them. A dozen parents, potentially as dangerous a touchline breed as could be found – the fathers were generally spiteful about the tactics employed by their sons' coaches, while the mothers were serial abusers of referees – travelled in their cars, parking them in the old colliery yard. It was a grey day, not ideal for a picnic, but they reversed into place, forming a circle, car bonnets facing outwards. The boots were opened and the parents ate their sandwiches and pastries, sipping wine, cracking open the odd can of lager, and for the moment kept their views to themselves. This experience promised to be all too typical of the Babcock Cup, whose worth they seriously questioned as it hardly replicated anything their offspring would encounter in their elite rugby careers. The fathers raised a toast to a professional performance and safe passage to the final, where they would at least be on familiar ground, the Millennium Stadium, and in more appropriate company, facing the winners of the clash of the Gulags of the West.

They drank again, and then again, pushing themselves into the parental frame of mind from which they could be even more fully supportive.

The mothers, allocated drivers on semi-final day, shivered as they watched the line of home supporters coming down towards them. They viewed everyone in – and every square inch of – this godforsaken place with grave suspicion. The whole point of attending the academies was to leave these ghost villages far behind. What was the point of signing up to the process of regenerating Wales when the reward was to stand and be gawked at by these savages coming down the mountain?

'Look at them,' said Margaret Ellis, the mother of Johnny Ellis, Stalag 2's second row.

'Like snot from a runny nose,' sighed Anne Williams-Thomas, mother of Dom, the captain of Stalag 2 and the Wales Under 20 team.

The mothers laughed and braced themselves to be abused as the line went past. All that came their way was good cheer and an invitation to the clubhouse after the game. The Widowers walked past holding plastic buckets that would be passed up and down the touchline, the closest thing there was on the day to a paying gate. Dario limped over to the circle of visitors and asked if he could take a snapshot of them in their 'circled wagons'. The parents obliged and stood in the middle. They smiled into Dario's lens with a slight rictus of forced bonhomie.

The progress of the march had been widely reported in the media every day. The pause in Builth had taken it out of the headlines, but as it neared Cardiff a sense of curiosity grew, especially in the Welsh-speaking pockets of the city. In these households in Pontcanna, the picnic rugs were already being neatly folded in preparation for a welcome party for the marchers, and the hampers packed as the hosts of Cardiff, presumably from a comfortable viewing position in a leafy park near the castle, or in Cathays in front of City Hall, prepared to add their voice to the campaign to save the language.

Little did they know on this Saturday afternoon that marches of a very different kind were heading their way. The stone-throwing, fire-setting troublemakers of Newport and Swansea were on the road. Encouraged over social media to join a fight-party in Cardiff, or taunted by the same means of communication that they had no stomach for conflict, the battalions formed in the cities that flanked the capital to the east and west. Hadn't it been a declared aim in Caernarfon to raise hell? There was then a shared ideology. But there was also a difference. What on the long march from the north was a cultural ache – a longing born of love for the mother tongue, but eased by song and good cheer along the way – was simply the lust for a ruck among the raiding parties on the two new fronts. When Newport had hinted they were heading for the Westgate, it was decoded as the Westgate Hotel in their own city, but now it seemed they were aiming for Westgate Street in Cardiff. What had been simmering in the cities of south Wales was about to erupt in the heart of the capital.

Academy players knew about the trappings of a professional rugby career as a classroom exercise. As products in the making, they were deliberately kept away from a life of riches. In fact, they were ritually reminded by their coaches of their lowly status, subjected to a midweek routine of menial tasks to reinforce their humility, to test their determination to stay the course. Slammer Watkins on this front was a model student, a willing workhorse with a mop and scrubbing brush. But on match day Slammer failed the bigger test. He would not graduate from Stalag 2 and he knew it. Incurious by nature, he could not begin to analyse the processes that transformed him from uncomplaining midweek slave into a maverick liability on match day. All he knew was that when subjected to the stresses of fatigue and the heat of the contest, time and time again something flicked in his head and before he knew it he had done something heinous. The red mist claimed him and Slammer was going to join a long list of rejects, players who had never quite been able to marry mind and body on the rugby field. He was a striking physical specimen and completely flaky.

Vanguards from Swansea and Newport arrived by train, spilling out of Cardiff Central Station and starting to fight amongst themselves on its front concourse. A ceasefire soon ended this preliminary skirmish as the incomers joined forces to take on locals who rushed in from Grangetown and Splott to defend their city's fighting pride. Shoppers in the centre scattered as the fighting spread down The Hayes, into the St David's 2 precinct. The police now arrived in force and a second truce was called as the rioters found a new common enemy. The first plate-glass window to shatter seemed to be an intoxicating sound, fuelling the fighters. Soon, glass was raining down on the retail quarter, drawing looters out of the shadows. They slipped in and out of the flailing limbs, stealthily working their way through the shops as the battle raged.

This first train-using wave was behind enemy lines, but columns of reinforcements were coming along the M4. The police set up emergency roadblocks and closed the motorway, following guidelines put in place after the Battle of Brynglas Tunnels. The motorway sat empty, but its clearance diverted the traffic through Ely on the west side of Cardiff and Llanrhymney on the east and here in the outer suburbs, defensive lines formed, gauntlets that cars and coaches had to run. Their sides chipped and dented by stones, their windscreens cracked and opaque, the vehicles soon ran into barricades thrown up before them. At these roadblocks the first fires started as Molotov cocktails were casually lobbed into the jams. Passengers and drivers fled and running battles continued up and down the streets, pulling and pushing the combatants in the general direction of the city centre.

'I'm sure it's safe to leave the cars here,' whispered the mother of Felix Williams, Stalag 2's left wing, as Dario hobbled away. 'Don't you think?'

The fathers did not answer. The wine was loosening their tongues and the first doubts about selection slipped out.

'What's Mewson doing, travelling with thirty-five players and not announcing the team till they get to the ground?' said a father.

'Just had a text saying Slammer Williams is on the bus. The constitutionally reckless Slammer...' said another.

'Reduces the skill in the back row. Dilutes one of our areas of strength – we've got to be able to outplay this lot,' said a third. 'He'll never pick him.'

The only wonder in Slammer's mind was that he was on his way to the game. He had missed every round of the Babcock Cup, and in training for the semi-final he had been given a bib that placed him once again on the cannon-fodder side of the preparations. Only just back from an eight-week suspension for kneeing his old mate, Codliver Jones, in the back during a Development League match, and fully aware that he did not fit into any of the plans for the remainder of the season, Slammer thought he must be here to carry water. When Mr Mewson called him to the front of the bus, Slammer expected to be handed the bottle-holder.

'It's the end of the road, Slammer, I'm afraid,' said Gareth. 'Your time with us, regrettably, is nearly over.'

Slammer dumbly kept his head low.

'Nearly over. But not quite. You have two things left to do.'

Slammer looked up, feeling a flush of hope, a prickle of excitement. Gareth checked nobody was listening and leant towards Slammer and whispered his instructions in his ear.

Coming in from the north through the gap where the mountains on either side of the Taff Valley ended, passing underneath the M4 that would grow eerily quiet even as they left it behind, and keeping to the eastern bank of the river, Meirion's marchers advanced into Cardiff almost unnoticed. Their police escort nervously kept them up to date with the running battles in front of them and to the sides and tried on four occasions to make Meirion stop, for everyone's safety, including the officers'. The Sage marched on, leading his force on the last leg, rejecting the counsel of his escort. They were going through parks and over playing fields, meeting nobody but well-wishers. They came through Llandaff North and if they suddenly became agitated it was only to jeer at the old headquarters of BBC Wales, rising above them on the opposite bank. They made their point to the broadcasters who were cutting back on Welsh-language programming and walked on, through Llandaff village and past the cathedral.

Shortly afterwards, they had to cross the A48, the old main road that ran the width of Wales, from Chepstow to Carmarthen. This, like the M4, was closed, but instead of an eerie silence, the road echoed to the distant sounds of trouble. The marchers now heard for the first time the wails of the sirens. The three police officers tried again to stand in the way, but the line of walkers pushed on, straight across the empty road and down the long tree-lined avenue between Pontcanna Fields and Llandaff Fields. Despite the growing sounds of confusion ahead as they neared Sophia Gardens, the procession could still see football games to their left and rugby to their right. The players paused briefly to watch the procession go by, but soon returned to their games. On went the pilgrims, past the Test cricket ground and on towards Cardiff Castle.

'If Mewson picks him, it's for one specific task,' said a fourth father. 'To live up to his name. To slam Gonzo Davies. He's the only weapon they've got.'

'It's too much attention paid to one old has-been,' said the first father. 'Christ, he's as old as me. Mewson should be thinking of what we're going to do, not what these tuppeny-halfpenny villagers are going to try.'

'Somebody might have used those very words in the last round,' said father three. 'Look what happened there.'

'It was a fluke. Won't happen again.'

'Lightning never strikes... and all that,' said father four. He looked around. 'Although it seems to have struck this place five or six times.'

'It's not a wind-up, sir?' asked Slammer when Gareth had finished his briefing.

'No, Slammer. It's not a wind-up.'

'For real, then.'

'It is for real and there will be a reality to face after it.' And Gareth leant back towards the willing ear of his forward. 'Which is why,' he whispered, 'If you do this thing that must remain strictly between you and me, you will walk away with five thousand pounds.'

It never struck Slammer that he was suddenly a professional rugby player, although one thing did occur to him.

'It's a bit out of the blue, isn't it, coach?'

'What's that?'

'You, asking me to do this. Goes against everything you teach, like.'

Gareth was thinking that this was anything but out of the blue, that this was a replay of times past.

'Don't you worry yourself about me, Slammer. Are you in?'

Slammer nodded.

'Right,' said Gareth. 'But only on my command, remember.' Gareth held out a hand. 'Congratulations. You've just been selected.'

They stopped briefly at the Castle. Behind them all seemed calm. Hazel's van was parked under the chestnut trees by the National Sports Centre, and Brian was pouring tea as fast as he could. The only change to the familiar routine was that instead of music coming from the Nissan's radio, there was live coverage on Radio Wales of what lay ahead. The scale of the battle was now apparent. Fighting from the centre had spilled out into Castle Street and was heading towards Cardiff Bridge. From the other direction, down Cowbridge Road came the sounds of the western front, the Swansea flank, fast approaching. Over the police escort's radios came the update that the Newport front was already in Splott and heading for Westgate Street. The eastern flank would soon reach the other rioters. Instead of trying to stop the marchers, Meirion's escort now urged them to keep going. Brian and Hazel pulled up the shutters on the van and reversed deeper into the cover of the chestnuts.

Meirion kept to the path under the bridge and slipped through, barely glancing at the Millennium Stadium as they hurried past. Half an hour later – and for the first time – their route was barred. Butetown was preparing its defences, but only against the police. Recognising the march as part of the uprising, the builders of the barricades at the points of entry into the area between Cardiff city centre and Cardiff Bay let it through. Once they were into Butetown, it was harder to pass out on the far side. The southern checkpoint was reluctant to let them through, partly because Butetown wanted to know why fellow rebels wouldn't want to stay and fight, and partly because by now the enemy was in sight, and anyone outside the barricades would be vulnerable.

The parents chuckled and filled their glasses. 'To our lads... '

Father one paused after drinking. 'You know,' he said, 'He might be called Slammer because that's where he'll end up, rather than what he does...'

They chuckled again. At that moment Annie Thomas and Meg Powell strode over, carrying the buckets they had just eased out of the hands of the Widowers.

'Just in case we don't get round to your side of the ground...' said Meg, rattling her bucket.

'Would you like to pay now to get in?' said Annie.

They stood in their long coats and wellington boots and looked the mothers up and down. The mothers looked at the fathers who began to reach for their wallets. At that point Meg released her trademark cackle, startling all before her.

'Only joking, my lovers,' she shouted.

'But honest now,' said Annie. 'You want to do as them lot said, and come up the club after.'

'There'll be a meal for your boys.'

'You dads can talk about the finer points of the game.'

'And by the way,' said Annie. 'May the best team win.'

'And you girls can come and have a drink with me and Annie.'

'We'll be having a right fuckin' knees-up.'

'Which, to be honest, is what some of you look like you could do with.'

'S'only a game, remember.'

'Aye, aye. That's what we always say, isn't that right, Annie?'

'It truly is, Meg, my love. Only a silly old game.'

Trouble was following the march. Cardiff and Swansea had met at Castle Bridge, but instead of clashing, they had turned south as one. Without a word of parley, they seamlessly formed harrying parties to disrupt the tactics of the police, who seemed to be taunting them, charging and then withdrawing, corralling them in Riverside. Meirion's marchers stuck to the riverbank, but closing in on them in the streets to their right was the mob, prodded by the police. The size of this pursuing force was now so large that the riot vans did not hesitate to drive beyond Riverside, into the streets of Grangetown, where they normally proceeded with extreme caution.

The Newport reinforcements had joined up in Splott with what was left of their vanguard. They had been aiming for the castle but they were redirected by social messaging to a new hot spot. The whirlwind on the other side of the Taff was moving towards Cardiff Bay, and Newport abandoned Westgate Street as a destination and swung left towards the renovated docks area. These raiders from the east stuck together tightly, more watchful than riotous now. Nobody stood in their way, but there had been a shift in the sense of control. If they had apparently been free only a few minutes earlier to make their own choice and make a sudden change of direction, now they recognised that they were being channelled according to the will of the police. They could walk towards the docks, but only towards the docks. As they travelled through the grid of long empty streets they could sense a parallel presence, glimpses of uniforms, moving at their same walking pace. If they broke into a jog, the shadow sped up too. A small group tried to go back the way they had come but were forced to do a second about-turn when they ran into six dog handlers, each with a German Shepherd straining at the leash. A group of Pill youngsters, well versed in ducking and diving through similar streets in their own city, volunteered as scouting parties to the side. But, however carefully they picked their way from house to house, they were soon seized by unseen, strong arms and thrown into the back of the first of ten large prisoner vans bringing up the rear of the police operation. The Newport mob was being picked off even as it was being shepherded into the Bay.

Capper was useless, his fears about the effect of love on athletic prowess proving to be a self-fulfilling prophecy. He could not escape his daze of the past few days, despite slapping himself around the head repeatedly and telling himself to snap out of it. Elsewhere, Useless was useless, too, sent scurrying hither and thither by the shrewd kicking game of the academy players and left too exhausted to run from full-back in attack. The Twins in the centre had the excuse of being up against opponents who were bigger, faster and more accomplished, with experience already of top regional rugby and earmarked for selection for the full Wales squad. Mystic struggled on bravely against tall, athletic jumpers who led him a merry dance at the line-out, teasing him into one position and then throwing somewhere completely different. On Mystic's own throw, he fell victim to Capper's distraction and inaccuracy. The Professor was the worst of all, abandoning his position on the wing and hovering too close to the forwards. There, he simply disturbed the routines of Daff at scrum half. In short, the old brigade of the team went to pieces on the big day.

As Gonzo had walked on to the pitch, he had seen Gareth Mewson. Of course, he had known the moment would come, but the sight of one of the agents of his downfall hit him harder than he expected. He did not fear for himself, although for the first time he realised that he might be in danger. If Mewson was here in person, then Martin Guest was here in spirit. Gonzo feared for Grace and at the time when he should have been thinking exclusively of the eighty minutes ahead, he found himself scanning the ground. He could not see her.

When the match started, a roar as never heard in the village went up. But Gonzo was not there. Or rather, he was there only in body, too old and slow to be a one-man team against some of the most promising players in Wales. He was there on the field, running as hard as he could, only to be scythed down by Slammer Watkins, allowing others to swoop after the initial tackle and deny him his passes of old out of contact. Deliberately and cruelly, the young academy team gave their elders a lesson, building up their lead with penalty after penalty – four of them, to give them a 12-point advantage. Then came the enterprise, the expansion of the game against a weary defence. By the end of the third quarter they had scored two tries after sweeping movements, finished with the flourish of a dive to one corner and then the other. Going into the last twenty minutes, the village trailed by 22 points to nil.

The *Plant* refused to give up. Playing against their peers, the best of their own age group – the privileged elite of their own generation – the children were on a mission. They had stayed calm before the game, but now, as it was slipping away from them, their frustration and anger began to show. Moss and Buddleia almost barged the Twins out of the way to tear furiously into the elegant centres of the academy and stop dead a move that was heading for a third try. The crowd, growing more subdued with every passing minute, was stirred back into life.

Daff gave the Professor an elbow to the chin. 'Fuck off, Professor, back to your wing,' the young scrum half said. The Professor, stunned, obeyed. Daff shook his head and managed to scramble a difficult pass to Tulip, who, left with no other option as he caught the ball behind him and above his head, turned and dropped a goal from thirty-five metres. The village were off the mark. Stalag 2 increased their grip up front, shoving Capper into the air at a scrum and stealing a put-in against the head. The three-quarters sprang into life behind the dominant pack and Dom Williams-Thomas threw the long pass that would lead to the third try and seal the game. Fungus was stranded in defence, caught in the terrible confusion of not knowing which attacker to target.

But the long pass seemed to rise invitingly and he launched himself not at a player, but at the ball. He intercepted it and ran sixty metres to score between the posts.

Three minutes later, Gonzo stayed down after a ruck. Gareth Mewson checked his watch and looked for Slammer, to see if he was responsible. The wing forward caught his eye and shook his head. Gonzo rose to his feet, slowly turned the shoulder that he had slightly wrenched and prepared to carry on. The ball squirted, after a sudden loss of control at a maul, Slammer's way. He dropped it. The posse of parents – Slammer's had never come from Port Talbot to see him play – groaned, as much in annoyance at the general sloppiness creeping into their sons' play as at the single culprit.

The Bay was empty when Meirion's march arrived at journey's end. Word had spread among the visitors and locals that the troubles they could hear, even far away at the top end of Bute Street, would not be confined to the city centre. Without panic, the strollers and tourists had melted away. In the distance lay the barrage that kept the tide in the old coal port permanently high. Penarth to the right rose pleasantly above the entrance to the harbour, while to the left the cranes of the docks hung still in the air. The marchers stopped outside the Pierhead Building. Everything was quiet. They knew they would not be alone for long, but there was no sound yet of the pincers closing in on them.

'So, what do we do?' asked Cosmos, edging close to Meirion.

'We were invited to the Senedd,' said Meirion. 'And here we are.'

It was not an inspiring welcome. A ring of fencing had been placed around the Welsh Assembly Government building. There were untidy gaps in this temporary defence. Not all the feet of the steel posts sat in their concrete bases. It was as if the last couple of guards had made a token gesture at protection and left their post. There was no security visible now, beyond a white van parked inside the fencing. It seemed that everybody in the Bay had found a bunker.

The mob began to arrive, running from building to building, seeking shelter or objects to hurl at the police. The Newport side met the larger – and most unlikely – joint force of Cardiff and Swansea in front of the Millennium Centre. They filled the plaza and some shook hands. They turned to face their pursuers. The police vehicles crept into view on all the roads serving the Bay. Officers in riot gear piled out of their vans and stopped, a few tapping their shields with their batons.

A little further away, on the other side of the Pierhead building and on the edge of the wharf, Meirion faced his pilgrims and told them to head away from the Senedd and congregate outside the Norwegian Church. Reluctantly they followed him, the Carmarthen farmers in particular feeling that they should not be taking a backward step.

'But is this our fight?' Meirion asked.

'Too bloody right it is,' said all the farmers.

'Fair play, Slammer's done well…' said the first father.

'But he's knackered. He can't be match fit…' said the second.

'Time to get him off…'

'May as well. Gonzo Davies has had it by the looks of it,' said the third, as Gonzo winced as he turned his shoulder again.

'Come on, Mewson,' shouted the first father. 'Let's nail this game down. Send on fresh legs.'

The mothers sensed the urgency in their husbands. It alarmed them.

'You're a joke, referee,' screamed Margaret Ellis, as the referee correctly awarded the village a scrum for Slammer's knock-on. 'You're a cheat.'

Gareth ignored the parents. He hated them. Instead, he looked at Slammer and gave him the nod. Slammer nodded back.

Suddenly there was a movement on the other side of the Millennium Centre. The locals of Butetown had left their barricades, curious to know what was going on. Caught between the Bay and the centre of Cardiff, they knew their stretch of high and low-rise apartment blocks were viewed as a sort of no-man's land, and it frustrated them that once again all but the innocents of the march had passed them by. The energy that had gone into building Butetown's defences had turned into something more offensive now, with the police the obvious target. The Butetown militia formed a line, sandwiching the forces of law and order between themselves and the combined units of Cardiff, Swansea and Newport. The sound of stick on shield stopped.

Butetown edged forward and Cardiff, Newport and Swansea braced themselves to surge forward in support of the attack of the latecomers. The Carmarthen farmers surrounded Meirion: 'Give us the word… Damn it, we're going anyway.' And they began to move away from the Norwegian Church on the quayside, towards the Welsh Assembly Building and the battleground on its far side. Some of the original marchers from Caernarfon sat down in despair, and the Trelawnyd choir formed a sad huddle, discussing what they should do. It seemed that the majority of the marchers remained defiant and were prepared to follow the farmers.

Meirion's legs gave way and he was helped to a bench on the edge of the quay. The Sage suddenly felt all control desert him. The journey overnight to Merthyr from Brecon and the continuation to Cardiff with barely a break had suddenly caught up with him. He ached in his limbs and back, and now his spirits were crushed. This had never been his plan, to see his campaign against cultural vandalism consumed by a riot. He remembered the scorn he had poured on the first outbreak of the Troubles, his conversion to the cause halfway down Wales and his elevation to leader. Hadn't he even exploited the Welsh Hell, a phrase born of sarcasm, to keep his pilgrims on track? And here they were, at the bitter end, where all would be smashed to pieces. What should he do? What place would be afforded to the efforts of the marchers when the history of this day was written? Meirion rose slowly from the bench and in a loud clear voice ordered the farmers to stop.

'If you want to do something useful, find one of those television crews and tell them to meet us at the Senedd,' he said. The farmers stopped and turned. They nodded and began to move.

'Our place is not in a pitched battle,' continued Meirion. 'Our place is there.' And he pointed at the Senedd, two hundred yards away. 'If it's empty, so be it. That in itself says something about our hollow democracy. But that's where we'll be raising hell. Our role is to stand tall on those steps and be heard. In Welsh.'

The professor stood reluctantly on the wing. He was as distracted as Capper – not through love, though, but guilt. He, too, had watched Gonzo go down and feared the worst. He sensed time was running out. He edged closer to the forwards and Daff shook his fist at him. The Professor retreated to his position.

Slammer did not even try to be subtle. He had reached the point of the game where everything normally went wrong for him and the only thing that registered clearly was that he had received the signal to take out Gonzo Davies. He had reached a certain point in his life, too. His academy days were over. Slammer was going to go out in a style that would at least silence the mouths of the bastard parents on the touchline. He stood and waited. He let somebody else at last tackle Gonzo Davies. He watched as the veteran disappeared beneath a pile of bodies, all parts of him buried, apart from his head. The ball was moved away, and the referee and all eyes followed it.

In a way, Slammer had a certain respect for the old guy in front of him. Strong man, brave. Not that it mattered. Slammer took a breath and ran in, aiming to kick Gonzo as hard as he could in the head.

The marchers rallied one last time. They gathered themselves for the last, short leg of their journey. The folly of their gesture, in the shadow of a full-scale riot about to be unleashed, was not lost on them. But they felt a dignified detachment from the stand-off a few hundred yards away. They had a mission to complete. The Trelawnyd Choir took a massed breath. And then the bomb went off.

The 'children' ran a blitz defence against the academy attack, Tulip pulling the Twins forward as never before. They usually opted for a drift defence, a slide across the pitch rather than this charge, but they were possessed, screamed on by the demented Annie and Meg, whose shrieks cut through the roar of the rest of the supporters. Fungus came in from his wing too, clattering into Felix Williams. The ball went loose, to be picked up by Moss who slipped it to Buttercup, who crossed the goal line and touched down.

Gonzo saved himself from the full effect of the first kick. Slammer gave himself such a run-up that there was time for the victim to watch and prepare, and enough space for him to move his head at the last instant and avoid full contact. The boot still landed, stunning Gonzo, and there was nothing he could do to avoid the second attack. Slammer stood over him and prepared to stamp down, just as Danny Mewson had, all those years ago. Gonzo shut his eyes and waited.

It wasn't the biggest explosion on mainland Britain by any means. It was more a big bang than a violent scattering of lethal material. There were no nails or ball bearings, but the detonation in the back of the white van blew its back doors off and created a shock wave that shattered all the glass on the front of the building. The noise was deafening and rolled around the Bay, rebounding off the dockland buildings as a first echo and bouncing back to the Cardiff waterfront from the Penarth heights as a second. The vast stretch of water between the wharfs and the barrage at the entrance seemed to quiver. Alarms in cars and buildings hundreds of feet from the Senedd were set off.

All eyes had followed the ball into midfield, where Fungus made his tackle and where the village's second try started. The noise as Buttercup sprinted away would have reached the furthest faces at the end of the deepest tunnel into the Garw Seam. All eyes followed the ball, except two pairs. The Professor never took his eyes off Gonzo. He saw Slammer's first attack and as the assailant's boot was raised for the second, the Professor launched a blitz defence of his own, cutting in from his wing and launching himself horizontally. The Professor's head hit Slammer full in the face and they both fell unconscious to the ground.

The second set of eyes belonged to one of the two neutral touch judges, appointed for this special occasion. They weren't the most experienced of officials, and the touch judge in question at first had been unable to stop himself from letting his gaze wander after the ball. But he suddenly remembered his protocols about supervising likely hotspots off the ball, and turned his attention back to the remains of the previous engagement. He had missed Slammer's initial assault and from the other side of the pile of bodies could not see the boot raised for the coup de grace. What he did see was the Professor's launch of himself as a missile and the sickening impact as he struck Slammer. The touch judge held his flag out and pulled the referee away from Tulip's conversion.

The referee disallowed the try, awarded a penalty against the village at the scene of the crime and showed the Professor a red card. Only Gonzo knew the full story, but for the moment he was clearing his head beneath a stream of cold water from one of the Widowers' collecting buckets, hastily emptied of its coins for use in the first-aid emergency. Most of the primary medical care was reserved for Slammer and the Professor, but since they were hors de combat – and once Gonzo had shaken his head one last time and pronounced himself sound – the game resumed. Now it was Stalag 2's fifteen players – with a replacement, as previously demanded by the fathers, on for Slammer – against the village's fourteen. The academy led 22-10 and time was running out.

If there was an immediate outbreak of noise after the explosion, soon everything stopped. On the battleground in front of the Millennium Centre there had been little enough movement after the police formed a rough square and faced the mob surrounding them. The last sound anyone remembered was the aside of a hardened sergeant, who muttered, 'Just like Rorke's Drift', through his visor, seconds before the explosion. After it, the scene froze, as if the 'Pause' button had been pressed. Light debris began to flutter down before there was any movement on the ground. And then, slowly at first, the mob parted to allow the police within their circle access to the Senedd. The police took a second to react but then, clumsy and weighed down by their riot equipment, they began to run towards the scene of the explosion.

The mob did not just part and stop. It carried on peeling away, the gap becoming a general dispersal, the units melting away into the streets down which they had been steered. The Butetown militia was home almost before the police reached the Senedd. The rest walked at first, but then broke into a run and did not stop, stampeding to reach home in the city, or the vehicles that would carry them back to Newport and Swansea.

Just before play restarted, Capper grabbed Gonzo's arm and pointed to the moorland. On a rock, hundreds of yards away, sat Grace and Our Marnie. Gonzo felt a surge of relief and something else, a rush of exhilaration. Capper still seemed distracted. They faced the penalty and watched the attempt at goal miss by a whisker. The village worked their way back into the Stalag half, but knocked on. Stalag were awarded a scrum.

'Right,' said Gonzo to Mystic. 'Swap.' Mystic stepped aside and let Gonzo take his place in the second row. From there he slackened his bind, slipped his right arm into the scrum and punched Capper in the face. Capper roared.

'At last, you bald old bastard,' said Gonzo.

Capper, dripping blood from his nose into the tunnel of the scrum, bent his back as the ball came in and the students' front row buckled and shot backwards. Their teammates behind lost control of the ball in the ensuing chaos, and Gonzo picked up and ran in from twenty metres. Tulip converted. With two minutes to go, the village trailed 22-17.

Straight from the restart, Mystic was lifted into the air and caught the ball with two hands. From the top of his leap, he dabbed the ball down to Gonzo who stormed upfield and slipped the ball to Daff. The children finished the last move of the game, with Fungus plunging over in the left corner. He slid three yards over the dead-ball line but had safely grounded the ball. The wing jumped to his feet, his arms held aloft. From the tips of his fingers to the toes of his boots he was coated in the black filth of home.

Daff stuck a kicking tee into this coal-stained glue and converted from the touchline, a soaring flight that triggered an explosion of noise. The whistle blew for the end of the game, a shrill blast completely lost in the sound of the village going, as Capper had predicted, mental. They nearly managed to post 24-22 on the peeling scoreboard, but the keepers of the tally couldn't resist joining the pich invasion and the final 2 swung off its nail and dropped to the ground. 24-2 would stay there for weeks to come.

Not a fist had been thrown, not a baton wielded at the Battle of Cardiff Bay. The Welsh Hell, however, was not quite over. As the police came to the Senedd they found the marchers dazed but defiant before them.

'Bastards,' shouted a Carmarthen farmer about nobody in particular and lurched forward.

Meirion, his eardrums pierced, staggered towards the police and tried to hold out a conciliatory hand, but he was clubbed to the ground. The police fell on the marchers, and the pilgrims were soon packed as prisoners into the vans that had stalked the mob through Splott.

It took half an hour for the team to leave the pitch. They were swamped at the end of the game and the invading crowd kept them surrounded on lap of honour after lap of honour. Finally, their backs and shoulders aching from the game and stinging from all the backslapping, the players managed to work their way through the crowd and head for the battered old changing room beneath the stand. The supporters quickly formed a line and strode towards the moorland and the path that would take them up to the clubhouse. They passed Grace and Our Marnie, who hadn't moved from their rock. The Widowers gently reminded the steward there was a bar to open.

'They'll be up soon enough,' said Malc. George and he offered an arm to Our Marnie and Grace, who took hold and joined the throng going uphill.

Stalag 2 were already gone, the team and replacements, coaches and back-up staff barely pausing to pack up their electronic gadgetry and collect their kit bags and climb on board the bus, where Slammer was already slumped, an ice-pack pressed to the bridge of his nose and against eyes that were too swollen to open. The bus bounced slowly across the old colliery yard and disappeared. The parents were hot on its heels, their cars turning south at the first junction, away from the village, away from the clubhouse where Annie and Meg's right old knees-up, as soon as they changed into their party clothes, was about to begin.

Inside the changing room all was quiet. Three cases of lager had been placed on the benches and the players opened a couple of bottles each and drank deeply and silently. From all the vibrations generated in the grandstand above, a plasterboard panel had come off the ceiling and lay in the middle of the chipped tile floor. The dust from the exposed cavity mingled with the steam from the shower where the Professor had stood disconsolately after being sent off. There was no sign of him now.

'What have we just done?' said Capper. 'What have we just fuckin' done?'

The lull broke. The players burst into laughter and the old guard led a round of formal handshakes. The *Plant* went for high fives. Everyone clinked bottles.

'It's tragic,' said Fungus. 'But we might give the clubhouse a go tonight. What d'you think, boys?'

The rest of the children nodded: 'Let's get at it.'

And they all began to strip, wet shirts and shorts, strapping and bandages piling high on the fallen plasterboard. The showers were turned on and thick steam billowed into the changing area. Nobody saw the door open, although the mist was sucked towards the cold air beyond it.

'Fuck, sorry,' said Capper, tripping over the board and falling against a figure in his ten-year old club blazer. 'Fuck me, Professor…'

There was silence again. Useless turned the showers off. The team, all naked, gathered around the wing.

'Are you all right, Professor?' asked Gonzo.

The Professor said nothing, but held up his hand.

''Cos we don't care…' began Capper, before the Professor stopped him by raising his hand higher.

'I have something to tell you,' he finally said. His eyes

were red, bruised by his flying head butt and filled now with tears.

'Has that bang on the 'ead got to you?' said Capper. 'You've already told us. We already knew.' He pointed at the naked team. 'Look, it's not as if the boys are bothered...'

'I have something else to tell you,' interrupted the Professor. And he told them his secret. How he worked for Martin Guest. How he had revealed the identity of Grace's lover to his employer, what Martin had commissioned the Mewsons to do to Gonzo, and how Martin knew Grace was back now and how Gareth and Slammer had conspired to make history repeat itself.

'I have betrayed you...' the Professor concluded. Nobody spoke.

'Except history wasn't repeated,' said Gonzo finally. 'You stopped it.'

'But it doesn't undo the guilt... the years of treachery. And he'll try again.'

'Maybe. But not through you. He's got no hold over you now, has he?' Gonzo took hold of the Professor's chin and made him look at him. The Professor looked terrified, as if he thought Gonzo was going to hit him.

'Has he?' Gonzo repeated. And he took his hand away. The Professor looked down.

'I must go,' he said.

'You must not,' said Gonzo. 'You should have told us earlier... about everything. That's true. But what's done is done. And we'll get through it together. Because that's what we do. Right?'

'Fuckin' right,' said Capper.

'So you stay right there Professor. And you come with us up to the club and you stick with us. Right?'

The Professor nodded his head, sat on a slatted bench and did not move. Capper thrust a bottle into his hands. The showers sprang back into action.

'Amazing flying head butt, by the way,' said Mystic, tapping the Professor on the shoulder.

Steam filled the room and the players sank into its folds. When Gonzo finished dressing and went to find him, the Professor had gone.

75

Brian had paced all through the afternoon beneath the chestnut trees. Now he stood outside Hazel's van – its shutters were up, its doors closed – and strained his ears to hear sounds from the city. All was quiet apart from a brush of the wind through the trees and the flow of the river Taff behind him. No sound carried to him from afar and he certainly didn't hear the gentle hiss of gas inside the van, an escape through a faulty valve and a poorly threaded connection. Brian had been in too much of a muddle all day to give health and safety his full attention. He had seen his marchers – his family, as he saw them – disappear down the river, and had heard the single muffled thump from the Bay. Hazel and he had no idea what had happened until Radio Wales began to carry unconfirmed stories of an explosion outside the Senedd. Later they heard that the police had dispersed a hostile crowd in one zone and made multiple arrests in another. Calm had been restored.

Gas inaudibly continued to flow. Brian sat heavily on the step of the van and prepared to spark up his pipe. Hazel came up to him and shoved him to one side as she prepared to open the door. Brian had his hand on the match; Hazel had hers on the handle. They both stopped at the same time.

'Come on,' said Hazel. 'It's over.'

'You're right,' said Brian. 'Let's be going.'

The match remained unstruck and the door did not open. The gas cylinder ran out halfway to Welshpool and by the time they stopped outside their home – their house of bricks and mortar – the only lingering smell in their mobile diner was the familiar day-old aroma of bacon and burgers and onions. Soon, the diner would be back in its layby, promoted not as Hell's Crossroad, but as Hazel's in pink lacy scroll on a blackboard.

As Brian and Hazel were driving through the night, Martin stood in his flat and looked down on the Bay, still ablaze with the lights of emergency vehicles. The show that had been staged beneath his gaze had surpassed expectation. To steer the combined mobs of three cities into his backyard had strained his powers of organisation. Anything could have happened along the way. He had fully expected to live his revolution vicariously through the messaging of those on the streets, but these people – these followers of his – had come his way, as if lured by the force of his will.

What had happened then was beyond reason, beyond his wildest dreams. The explosion. It made up for the news

that Gonzo had survived. Martin had been dejected until –
boom. A bomb, a stroke of genius. But not his. Why had he
not thought of such a *coup de théâtre*?

It was not too late for a finishing touch of his own. With
great deliberation he reached out with his arms and held the
curtains, taking the trace of Grace in his hands. He tried
to close them and draw himself ino the shadows, but he
could not move his arms. Nothing responded. Instead, in
his ecstasy he continued to stare down at the scene below
until his shoulders ached, and then he sank to his knees and
pressed his face against the cold glass that had shaken but
not broken when the bomb went off. He reached out and felt
for his Danny phone. He texted his delivery boy: Proceed.

76

The single bulb outside the clubhouse burned deep into the
night. The players went through the motions of saying the
job was not yet done and that there was the final to come,
and that they should not overdo the celebrations, but it was
only token resistance. They drank and drank and sang and
the club bounced at the end of West Street until slowly,
staggeringly, it began to empty. The Widowers were the first
to leave and Meg and Annie the last, tottering away into the
early hours of the morning, their coughing and cackling
slowly fading and bringing the curtain down on the village's
finest day.

Capper was the first to crash, stumbling up to bed in Our Marnie's flat. Into the bar below came the rumble of his snoring, announcing that he was out for the count. Gonzo pushed Grace up the stairs not long afterwards. She said she wanted to finish the job of tidying up but he insisted. She nodded and with a yawn told him not to be long. Their couch awaited.

Gonzo loaded the glass-washer while Our Marnie collected the last of the pints and put them on the bar. She held up Meg and Annie's port and brandy glasses, lipstick smeared around the rim.

'These might have to go through twice,' she said.

Gonzo glanced up. She was looking at him.

'Gonzo, look...' she started.

'It's ok, Marnie. Everything's fine.'

She didn't move for a moment.

'Go and stop Sleeping Beauty's fracking up there,' he said, nodding upstairs. The snoring was louder than ever. Our Marnie nodded and left, leaving Gonzo on his own behind the bar. 'I'll finish off down here,' he said.

Danny Mewson sat in the back of his van on West Street and did not move. He had waited for night to fall before parking at the emptier end of the street, under one of the streetlights that had not shone in forty years. He did not have to look out of the pinhole drilled into the rear metal panel to know that the rugby club was in full swing eighty yards away. He lay on the mattress and caught the waves of party sounds that floated his way whenever the front door of the club opened. The odd person or couple went by, quietly in the one direction, louder in the other as the party began to break up and the village's inhabitants headed for their homes. He heard the last pair of heels go noisily, unsteadily past.

An hour after all went silent Danny did look through the spyhole. The light was off outside the club and he saw nothing. Heard nothing. He checked his watch and lay back on the mattress. He shut his eyes and slept for two hours. At four o'clock he awoke and softly opened one of the rear doors, climbed out and let it swing back against a piece of blanket over the catch. He walked to the club, his rubber soles making no sound. The petrol can had a length of hose attached and was ready to pour. He inserted the end through the letterbox and tipped the can. There was the faintest glug of liquid in the container and the slightest splash on the floor on the other side of the door. Personally, Danny thought, he'd have torched the empty stand at the ground first, while the clubhouse on West Street was full of people celebrating. That would have caused a mass exodus from the top of the village to the bottom. And he could have set the headquarters ablaze while they were firefighting below. A double blaze. They wouldn't have known which way to turn.

When he had broken into the Courtney house down on the Usk, Danny had learnt to appreciate points made in pairs. This time Mr Guest had wanted a human element, a face at an upstairs window as the flames licked at the curtains. It couldn't be faulted, of course, but there was something about a point made twice. As he had smeared shit over the walls of the master bedroom on his second visit he had felt so alive, his every sense on full alert.

The can was nearly empty. Danny started to withdraw

the hose and felt for the lighter and the rag in his pocket. He soaked the rag in the last of the petrol and lit a flame. And in its flickering pool of light saw the feet of Gonzo Davies step out of the darkness.

'Never too warm for a good fire, eh?' said Gonzo. 'How've you been, Danny?'

77

It didn't take long for the questions about the Battle of Cardiff Bay to turn from what into why. Nobody had claimed responsibility for the explosion, apart from a familiar group of cranks. And after four days the lines of inquiry were running into some solid stonewalls. Where, the police wanted to know, was the CCTV footage of the area around the Senedd? How could it be that from the middle of the night before, the recording machines at the building at the very epicentre of what was happening in Wales had been programmed to go into stand-by mode? Only a pair of cameras on nearby buildings offered grainy, wide-angled recordings of the Assembly building. These images revealed general scenes but no close-ups. Who, furthermore, had placed the order for the security fencing that arrived on the Saturday morning, creating a hubbub of activity that allowed the white van to arrive, and its driver – in a hard hat like all the other contractors on site – to mingle with them and slip away, leaving his bomb behind? Who had ordered the bulk of the security staff at the Senedd to swap their posts at the most visible public building in Wales for the nearby 1, Caspian Way – Welsh Office space that had been decommissioned years previously? Had it not struck the staff as highly unusual, if not entirely irregular, to be redeployed at a moment's notice to a building that was standing empty? The security firm inevitably retorted that it was not their role to question orders to respond to a 'credible threat', not if these instructions came their way down channels they had no reason to presume were compromised. Had they checked the chain of command? They had not. An invisible authority had breached the security firewall. But whose hand? And why?

On day five after the bomb, the detained protestors were released without charge. Meirion could still not hear properly and made only the briefest of statements about needing time to reflect on what had come to pass in Wales. Far from standing proud and loud on the steps of the Senedd, he asked for a period of contemplation. He stumbled with his words, even when asked by *Y Cymro* to express himself in Welsh.

'I have been foolish… a foolish man on a long road to this… nowhere…' were his parting words. And he stumbled with his steps as he left Cardiff and headed for home.

In dribs and drabs the other protestors were set free. They limped away with not a spark of defiance, not even from Cosmos. The hippies retreated to their simpler, quieter life in the western woods. The Carmarthen farmers went west too, with not a word of complaint about the heavy-handedness of the police response. Their sole aim was to be back on their land. The Trelawnyd choir did not emit the notes that had been swelling in their chests. They had marched from a tragedy at one end of the country to a disaster at the other. There was nothing to say and no sad song to be sung.

In the light of the security meltdown, nothing electronic worked in the chamber of the Senedd. 'We shall run Wales by semaphore if we have to,' said the Assembly Members. Their most important motion – unanimously passed – was to promote a return to normality across the land. And with that in mind, and much to the disapproval of the police, who did not want to see any large body of people coming to town for the foreseeable future, the go-ahead was given for the final of the Babcock Cup to take place at the Millennium Stadium the following Saturday.

Nobody had to spell it out to the police officers on the ground, going from door to door in the capital and watchfully patrolling the streets of Newport and Swansea, that softly, softly was the preferred method now. For the first time since the patrol car was rocked in Guildhall Square in Carmarthen, community leaders were consulted on the mood, the temperature in their neighbourhoods.

In Cardiff, police traffic between the city centre and the Bay flowed heavily, but not blaringly, through Butetown. From the Castle to the Barrage there was work to do and anything else would have to wait. On the Thursday morning after the explosion – Bomb-day plus five – they took delivery, however, of a package. The desk sergeant at Cardiff Central Police Station on the edge of Cathays Park turned his back for twenty seconds and suddenly there was a box on the counter he had so briefly left unattended. CCTV revealed a motorcycle courier, complete with leathers and a helmet, walking in, placing the package and departing, all in the space of seven seconds. The courier could be tracked to his or her bike – the gait suggested a male – parked outside the Cardiff University School of Journalism, its registration plate unreadable. The rider and motorbike were gone, heading north and out of camera range, within three minutes.

The sergeant immediately had the package checked for explosives and when the tests proved negative had it taken upstairs that afternoon to CID, and left the job of finding the addressee to them: the officer in charge of Serious Fraud. By Bomb-day plus nine, the package had been sent – by legitimate courier – to the Serious Fraud Office. Inside, in meticulously arranged files, lay the bank records of Martin Guest, the entire canon of his personal, business, Swiss and offshore accounts covering a dozen years. Hundreds of transactions had been highlighted with a marker pen, and at the end of each unerringly straight yellow line, a handwritten number had been added in black ink. In a red folder lay a sheaf of papers, bound together by a yellow ribbon. Each sheet of paper had a single column down the left side, containing the index of numbers. Against each set of digits, in tiny but perfectly legible handwriting, was a guide. The recipients were named, the flow of outgoing money was explained, the source of any incoming revealed. Bribes were exposed, undeclared profits by the hundreds of thousands of pounds unveiled. Martin's old covert business practices were stripped bare.

The yellow file seemed dedicated to domestic business, Martin's businesses in Wales, or at least those that predated his sale of Steel-Ag. There was no mention of this last deal: no index number, no yellow highlighter. But three payments of half a million pounds had a blue line over them in the Swiss accounts – with no adjoining index number. No explanation.

The author of the exposé could not be found. The Professor made his drop at the police station and rode away on his motorbike. He headed north and then cut west, heading on the open road for the Cardigan coast and the sea.

He missed his disciplinary hearing. The club was slightly taken aback to find that a George Charles Wainthorp, having been sent off for an act of foul play, was summonsed to appear at the Welsh Rugby Union in Cardiff. The village knew the Professor only as the Professor, to the extent that the last time – a full decade earlier, when it had been part of rugby's protocol for teams to be published in the local press – they had put PR O'Fessor on the wing. Nobody remembered asking what the Professor's real name was.

Gonzo consulted the Widowers and they agreed that they should wait until the last possible moment before responding, giving the Professor, who was not answering his phone, time to decide for himself how he wanted to proceed. A day before the deadline, Gonzo received a text from a withheld number: 'Plead Guilty.' The WRU were informed and a sentence was delivered. The incident ranked at the top end of the scale and the disciplinary panel worked its way down from a sixteen-week tariff, knocking off time for a previously unblemished record and the miscreant's good character. There was also a feeling on the panel that there was more to this incident than had met the eyes of the officials, and they would have liked to question the offender in person. Despite his decision to remain *in absentia*, they responded to their gut feeling and knocked off another week. Even so, the Professor was banned for twelve weeks.

The village, still dissecting the game blow by blow around the tables of the café in the square, already knew they would have to go to the grand final without their wing. His head butt had been the blow of all blows and not even if Meg and Annie had been put on the sentencing panel would the wing have been allowed to play against Gulag 2, victors over Gulag 1 in the other semi and now the village's opponents in the last game of the season.

Capper had to think of a name for Ashley Watts, one of the replacements recruited by the *Plant* for the semi-final, and now elevated to the starting team in the Professor's position.

'Is he young enough to be a plant?' he asked Gonzo.

'Young enough to be your son, Capper.'

'Be a bit fuckin' boring if we ended up calling him Ash, wouldn't it?'

'Why's that?' said Gonzo. 'Think of it as an energy-saving device. Saves you having to think, and saves him ending up being called something like Ragwort.'

'Nice one, Gonzo. Fuckin' Ragwort it is.'

On B-Day plus eleven, Martin was arrested in his flat. The police found him sitting in Grace's old workroom. It was completely empty, all his wife's possessions having been put in a skip and taken away. Grace was landfill to Martin. All that remained in the room was a box, full of mobile phones, their SIM cards removed and destroyed. Martin was perfectly civil with the arresting officers and agreed to accompany them to the station without ado. He imagined Danny had spilt the beans.

'May I ask what this is about?' he nevertheless asked.

'I'll answer that if you answer my question,' said one of the arresting officers.

Martin nodded.

'Why all the phones?'

'I'm a businessman. I was thinking of investing. Telecommunications. Very important.'

The policemen looked at each other. 'The answer to your question is: we'd like to ask you some questions about your business.'

'That's a lot of questions in one sentence, officer.'

'Questions, questions. It's what we do, sir,' said the first.

'Here's another,' said the second. 'Mind if we take that box with us, sir?'

'Be my guest,' said Martin.

The phones, unlike the bank statements, revealed nothing. Martin recognised the hand of the Professor immediately – his actual handwriting for a start, and the hand of the man who would have his revenge. Martin knew that the work would be thorough. He said very little during his first interview, but on B-day plus 12 he returned to the station and agreed to a deal. In the presence of his solicitor he would make a full confession, and in return – the Crown

Prosecution Service had already intimated their approval – would be handed a reduced sentence. How very white-collar and civilised, they all thought. Martin was allowed to go home.

The next day he went to the waterfront, texted a message and dropped his phone into the bay. He returned to the flat and saw that the door to Grace's room was open. Martin knew that he had shut it before leaving. He found a box on the floor, roughly the same size as the one the police had taken away. Had they returned the phones? He opened the box and recoiled before the smell coming off a crudely wrapped parcel of newspaper. Martin very carefully peeled open the pages and saw a lump of flesh. From his time spent staring at the animals being butchered in Merthyr, he knew instantly what it was. A severed cow's tongue.

On a piece of paper stained with dried bood was written a line in blue ink, exactly the same colour as the highlighter pen through the three transactions on his statements: 'Do not light the blue touch-paper.' There was no signature but Martin knew that Konstantin Mordashov had sent the message.

When the police broke down his door, Martin was gone. He was sitting in the cabin of a luxury forty-foot cruiser, three hours out from Penarth Marina. He had a suitcase of cash, false identity papers and more accounts in Europe than the Professor could find in a hundred years of treachery. He felt alive for the first time in years. He was reborn, reanimated by this Mafiosi melodrama. He popped his head into the open air and ordered a southerly course to be set.

'Where exactly, boss?'

'Destination unknown, Frank.'

Gonzo did no work in the first few days after the semi-final. Capper was even more out of service, his lower back having gone into spasm and leaving him solidly locked, listing at a five-degree angle to starboard. He had done himself the injury leaping out of bed just after Danny's arm crashed against the front door of the club. Gonzo had kicked it there, and the lighter had gone out. As had Danny's lights in his brief encounter with the man he had stamped on all those years ago. It wasn't a gentlemanly settling of a score, but a vicious assault. Capper had come clattering down the stairs, run to the door, skidded on the petrol and done a backward flip, twisting his lumbar region in the process. He had managed to regain his feet, his fear of what Gonzo might be doing driving him through the pain.

'Enough, Gonzo, enough,' he shouted after throwing the door open.

Gonzo picked up Danny by the shirtfront and punched him one last time square in the face. And then dropped him to the ground. Danny's head bounced on the tarmac. Capper had stumbled out in the darkness and there was no light in the street, and no sound.

'Fuck,' he said. 'Is he dead?'

'I hope so,' said Gonzo.

A warrant was issued for the arrest of Martin Guest, and the police rather wearily put him on a to-do list. As if they didn't have enough on their plate, without being diverted to look for somebody who'd paid a few – well, many – bungs back in the day. But then somebody put the name of the businessman to the face of the failed politician and a connection was made between the current void and the vanished man of Welsh politics. Martin became something of a fantasy figure – the man who had it all, now on the run. Contrastingly, as the police picked their way through the records delivered by the Professor, a demoralising story of systemic corruption unfurled. The venality of local-government officers, the easy purchase of planners, the sheer greed at all levels of the operations that kept Wales running on a daily basis coincided with the soul-searching that followed the Bomb. The Welsh were already in a state of complete bewilderment. Day after the day the question was posed: how had it ever come to this? Perhaps here was the start of an answer. Far from being the compilation of figures and unimpeachable analysis that nailed an individual wrongdoer, the Professor's manuscript became a treatise on how a nation can rot from within. And the status of both the whistleblower and the fallen criminal mastermind grew more legendary as the whereabouts of the pair of them remained a mystery.

Trouble after B-day did not flare again. Recalcitrant Wales seemed to have accepted the restoration of order in the pack and the Westminster government now thought of what the top dog might offer by way of reward. But what? They noted that the project to build the M470 the length of Wales had been abandoned. They reviewed the costs and decided that this was a reward too far. The Welsh spinal column stayed in the bin.

Far less demanding on the public purse was the Welsh tongue. After a brief meeting with the Culture Secretary, a phone call to the Director General of the BBC – who quickly passed him over to the Controller of BBC Wales – and with a sweep of his pen, the Home Secretary put a line through the decision to reduce the hours of Welsh-language broadcasting. Caernarfon had not protested, and Meirion had not marched, in vain. His eardrums had not been ruptured and his heart had not been broken for a doomed cause after all. He did not celebrate. At least, he made no public utterance. No gratitude for a trifle would be pathetically expressed. But on B-day plus 14, his wife, María Jesús, shooed him into the car, saying she had to get him out of the house and, for want of being able to think of anything more convincing, told him a half-truth – that tapas would do them both some good. They drove north and in the Wal Bach Spanish restaurant in Caernarfon were reunited with the Sages and as many of the marchers as could be mustered at short notice. There, in their own company, they drank not to the antiquity of their language, but to its future.

The police eventually tracked Gareth Mewson down to the University Hospital of Wales in Cardiff. A pair of constables found him sitting by his brother's bed.

'What's been going on here, then?' asked an officer, genuinely interested in the condition of the patient, who looked as messed up as any trauma victim he had ever encountered. And he had seen a few along the way, especially in high-speed road-traffic accidents up and down the M4.

'None of your business,' said Gareth, reverting to the youngster he once was, not the educator he had become.

'It's going to be like that, is it?' said the second officer.

'I'm saying nothing,' said Gareth.

'And neither is he, by the looks of him,' said the first policeman, nodding at Danny.

Gareth grudgingly agreed to attend an interview at the police station. True to his word – and even when he discovered that he would be interrogated about his dealings with Mr Guest, rather than about what had befallen his brother – he did not say a thing. And, when he was discharged from hospital three weeks later, neither did Danny. The Mewsons would not be the key to solving the mystery of Martin.

Gonzo finally returned to work before the final, and told Capper that if the hooker was to have any chance of regaining sufficient flexibility to play on the big day, he would have to do something physical beforehand. Gonzo set to work at the bottom of the valley. The stand and everything under it would not be used again that season, but he felt the changing room ceiling should be repaired sooner rather than later. Otherwise, it would just become one of those jobs they kept putting off – like the gable end of the clubhouse. He dispatched Capper to do a proper inspection of the wall at the end of West Street, despite finding that he could have done with a second pair of arms to help him put up the new plasterboard on the ceiling. On the other hand, holding plasterboards above his head might have scuppered Capper's slim chances – as Gonzo saw it – of playing.

Capper looked at the wall and tried to stretch his back.

He winced and reckoned his chances of playing were non-existent.

'What you need,' said Our Marnie, making him jump, 'Is a good massage.'

'I'm fuckin' locked tight.'

'Come on, you. Upstairs.'

Grace had been shopping in the village. When she came back to the clubhouse she noticed Capper's boots at the bottom of the stairs. There was a rhythmic pumping coming from above, the sound of Our Marnie jumping up and down – her feet were the only bare bit of her – on Capper's back. Grace thought otherwise. She sighed and smiled and left the club. She walked down the moorland path to the playing field and found Gonzo struggling with his plasterboards in the changing room. She joined him on his makeshift rostrum, stood in front of him and held the board in place, her arms above her head, her back arched. Gonzo began to hammer in nails. Together they put the ceiling back together.

'I'll skim it tomorrow,' he said as they contemplated their work. 'What's Capper up to?'

'Oh, he's getting on with it.' Grace slipped her arms around Gonzo and stood on tiptoe. 'Take me back to the cottage,' she whispered in his ear.

Ten minutes later they were lowering themselves to the old mattress and with infinite tenderness were making love for the first time since Grace came back to the village.

78

The return to normality in Wales, as symbolised by the descent on Cardiff of a rugby crowd, came with certain conditions. The village would be escorted in and out of the city, with the police encouraging everyone to use the special three-carriage train service that was to be laid on from Ebbw Vale. From nine o'clock on the morning of the final, this Babcock Express went up and down the valley ferrying every man, woman and child – even the Yuppies of Edgar Street and Straight Row – to the capital. The streets of the village would be emptied and the silence of a ghost-town would descend for the day. S4C television, keen to show something other than endless updates from reporters still unable to give even the slightest hint of an answer to the big question – who planted the bomb? – bid at the last minute for rights and announced that they would be providing live coverage of the game. The doors were open at the Colliers' Arms and the café, and their televisions were tuned in, but there was nobody behind the counter in either establishment and nobody came in to be served.

The Gulag brought only a handful of supporters, who came by road, surrounded and outnumbered by their police convoy. The last census was consulted and a quick calculation revealed that if the entire population of the village were added to the paltry number of Gulag supporters, the Millennium Stadium would be one hundred and forty times below full capacity. The police began to think they might be guilty of overkill – not that they used the word – and dared relax a little behind their riot shields. Even so, they formed a formidable corridor down which the village supporters had to travel between Cardiff Central Station and the Millennium Stadium. Meg and Annie, arriving on the mid-morning shuttle and already in their highest heels in anticipation of a day out in the city and dry conditions beneath the closed roof, invited the entire corps of police officers to beat them mercilessly.

In the end, the prospect of a public event – the first in a fortnight – attracted a crowd of nearly 8,000 to the stadium. The security clampdown since the Bomb meant that there was precious little else on offer in Cardiff, and at least, on a day of constant rain, the stadium offered its bars and its roof. Service at the beer taps functioned without a hitch and the crowd was in good cheer throughout. Overhead, however, there were problems. The ancient motor driving the roof's sliding operation gave a last blue flash and died. The roof remained half-closed – or half-open depending on the view of which team might adapt better to wet conditions – and the rain fell as a fine mist on the final.

The crowd was placed in the lower and middle tiers of the east side of the stadium, a compacted army of extras opposite the television cameras. Our Marnie and Grace sat in the middle of the throng. Our Marnie's feet and hands were aching from the hours she had spent trying to decontract the muscles in Capper's back. He was straight again, but would he be able to bend himself into the scrum? Grace held Our Marnie's arm and swayed with the singalong all around them. She worried only that there was some truth in Capper's theory about love and rugby not mixing.

'Don't worry, my love,' said Our Marnie. 'He'll rise to the occasion.'

'Yes,' said Grace. 'He always seems to.' Our Marnie nudged her in the ribs.

Gonzo sat deep beneath the stands. The village were in the Home changing room and he felt himself drawn back to the last time he had been here, about to face England in the game of his life. He remembered what he had done to prepare for that day. And he quickly put such memories to one side. Today was different. Today he had to navigate his team through the emotions of the biggest day of their lives. Even the most nonchalant of the *Plant* had seemed affected by the journey under escort on the last Babcock Express of the morning. Every mile they travelled from their patch seemed to increase the strain on their young faces. The old guard seemed settled but the Professor was not among them and Capper was possibly not going to last very long.

It was true that the *Plant* were collectively fretting. They looked at Gonzo in the changing room. And so did the elders. Even the Twins needed a little reassurance, as did Mystic and Useless. Thirteen of the team looked at their best player, but he had lowered his head and was staring at the floor.

'Give 'im five,' growled Capper, trying to stretch his back. He too would have liked a little word of encouragement.

The gulls released Gonzo's head in order to peck at each other. He landed in Cardiff Bay without a splash and bobbed up under a wharf, close to the place where he had once lived.

Above him now stood Martin Guest, in front of a crowd. He was about to address them, about to enjoin them to be baptised. He pointed at the water and turned to stare into its depths. And saw Gonzo. Martin's face froze in horror. He toppled into the water and vanished.

Gonzo opened his eyes and stood up. The referee came into the changing room and told them it was time. The players were all still looking at Gonzo.

'Follow me,' he said.

The Gulags of the West had fought out a semi-final that had been declared 'a classic of its kind' in the *South Wales Evening Post*. But the showcase for all that was fruitful on the production line of Welsh talent had also taken its toll. Three of the winning team had gone into the academy derby with injuries and had exacerbated them. They had spent two weeks in rehabilitation, receiving extensive treatment from the best experts and equipment that money could buy, but they were not fully recovered. And four other players had picked up fresh injuries in the semi. As they lined up for the anthem, the young stars of the Gulag looked the part but feared that they were vulnerable.

The village's physiotherapy had been confined to Our Marnie working on Capper's back. She had kneaded him physically and given him a psychological pounding by withdrawing her amorous favours until the final was over.

'You're going celibate for ten days,' she had told him.

Capper was still fidgeting with his back during the anthem. Everybody was twitching and shuffling, making it hard for the cameraman doing a pan along their faces to keep a steady shot. Only Gonzo did not move. He had found Grace in the crowd and was fixed on her. When the last note became a wall of roaring, he smiled and gathered his team around him.

'No more fear,' he shouted. 'No more nerves. This is our day.'

And it was. Gonzo parted the curtain of rain with his running. He produced a non-stop performance of mature power and intelligence and subtle skill that had the commentators purring about the years being folded back. The Gulag was the future but on this one day the past would be honoured. They urged everyone watching to sit back and admire a master at work.

Capper made it to the start of the last quarter and left to a standing ovation. The Twins scored a try apiece and Ragwort finished the job with a forty-metre run and a sliding dive that went on for twenty metres more. The village won 35-27. With a sudden awareness that the effort had drained him of all his energy, Gonzo stepped wearily forward to receive the Babcock Cup. It was given to him by the Welsh Rugby Union's special guest, Conrad Thomas, who had been sitting alongside Murray Collins. Gonzo took the cup, but handed it straight to Capper and wrapped his arms around his old New Zealander coaches. Capper waited, but Gonzo told him to raise the cup.

In the changing room there was a brief moment of madness, but the team was more interested in getting back to the village. Even the *Plant* were heading for the clubhouse again. The last Babcock Express was awash with beer and lager and villagers who wanted to share the journey home with the players. Cans and bottles and the helmets of the police escorts went back and forth over the heads of passengers crammed into the three carriages. Each helmet was returned dripping in prosecco. At Ebbw Vale there was a wait in the rain that continued to fall, but nobody seemed to mind. Eventually the fleet of coaches and minibuses reappeared to shuttle the last groups back to the end of West Street, where the real party began in earnest.

Gonzo spent much of the night changing barrels and pouring beer. Nobody was charged for the drinks. The ale ran free all night. Every now and again he went to find Grace, who was working flat-out, gathering glasses, emptying the washer, or stopping to take pictures of the party. She took a snap of Gonzo, bruised and slightly hot, coming towards her, a grin stretched across his face. He hugged her and they stood looking at the scene of celebration before them. Grace took Gonzo's hand and squeezed it.

Twin Tub took to the piano and pounded out the numbers. The wall behind the piano – the gable end of the club – sparkled from the crystals stretching out from the central line of the stain of Wales. Such was the noise that on the front wall of the clubhouse the single bulb quivered.

At one o'clock in the morning the party was still in full swing. Tub had started to slow down the tunes but the clubhouse was still packed to the rafters and the beer was still flowing. Suddenly Tub's fingers slipped off the keys. It was as if the piano had moved. He looked up, not so very

337

startled because he had had a great deal to drink. Nobody else seemed to have noticed anything, so he began to play on. But then the floor seemed to shift again. Or was it the wall? Tub looked up and to his amazement saw the stain of Wales moving, disappearing before his very eyes. Everyone fell silent and instinctively moved back from the falling end of the building. There was no loud crash. The entire wall simply seemed to slide down, landing with barely a splash in the puddles of the waste ground between the club and the moor, an area declared out of bounds by Capper while he did the repairs – work, what with one thing and another, he had not started. The silent avalanche just missed Dario and the Widowers, who had left the lounge to check there were no intruders lurking in the street or on the moor.

Tub jumped off his stool. Meg and Annie held on to the nearest table and, spilling not a drop of their drinks, pulled it deeper into the lounge. The piano followed the wall for a foot or two and then stopped, reluctant to go outdoors. Capper was the first to move, shuffling forward, his back ramrod stiff. He cautiously twisted his neck to look up at the apex of the roof, and then down at the ground, covered in debris.

'Fuckin' subsidence,' he said.

Outside, it had stopped raining. The clouds had lifted and the mountaintops were clearly visible in the moonlight. Stars shone above them and in the distance the orange glow above Newport and Cardiff made an arch in the southern sky. Light from the clubhouse now spilled over the moor and as figures slowly started to edge forward to examine the damage, shadows moved on the wilderness. Dario and the Widowers picked their way in through the gaping hole. Everyone was too stunned to speak. The sloshing of the glass washer was all that coud be heard.

'What do we fuckin' do now?' said Capper eventually.

Gonzo stuck his head out and stepped on to the collapsed stonework. He looked up at the night sky.

'We'll rebuild it,' he said. 'And better, too. A special place.'

He went to the piano and tried to move it. He winced as his aching body resisted.

'Come on,' said Daff, and the Plant came forward. They pushed and pulled the piano to safety.

'In the meantime,' said Gonzo, 'There's a celebration to finish.' And Twin Tub sat back down on his stool and struck up a ballad, mournful and yet rousing. The sound poured unobstructed out of the clubhouse at the end of West Street, where the lights didn't shine, and flowed down and over the village, out across the moorland and up to the very tops of the mountains.

The end